Help! My Dog Is The Chosen One!

Ronit J

Copyright © Ronit Jadhav 2023
Self-published by Ronit J
www.ronitjauthor.com
All Rights Reserved

Cover Art by The Hyphn
www.thehyphn.com
ISBN 978-93-6013-541-6

No part of this publication may be reproduced, stored in a retrieval system, or transmitted, in any form or by any means (electronic, mechanical, photocopying, recording or otherwise), without the author or publisher's prior written permission.

This book is a work of fiction. Names, characters, places and incidents are either a product of the author's imagination or are used fictitiously. Any resemblance to actual people living or dead, events or locales is entirely coincidental.

This book is entirely human-made. No AI tools have been used in the creation of any part of this book. No part of this book may be entered into an AI tool or platform with the purpose of replicating or imitating the author's work and writing style without written permission from the author.

FOR JOY,
And all the awesome doggos in the world.
You are truly us hoomans' best friends

TRIGGER WARNINGS

While this story is a light-hearted read, some elements in the book might make some people feel uncomfortable. I'm including these trigger warnings to ensure that no one is caught off guard.

This book contains depictions of mental health, trauma, and anxiety. Also includes scenes of mild violence, including violence involving animals, some frightening scenes, and death.

ACKNOWLEDGMENTS

First and foremost, I want to thank my wife, Gopi. Her never-ending love and support have been instrumental in my being able to realise my dreams. Also, without her, Joy wouldn't be in my life, and without Joy, this book would not have been possible.

Secondly, I want to thank Louann, Ashish and Saptarshi for reading my early drafts and having the patience to give detailed feedback. Not only did they help me improve my draft, but also gave me the confidence to believe in it.

I also want to thank Anmol, Aparna, Riddhi, Alisha, Farnad, and Vineet, all of whom have been extremely encouraging and supportive of my writing endeavours for years now. I wish I could express in words how important your love and support are to me.

A huge shoutout and gratitude to Satyam and his team at The Hyphn without whom my book's cover wouldn't be possible. Their talent, dedication and hard work have surpassed my expectations and realised my vision better than I had dreamt.

Another huge shoutout to my editor, Shreya, for her patience, punctuality, and diligence in working on polishing my manuscript, and making it publishable.

Last, but not the least, I want to thank my parents, who have always been supportive of my absurd endeavours.

I finally did it!

CONTENTS

	Copyright Page	ii
	Dedication	iii
	Trigger Warnings	iv
	Acknowledgments	v
	Contents	vi
	Prologue	1
1	A New Doge	9
2	Puss and Hoots	19
3	Landlord of Chaos	30
4	A Storm of Strays	41
5	Leviathan Shakes	52
6	The Blame Itself	67
7	The Colour of Tragic	85
8	The Pigeon at the End of the Lane	92
9	Chaidrinkers	112
10	The Rage of the Pigeons	127
11	Dunging Egg	135
12	Attack on Snaitun	143
13	Rendezvous with Yama	163

14	The Puppy War	179
15	Memories of Fright	213
16	So Long, and Thanks for All the Crises	232
	Epilogue	256
	About the Author	263

PROLOGUE

IN ONE OF MUMBAI'S EMPTY LANES, amidst the city's filth, a two-year-old dog opened his eyes. He looked around and felt his tiny heart race with fear. He didn't know where he was or where his friends were.

Alone, cold and hurt, he shivered in fright. He tried to cry but all he could muster up was a squeaky little whimper.

Suddenly, a sweet voice called out to him. Before he could open his eyes, he felt warm hands rub his head and belly. A cosy feeling settled in, melting his fear away as the hands picked him up. He tried to open his eyes, but was too tired, too hungry, too hurt to even care. He decided to trust the affection he received, hoping that it would take care of him.

Slowly, sleep took him. He dreamt of owls, he dreamt of cats and he dreamt of floating in a sea of stars.

The dog didn't know it yet, but the fate of the universe and more would depend on his tiny puppy shoulders.

*

Kunal suffered from crippling anxiety. It's fairly common in the modern age, except that Kunal had a whole cocktail of other issues that made his condition altogether unfit for adventuring of any kind.

After all, who'd want the fate of the universe to rest on the shoulders of a barely functioning adult with an intense affliction to socialising? A sadistic god who derives pleasure by interfering with the natural order of things just to see mortals suffer, that's who.

It all started that one fateful night, when Kunal's girlfriend Aisha texted him:

Aisha:
Hey, I need help.
Urgent.

Kunal was the kind of guy who would freak out at a contextless text saying, *'Hey, we need to talk'*. Naturally, his brain hit the panic button when he read the word 'help'. However, with time and practice, he had learnt not to react instinctively to such stimuli. Calmly, he continued the conversation without even a hint of the maelstrom of worst-case scenarios that played in his head.

Kunal:
Sure. What's up?

The worst part of such situations for Kunal was the wait. Luckily, Aisha was serious when she said it was *urgent*.

Aisha:
Abbu & I need to go out of town.
Work call.

Aisha's father, Dr Raza, was one of India's top astrophysicists. He was actively involved in various projects in and out of the country, including some confidential ones for RAW. Kunal and Aisha had an inside joke about how he worked on covering up UFO appearances.

Kunal couldn't figure out what an astrophysicist would want with Aisha. She wasn't a scientist, after all, just a trained archaeologist. Was she being called in to identify alien fossils?

As curious as he felt, his low self-esteem told him he wasn't worthy enough to ask for more details. So, he went with the less offensive follow-up.

Kunal:
Okay… so movie night cancelled?

Aisha:
Sorry…

That was bad, but not aliens-invading-earth-to-enslave-humanity-and-harvest-their-organs bad.

Aisha:
I also need you to do something.

Kunal hated having to answer urgent calls. But this was Aisha. He would gladly even socialise with strangers for her. So:

Kunal:
Anything you say, love.

A dog photo popped up in the chat. Kunal was about to type '*so cute!*' when he saw that Aisha was still typing. He erased his draft, not wanting to interrupt her.

Aisha:
I found this stray doggo today… about two years old.
I just got him vaccinated. Can't take him home though.
Could you please keep him?

Now here's the thing about Kunal, like most people on

the internet, Kunal loved dogs. Regrettably, he was also afraid of them. What if the dog bit him? He'd have to get a hundred injections, and he was even more terrified of needles.

But Kunal really loved Aisha, so naturally, he responded:

Kunal:
Of course!

Aisha called about an hour later, '*I'm waiting at the gate!*'

'Not coming up?' Kunal asked, making an attempt to emphasise his disappointment.

'*No, babe. Rickshaw's waiting. Please come no.*'

'Coming.'

Kunal lived in one of the backroads of Andheri East, and rickshaws were like endangered species in his locality, especially at this hour.

Kunal didn't want her rickshaw's meter to keep running while she waited. So, he grabbed his keys and went out of his apartment without even changing clothes or putting on shoes; Mumbai's roads were so filthy that Kunal always wore shoes instead of flip-flops to avoid getting dirt on his feet.

Kunal lived in an old apartment building that didn't even have a functioning elevator. He minded that, despite his apartment being on the second floor. He wished he could afford a better place, but the rent in Mumbai was like his anxiety—unreasonably and unjustifiably high.

Kunal rushed out of the gate and spotted Aisha across the road. She stood next to a rickshaw and looked like she had done a full day's work plus overtime. She held a huge pink basket in her hand and had a baby-pink backpack double-strapped to her shoulder.

Some kites circled the tawny sky. Half the windows of the high-rises had switched on their lights to mimic the scant twinkling stars that would soon show themselves. It would've been a magical sight, if not for the cawing crows and cooing pigeons performing a medley with the distant noises of traffic and construction that were a staple of Mumbai. To many it was the boisterously lively spirit of the city; to Kunal, it was noise pollution.

Aisha stood directly under a street light, the yellow casting a golden halo around Aisha's dark hair. Kunal wished he had a professional camera with him so he could capture that nearly perfect image of her.

Aisha waved back at him, 'There you are!'

Kunal continued to wave, not sure what to do with his hands, 'Hey! Where's the dog?' *I can see the basket. Do I really need to ask?* If only Kunal knew how to start conversations.

'Right here,' Aisha lifted the pink basket up.

'Does it have to be pink?' Kunal asked, and regretted it immediately. He loved pink, but society had deemed it a girl's colour and trauma made him care about that for some reason.

'Seriously, Kunal?'

'Sorry,' Kunal smiled awkwardly, 'Can I see him?'

She smiled back and opened the lid gently to reveal a sleeping Indian Pariah inside. He was tiny, golden-brown with a few white spots and a thin brown tail. He had a thin black collar around his neck, and underneath it was a string with a cracked pendant shaped like a fish.

'What's with the pendant?'

'He was already wearing it,' Aisha shrugged, 'It looked cute, so I let it be.'

'Sweet,' Kunal smiled, imagining how it'd feel to have his insides ripped out by this cute pupper. He sniffed and recognised the smell, 'Lavender?' Kunal loved the scent. All his room fresheners had lavender in them. He even liked to add lavender to his hot chocolate.

'The vet's given him all the necessary shots. I had him bathed too, so he shouldn't smell. All the major stuff's done, so you shouldn't worry about anything.' Aisha smiled. She took off the baby-pink backpack and handed it to Kunal. 'I'll take him home once I'm back. This has about a week's food, his feeding dish, some toys...'

'A week!?'

'I should be back by tomorrow, or maybe the day after. But it's never a bad idea to have more food, right?'

'Right...' Kunal nodded, convincingly hiding his regret at accepting this responsibility.

'I'll text you his schedule.'

'You already have a schedule for him?' Of course, she did. It would be surprising if she didn't.

'Expect anything less?' Aisha smirked.

Kunal shook his head, took the backpack and slung it over one shoulder. He tried not to think of how ridiculous he looked. *I am not ridiculous, society is.*

Aisha held his hand in both of hers, 'I know you have a lot of work this week... just try to take him for walks every day. Even if they're just for half an hour. Your apartment is small, so he's going to get restless. The walks should calm him down, okay?'

'I know. I'll make sure he gets everything he needs,' said Kunal, trying to sound more confident than he felt.

'Good,' Aisha smiled and kissed him on the cheek.

Immediately, Kunal's cheeks burned and his heart raced, not out of love, but fear. What if someone saw this and complained to his landlord? Kunal didn't get along well with Mr Tambe, and he needed the smallest excuse to evict him.

'Still nervous about PDA?' Aisha teased.

Kunal bit his lip, then said, 'Sorry...'

'You don't have to apologise!' Aisha lightly punched his hand, 'I just wish you'd learn to chill.' Her phone started ringing. It was her father.

'Have to go?'

'Sorry,' Aisha shrugged and then hugged him tightly. 'Thanks for doing this. Bye!'

'Bye,' Kunal said. He looked around to make sure no

one was looking, then quickly planted a peck on her cheek. Sadly, she hadn't seen him coming, and she had already turned; Kunal's kiss landed on her shoulder.

Aisha laughed and covered her mouth. 'Wow. Clumsy much?'

Trying to look cool about it, Kunal said, 'Just thinking out of the box.' He straightened and clenched his fist to calm himself, then added, 'Love you.' That was genuine.

'Love you too,' Aisha said and answered her phone. 'Yes, Abbu. On my way. Twenty minutes max.'

As the rickshaw grumbled to a start, Kunal suddenly ran towards it. 'Wait! Aisha!'

Aisha had just disconnected her call.

He approached her. Trying really hard to ignore the rickshaw driver's annoyed expression as he revved in place, Kunal asked, 'What's his name?'

Aisha looked at the pink basket, then shrugged, 'I don't know, Kunal. You pick.'

Kunal pursed his lips. 'Okay.'

'Can we go, madam?' the rickshaw driver asked rudely.

'Yup.'

The rickshaw driver zoomed away unceremoniously. Kunal heard Aisha's fading voice shouting at the guy to drive slowly.

He shook his head, then looked at the basket of responsibilities in his hand. *I can do this…*

As he walked back into his building, he saw the security guard look at the basket with suspicion. Kunal almost never did anything wrong. Yet, he felt like a terrorist hiding something every time he had to cross a security checkpoint.

In this case, he didn't have to get frisked or show his belongings. This was his home. The security guard was a kind old man who always smiled and waved at Kunal. There was absolutely no reason to be worried.

But no… there was.

What if the security guard informed Mr Tambe that Kunal had adopted a dog? What if Mr Tambe was against dogs? What if he kicked Kunal out for dog-sitting for just a few days?

With a palpitating heart, Kunal ran up the stairs like a thief and quickly rushed inside his apartment.

It's okay, he told himself. *It's just a day or two. What's the worst that can happen?*

Kunal placed the basket in a corner and went back to his work desk. Before he knew it, he was too engrossed in responding to the flurry of messages he had received in the ten minutes he had stepped away from his laptop. Work took up all his attention. So much so that he failed to realise the dark shadow that loomed over his window sill.

CHAPTER 1
A NEW DOGE

KUNAL HATED ADS WITH A VENGEANCE. Sadly, advertising was the only viable career option given his limited skillset. So, after some self-learning and scouring the internet, he bagged the role of a media buyer and strategist in an ad agency.

He didn't love his job, but he didn't hate it either. And in this economy, not hating your job was doing better than the majority of the workforce out there. It was a demanding commitment though, especially given that Kunal's company was based in the US. It was leagues better than his old job with an Indian start-up that had no idea what they were doing.

Of course, the new job meant Kunal's sleep schedule was all over the place. His work notifications were always buzzing.

In the ten minutes that Kunal had stepped away from his laptop, he had received 17 emails, 9 DMs and 208 messages on various channels.

There were no fires to be put out per se. No urgent requirements or tasks either. But Kunal's anxiety always fired up when he saw those notification bubbles. His survival mode kicked in. Kunal blamed his desi upbringing for making him feel like this. Even after a year of therapy, he was still struggling to overcome his deep-rooted subservience.

Most people wouldn't really care, but every incomplete conversation felt like an unlit gas stove that had been left on. The gas was filling in the room and threatening to suffocate Kunal. The only way to survive was to turn it off—which in this context meant replying to every single message with the hopes that the conversations would end soon.

Unfortunately, half of the replies lead to new ad hoc requests that bloated his existing to-do list.

Kunal had barely finished everything when he felt pangs of annoyance prick him yet again. His manager had tagged him in the one thread among twenty-three that Kunal had missed.

Don:
*@**KunalC** these creatives were approved last night. Why aren't these ads live?*

Kunal wanted to curse Don, but it wasn't Don's fault. Kunal blamed himself and started typing his response. Below the thread, it said: '*KunalC is typing…*'

Kunal hated that indicator. It made him feel pressured to reply instantly. He was done typing and proofreading his reply. He was ready with his explanation and was about to hit send…

And at that exact moment, the dog started barking.

He sounded frightened. Naturally, he would be. He had just woken up in strange surroundings in the company of an anxiety-ridden madman who seemed just as frightened of the dog as the dog was of him.

The dog barked from inside the basket, trying to get someone's attention. If only he knew that it was the worst way to get Kunal's.

Kunal started up, looking at the basket just as it toppled over. The golden-brown indie plopped onto the tiled floor and immediately darted towards Kunal.

Kunal watched the carnivorous animal rushing towards him with bared teeth. Panicking, he screamed and jumped to the side, crashing into his sofa-cum-bed. The dog slammed into Kunal's folding chair. Luckily, his folding desk only scraped to the side.

Kunal hoped the neighbours hadn't heard the commotion. He quickly rose to his feet and put his hands forward, 'Stay! Boy, stay!'

The dog turned around. To Kunal's horror, the laptop's charging cable had wrapped around the dog's leg. His laptop was still charging.

It was too much to expect the dog to know what a laptop is, or the proper protocol for when you have a charging cable wrapped around your leg. Kunal slowly made his way towards the dog. The dog, clearly unhappy with the advancing stranger, snarled threateningly and shot forward.

To Kunal's horror, the laptop slid off the desk. To his further horror, it crashed onto the tiled floor, folding shut rather loudly. Kunal's heart skipped a beat. *No...*

The laptop had cost him two months' salary from his old job. His entire life had been on that machine. All his work, all his side projects and hobbies, even his unpublished sci-fi epic...

Kunal ran towards the fallen laptop.

At that moment, the dog's survival instinct kicked in, and he zipped away right from between Kunal's legs. For some strange reason, the charging cord was still affixed to the laptop. Kunal barely had a split second to react before the laptop stubbed his big toe, and slid through.

Kunal fell to the ground and watched the dog run around the room, the laptop scraping against the floor behind him. The dog panicked, trying desperately to escape.

Kunal was panicking too for a host of other reasons.

At that moment, his phone decided to give him just

one more reason to panic. Kunal grabbed his phone to silence it but saw Aisha's name. Just then, he saw the dog crawling behind the sofa-cum-bed, its lean butt swaying like a model's as it tried to fit into the confined space. At least he was quiet for now.

Kunal answered the call, and immediately Aisha asked, '*Hey, did he wake up?*'

Kunal looked at the dog trying to chew the cord. 'Err… he's…'

'*Still sleeping?*'

'Umm…'

'*Well, when he wakes up, just give him something to eat, will you? He's probably gonna freak out. And he'll be hungry. Don't forget to put out some water for him.*'

'Of course…'

'*Sorry, I should've given better instructions. I was in a hurry—*'

'It's okay, love. Have you reached… wherever you were going?'

'*The site? Yeah. But they're going to confiscate my phone before I enter. Thought I'd hit you up before they do.*'

'Why? Are they making you identify alien fossils or something?' He jokingly asked. They would normally joke about Dr Raza's secret projects, but Kunal wondered how Aisha would react, now being involved with one herself.

To his relief, Aisha chuckled. '*Something like that.*' She cleared her throat, '*Once he's up, you're going to have to become his friend. Just pet him, give him treats. All right?*'

Kunal nodded, 'Of course. I'll manage, love. Don't worry. You deal with whatever alien fossils they've found, okay?'

Aisha laughed at that. It made Kunal smile. '*Love you, Kunal. Bye.*'

'Love you too. Bye.'

The moment the call was disconnected, Kunal slowly walked over to the baby-pink backpack. He found some treats and cautiously walked over to the dog.

The dog flinched and bared his teeth. Then he smelled

the treats in Kunal's hand and sniffed. Kunal watched his tiny button nose twitch. Slowly, hesitantly, Kunal proffered his hand.

He had never fed a dog from his hands directly. He'd always leave food on the ground while feeding street dogs. Unlike him, Aisha always fed them directly with her hands. He'd seen her giggle as the dogs licked the food clean from her palms.

He braced himself for the same, praying that the dog wouldn't bite him, or that the dog's teeth wouldn't cut his flesh.

He closed his eyes and winced. The dog sniffed at his palm, making sure that the treats were, in fact, safe. Once the treats passed the inspection, the dog gobbled them all with two quick chomps.

Kunal let out a sigh of relief as the dog audibly chewed on the treats. There was a thin film of canine saliva on his palm. He would've normally felt disgusted at it. But, at that moment, he was just relieved that he still had all his fingers.

Kunal wiped his hand on his pants. The dog swallowed, then looked at Kunal suspiciously. Its floppy ears flicked as he moved forward to sniff him. Kunal didn't move. The dog had to sniff him to trust him. He prayed to every god he ever knew that the dog wouldn't find him a threat.

The dog sniffed at his chest and legs. Deciding Kunal wasn't a threat, he sat back down and looked at him. For the first time, Kunal looked into the dog's beady puppy eyes, seeing a distorted reflection of his frightened self in them.

Kunal couldn't believe himself. How was he afraid of something so adorable?

The dog yawned widely, reminding Kunal why.

Still, he had to get his laptop. Kunal slowly raised his hand and hovered it over the dog's head. As if understanding, the dog raised his head to allow the pat.

Kunal stroked his furry, bumpy head. Lightly at first, then a little more lovingly. The feel of soft bristly fur under his palm was almost relaxing. He found himself getting used to the dog's presence.

For a second, he almost forgot about why he was trying to calm the dog down. *Okay, I think he's calm enough.*

He slowly reached for the cord around the dog's leg. The dog flinched. Kunal flinched.

'It's okay,' he said softly. 'Good boy...' he offered his hand and asked, 'Paw?'

The dog blinked at him in confusion.

Kunal quickly tapped at the wrapped paw and asked again, 'Paw?'

The dog blinked and looked at his paw, then slowly raised it, placing it in Kunal's open palm. He gently held it, feeling the dog's rough claws on his skin. Slowly, carefully, he unwrapped the cord.

'Good boy,' Kunal said, the cord loose enough now. The dog's tail was wagging gently. Kunal was surprised at that.

I did that... He looked into the dog's beady eyes, seeing a smiling reflection of himself. *He likes me!*

For the first time since getting the dog home, Kunal felt like he could actually befriend the dog. He wanted to hug it and pet it and give it belly rubs, but all in good time. Right now, he had work to finish.

Kunal petted the dog one last time, then quickly reached for the laptop and opened it.

The moment he saw his lock screen, he felt his anxieties soothe. There were no scratches or damaged pixels or anything. He quickly unlocked his laptop and checked some basic functions to make sure it was all right. The trackpad seemed functional. No issues with the keyboard either.

There were some scratches at the bottom and corners, but, as long as he didn't have to buy a new laptop, he was fine.

The dog raised his head and started sniffing the corner of the screen.

'No!'

The dog rose to his feet and continued sniffing the side of the screen.

'No! Bad dog!'

The dog ignored him.

Kunal snatched the laptop away and got up. The dog tailed him, whining softly like a baby.

Kunal grew annoyed. Couldn't the dog leave him in peace for just a few moments? He decided to ignore the dog, thinking that might work. He placed his laptop on his desk and resumed his work. The dog's whining grew louder as he circled around Kunal's legs trying to get his attention.

But Kunal's attention was on his message: his explanation for why he hadn't completed a task that was never assigned to him, an error that was someone else's fault but was conveniently dumped on him, a long explanation that was supposed to have been sent ten minutes ago.

There in that thread, Don had tagged him again asking: *@**KunalC**???*

Below the draft, the notification still said *'KunalC is typing...'*

Kunal hit send and proceeded to double-check each creative. As he was setting up the ad set parameters, the dog started barking at him again.

Clicking his tongue, Kunal shooed the dog away so he could work. He hated ad hoc requests and hoped that anyone who requested such tasks was condemned to hell.

Just as he was done setting everything up, he realised he had already set this up the night before. He was just waiting for the client's approval, which he now had. Without wasting any more time, he launched the ad set and leaned back.

Kunal cursed himself for not checking before. He had

done double the work for no reason. If only he hadn't been distracted by the dog.

The dog...

Kunal turned around to find the dog with his hind leg raised. It seemed like he was almost done with his business on the coffee table's leg.

'Damnit!' Kunal quickly responded to the thread saying *'launched'* and slammed the laptop shut.

'No no no no no no no no...' Panic gripped Kunal. Everyone knows that urine isn't an acid that'll melt through wood. But at that moment, Kunal's anxiety made him see it exactly as that.

He stopped right before the coffee table, pacing from one direction to the other. He hadn't wet his pants since he was eight. He had no idea how to clean up pee.

The dog started sniffing at the wet patch.

'NO!' Kunal shouted, making him flinch. 'Go there! Boy, go there!' He pointed to a corner, but the dog just blinked cluelessly. Kunal sighed and repeated the command with more clarity, 'Go there, boy!'

Flopping his ears, the dog finally obeyed. Kunal was glad that the dog was obedient at least.

'Okay, sit!'

The dog sat down. Kunal didn't think to wonder where the street dog might've learned that command. His attention had switched back to the pool of pee by his coffee table.

Kunal remembered that it was important to completely get rid of the smell. That way dogs wouldn't pee in the same spot again. He quickly fetched cleaning supplies from his bathroom and cleaned the mess as best as he could. At that moment, he was grateful that Indian homes had tiles on their floors instead of carpets.

Once the mess was cleaned, he returned all supplies to their rightful spots and washed his hands meticulously. He returned to the hall, finding the dog sitting exactly where he had been instructed to sit.

All crises dealt with, Kunal was finally able to look at the dog for the cute puppy it was. He exhaled and smiled. 'Good boy…' he paused. 'You need a name, don't you?'

The dog barked.

Does he understand me now? Kunal chuckled, 'Okay… what name should we give you?'

The dog blinked, then woofed twice.

Kunal scratched his chin, trying to remember his random conversations with Aisha. Hypothetical scenarios where they had adopted dogs and had to name them.

Around the forty-second name suggestion, he remembered he was still supposed to be working.

Kunal rushed to his laptop, hoping he wasn't fired. Luckily his account was still active. He reasoned with himself that no company would be unreasonable enough to fire him for being missing for fifteen minutes, at least not in a remote work setup.

Besides, he always clocked his hours despite his company being trusting enough to not install activity trackers on their employees' devices. Kunal quickly skimmed through each channel to make sure he hadn't missed anything, then turned and looked at the dog.

The dog wasn't where he had left him. Instead, he was pawing at the main door.

Kunal's apartment was cosy enough for Mumbai's standards, but those weren't high to begin with. He was used to living in cramped quarters, but a free-spirited animal? He couldn't do that to the poor pup.

He checked the time; it was 21:07. The streets would be relatively empty at this hour. So, Kunal conjured up the most childlike voice he could manage and asked the dog, 'You wanna go out, boy? You wanna go for a walk?'

He sounded ridiculous, but the dog's ears flicked erect. His tail began swishing from side to side. He barked in an infectiously happy tone. Kunal felt the dog's happiness embrace him, and he wanted to take the dog out. He wanted to do anything to make the dog happy.

Kunal found his leash in the backpack and clipped it on.

Kunal always wore different clothes for the outdoors unless it was a quick trip to the gate and back. He should've changed before putting on the leash. Because, throughout the five minutes that Kunal took to change, the dog barked and whined incessantly. Kunal's heart broke, not wanting to keep the dog from his fun time. Meanwhile, his anxieties spiked, fearing his neighbours would complain.

Kunal rushed through changing, put on his shoes, quickly grabbed the keys and almost darted out of the door.

The moment the dog crossed the threshold, he stopped barking. Instead, he sniffed at literally everything that he could find. Kunal struggled to close his door because the dog was too excited to go out. He kept pulling at the leash trying to run. To say that Kunal was taking the dog for a walk wouldn't be entirely accurate. It looked like the dog was dragging Kunal behind him as he ran restlessly in every direction.

Kunal was just a regular nobody in the city. He always dressed inconspicuously and minded his own business. The chances of him being stalked were almost zero.

However, something was stalking Kunal. Most people, even Kunal, failed to notice the stalker. After all, who in their right state of mind would think an owl would stalk them?

Who?

CHAPTER 2
PUSS AND HOOTS

KUNAL AVOIDED EYE CONTACT with the security guard as he exited the building with the dog. Luckily, the guard was watching a C-grade film on his phone, full volume without headphones. Kunal was glad that he was distracted. But as soon as he was out of the building compound, he remembered why he hated going on walks.

Mumbai is one of the most advanced cities in India. She offers everyone food, shelter and a chance to achieve their dreams. Yet, she lacks some basics, like hygiene. It doesn't matter if you're a poor worker spitting on the streets or a business owner dumping trash out of their luxury cars, everyone littered in public spaces without a care because they don't regard it as their problem.

Now imagine walking a dog on such a filthy street. Their curious noses bring them close to everything, from snack wrappers and decaying garlands to cigarette butts, *gutka* packets and *paan* stains or turds of unknown origins—the list is never-ending, just like the flow of trash.

If that's not bad enough, there's also uncollected garbage leaking its filthy fluids all over the place. And with the garbage come rats, flies, cockroaches…

Kunal was on high alert. Yes, this was a rescued street dog, but that didn't mean he should be allowed to eat trash again. No one should have to live amidst such filth.

At least the roads were relatively uncrowded at that hour.

The dog pulled in every direction, careless and unaware of all the dangers that existed around him. The cocktail of anxieties that brewed in Kunal's brain left him unable to enjoy the walk. His complete attention was on the dog, making sure he was walking on the footpath, not eating trash or insects, not running off into an oncoming car, all the while keeping an eye out for approaching strangers.

It was all incredibly exhausting.

Finally, when they entered an empty backstreet, Kunal felt some amount of relief. He looked around and the only thing he spotted was a stray cat sprawled under a bench at a deserted bus stand. Some kind Samaritan had left some kibble for it to eat, neatly piled atop a loose sheet of newspaper. Kunal wondered if anyone had been kind like that to his dog. *Can I consider him my dog?*

The dog suddenly started barking. Kunal noticed the barks were directed towards the cat under the bench. As Kunal pulled on the leash, he realised it wasn't just one cat, but a group of cats who were lying around the bus stand. Wild cats, by the look of scars and dirt on them, all glowing red and neon eyes pinned on the brown indie Kunal was walking.

Most people aren't scared of cats like they are of dogs. But Kunal wasn't like most people.

Immediately, his mind told him that these cats were going to maul him to death and feast on his corpse.

In an unfortunate turn of events, his mind was proven right.

The cats dashed straight at them. The dog barked louder, as Kunal ineffectively pulled at the leash. The leash was taut, biting into Kunal's palm. The dog raced forward, his claws and paws scratching against the dirty footpath.

But the cats were swifter. A huge black cat lead the pack. It leapt forward and scratched at the dog's face.

The dog flinched and whined. Turning around, he ran with all his might.

Kunal didn't have time to react. He was pulled along, almost tripping as he tried to keep pace with his fleeing mutt. It was strange how such a small creature could have such strength. Kunal tried to stop him but felt something touch his leg.

His mind told him it was a monster. But it was just one of the stray cats.

Kunal feared both equally.

Panicking, he kicked his leg in the air, sending the cat flying. It landed on its feet perfectly and bared its teeth.

The dog whined, still trying to scurry away. Kunal turned to walk away briskly, fearing that if he ran, the cats would chase him. Nonetheless, the stray cats approached him menacingly. There were four of them, and they were all capable of killing him. Or worse—scratching him with their diseased claws, compelling him to get painful shots.

Kunal hyperventilated, his hands gripping the leash tight enough to strangle it. His legs were frozen, refusing to move despite his conscious commands.

If he were attacked by a dog, people would pity him. But if the same were to be perpetrated by stray cats, he'd become the laughing stock of his neighbourhood. Even his friends and family would forever make fun of him. He could already see the news-articles-turned-memes: *Mumbai Man Almost Killed By Stray Cats. Cried While Getting Anti-Rabies Shot.*

Kunal swallowed the lump in his throat. He had to do something. He turned to the dog, hoping the animal would be of some help. 'Attack them, boy!' Kunal shouted, pointing at the cats, 'Go! Bite!'

The dog ignored him. He was probably as frightened as Kunal. Maybe more.

It had to be Kunal. He had to be the one taking

charge.

He decided there was only one way to do this.

He quickly picked up the dog and ran.

There are athletes who run with elegance whilst demonstrating the extreme limits of human potential.

And then there's Kunal.

His hatred for the outdoors meant he lacked a natural proclivity for outdoor activities, including running. The only time Kunal could even dream of beating a cheetah in a race was if the cheetah were actually a plushie.

Kunal had barely taken two strides before the strays were onto him. He felt one latch onto his leg, slowing his already sluggish movements. The dog whimpered, trying to shake itself free. A second cat pounced on Kunal's back and he felt its sharp claws pierce through his T-shirt.

Kunal was too focused on the cats stuck to him to pay attention to the panicked dog. Unfortunately, the dog's leash was still around his wrist. As the dog ran forward, he pulled Kunal behind him. Kunal tumbled, face slamming into the footpath.

The cats squealed and jumped away. The dog tried to keep running but wasn't strong enough to pull Kunal's weight.

Kunal managed to sit upright, wiping away the blood and phlegm from his face. His nose felt sore, salty blood dripping onto his lips and into his mouth. He spat and touched his face, worried his nose was broken, but it didn't feel like it. He needed to wash himself.

He didn't have time. The cats were already pouncing on the dog, scratching and biting him. Kunal went pale, worried that he wouldn't be able to save the dog.

The dog whimpered. Kunal's heart skipped a beat as he looked on helplessly at the dog, wishing he could somehow help it.

A hoot echoed in the air.

When crows or pigeons flap their wings, you can hear them. Owls, however, are silent assassins. Kunal wasn't expecting the grey-brown owl he saw sitting next to him, its saucer-like orange eyes piercing Kunal's shivering soul. *What the...*

Before he could react, a white blur shot from overhead. He flinched, seeing another cat, a white shorthair, dart towards the struggling dog.

To Kunal's surprise, the white shorthair attacked the other cats. With surreal speed, it managed to knock two of them away, giving the dog an opening to take care of the two on top of him.

Frightened, yet curious, Kunal rose to his feet.

The white shorthair attacked its adversaries, making sure each blow landed on its victim. The remaining two had redirected their focus onto the shorthair; the dog trotted up to Kunal with his tail between his legs. Kunal held him, trying to calm him down.

That's when he noticed the owl staring at them.

Kunal got up and tried to walk away, but the cats rolled into his path. They weren't trying to stop him or anything, they just fell where the shorthair had thrown them. By the looks of it, the white shorthair was completely destroying them.

Strays fight like there's no tomorrow, probably because that's true in their case. The cats' brawl was brutal. The dog snarled but was too afraid to join the fight. Kunal kept watching the clash with the curiosity of a wildlife documentary viewer. As if something miraculous were to happen.

And then it did.

The white shorthair stood on its hind legs, fore legs bent in a martial arts pose.

'What...?'

Kunal rubbed his eyes, but the shorthair still stood in perfect posture. It manoeuvred itself gracefully, grabbing one stray by the ear, kicking the second and throwing the first into the remaining two. Before they could recover, it pounced on them with fangs and claws bared.

A few near-fatal scratches later, the strays darted away, and the white shorthair dusted its front paws.

'What the…?' Before Kunal could finish that sentence, the owl attacked his face.

Kunal tried to grab it but lost his grip as he fell to the ground again. He felt something coil around his neck. His mind yelled, *SNAKE!*

Beating his arms around, Kunal started rolling on the ground, the leash wrapping itself around him. The dog barked as it got pulled into Kunal's crazy defence. Maybe it was just responding to Kunal's shrieks.

Finally, the owl took flight, disappearing into the night.

When no sound or touch affected him, Kunal realised he was safe. He lay flat on the ground revaluating his life choices. His clothes were dirty, his back stung, probably from the stray cats' scratches. Now even the owl had scratched his face up. Kunal had to fight his mind to avoid thoughts of needles and burning antiseptics.

The dog was pinned under Kunal's leg somehow.

'Boy… I'm so sorry…' Kunal quickly detangled the leash and pet the dog to calm him down. He wished someone would pet him too. He had almost died. His heart pumped like an overheating piston in a race car engine. He held his chest as he felt some discomfort. *Not a heart attack… please…*

The dog whimpered and licked Kunal's hand.

'Boy…' he began, but paused, realising that the dog was completely unscathed. No scratches, no bite marks. Only some dirt from the road had rubbed off on his fur. Kunal looked confusedly, wondering if he had dreamt of the assault.

'Are you okay?' a voice called out.

Kunal froze. He hated the fact that someone had seen him in such an embarrassingly vulnerable position.

Kunal turned to find the source of the voice.

It was the owl; a dusky eagle-owl commonly seen in Mumbai, the key difference here being that Mumbai's owls weren't the talkative kind.

It's not every day that an animal talks to you. Most people would think they're drunk or dreaming. Kunal thought he had hit his head so hard that his brain was damaged.

'Don't be frightened...' the owl said. Owls didn't have the right muscles and organs to produce human speech. But the owl was opening and moving its beak. Was this really an owl? Was it telepathically communicating with him?

Maybe it had a nanochip implanted in its brain.

Or maybe this owl was a host to some alien parasite, possibly looking for a more advanced host.

Kunal's throat went dry.

'Breathe. You need to stay calm.'

Of course, it wants you to stay calm.

'We need to get out of here...' another voice said. A female voice.

It was the cat. The white shorthair's fur was dirty and beaten. She strode on all fours like a tiger on a hunt, her eyes deep and brooding.

I need to run...

'Adira, let the boy breathe,' the owl said, spreading its wings to stop the cat.

'But Guru,' Adira, the cat, said sitting down, 'they might return.'

'Not immediately,' Guru the owl said turning to Kunal, 'But it would be wise to make haste.'

The dog barked at them continuously, but the speaking animals were unmoved.

In all this chaos, Kunal had forgotten that they were in public.

'*Beta*! Are you okay?'

Kunal looked up to find a mean-looking middle-aged woman in a nightgown leaning out of her window. Why couldn't Mumbaikars just let a stranger get mauled to death by stray animals?

Kunal shook his head 'Yes, auntie! All okay!'

'Stupid boy! Stop making noise and go home!' she shouted and went back in.

Kunal turned to look at the owl and the cat. Guru and Adira. 'I hit my head real hard. I need to…'

'We need to go somewhere safe,' Guru insisted, hopping closer to him. 'Please… Snaitun is looking for us, and he's probably looking for you too…'

His voice sounded genuine. Kunal gulped, feeling a resistance in his throat. He reached out and found a string with a fish pendant tied around his neck.

'Don't remove that…' Guru said flapping closer, 'It helps us communicate with you.' Kunal noticed that the owl was wearing a similar pendant.

The dog…

Kunal looked at the dog, who was busy sniffing at the ground, walking in circles. *How come he's unhurt? I'm sure I saw the cats attack him…*

'Get up, boy!' Adira snarled, grabbing his attention. 'We need to leave!' Kunal usually found cats cute, but he'd seen this one hold her ground against four brutal strays.

Kunal wanted to protest, but he also didn't want to take any risks. Obeying felt right. That's what he had always done with his parents. Despite years of therapy, his survival instincts kicked in. He rose to his feet, 'Yes ma'am!' He noticed the dirt on his clothes, 'But first, I need to change.'

Adira facepalmed. Facepawed?

Guru flew up towards Kunal. Instinctively, Kunal raised his hand and Guru landed on it. 'Boy,' the owl's voice sounded full of concern. Kunal had rarely heard such a tone, except when his parents wanted something from him, 'I've seen where you live. It's not safe.'

'But… I need…'

'We can hide there temporarily, but we need a safer location. All our lives…' Guru leaned forward, and said in a grim voice, '...the very fabric of this reality... all is at stake.'

Kunal's mind suddenly flashed through all of the epic science fiction and fantasy stories he had consumed over his lifetime. It even skimmed through his own half-baked attempt at a sci-fi masterpiece. Was he really a part of one now? Reluctantly, he asked, 'You're asking me to join you... on an adventure?'

'No,' Adira said with a snarl, 'We're trying to save your life. Snaitun's gaining power, and if he finds us...'

'Aha!' Kunal shouted. Unfortunately, he pointed with the hand Guru was resting on. Guru flapped away and landed next to Adira. 'Snaitun! That's the dark lord... call to adventure... this is...' He was certain he had some brain damage. 'I'm going to my apartment. You can follow me if you like.'

'Okay,' Guru said, 'we can explain...'

'No need to explain. It's all in my head, isn't it...?'

'What?'

'Come on boy!' Kunal tugged at the dog's leash but was met with resistance. The dog was squatting next to an open gutter, pooping. He looked at Kunal with his beady eyes, mouth closed in concentration. Once he was done, he shook and walked up to Kunal, tongue lolling on the side. He looked relieved, almost happy. Did he already forget about the stray cat attack? And the magical talking animals? And the poop?

Kunal looked at the poop and sighed. It was bad enough that he had to pick it up. But to pick it up from an open gutter where people threw trash and spat *paan* and whatnot—a shiver ran down his spine.

At least he had a new bottle of sanitiser in his pocket. Many dog owners and dog walkers in Mumbai didn't even care to clean up after their furbabies. Kunal was better than them.

Adira and Guru watched as he made a glove out of the poop bag and picked up the turd before dumping it into the empty trash can five inches next to the gutter.

At least the trash can was close by.

Kunal took a generous amount of sanitiser and rubbed his hands. He regretted it instantly as his scratches burnt from its sudden contact. He yelped in pain and shook his hands to force the alcohol to evaporate faster. Once the stinging receded, he tugged at the dog's leash. 'Come, boy…' He started walking back home. The dog followed, wagging his tail.

'We're coming too,' Guru said calmly.

Kunal ignored it. He didn't have to respond to his imagination, did he? Would that be rude?

'Will you at least listen to us?' the owl persevered, 'The fates of your world and ours are at stake.'

Kunal snorted, 'Yeah right, and you're really a man stuck in the body of an owl…'

Guru flew up to him and landed on his shoulder, 'Correct! Except, I'm not a man.'

'Okay… sure… So, what are you?'

Guru shook their owl head, their feathers ruffling. 'I'm a high mage. We're neither male nor female. Doesn't your reality have alternate genders?'

Kunal looked with utter confusion. He didn't know if he wanted to pull on that thread. 'So… you're a non-binary owl?'

'I don't know about that,' Guru said, 'Where we come from, high mages have to shed every bit of their mortal identity when they…' Guru shook again, 'I'm sorry to push you like this but we really don't have time. We need to hide.'

Kunal decided to play along. 'Because the fate of our worlds depends on us?'

'Yes! Exactly!' Guru exclaimed.

'And you're here from a different reality because…?'

Guru sighed. 'It's a long story…'

'Let me guess… this *Shaitan* person you keep mentioning made a deal with the devil,' Kunal thought of all the sci-fi fantasy books he had read which had similar premises. 'And, for some absurd reason, I'm the only one who can stop him. I'm the chosen one, right?'

Guru was at a loss for words.

Adira snapped, 'Not you, idiot!'

Kunal stopped in his path. 'Sure. If not *me*, then who?'

'Burfi,' Guru said as if that were common knowledge.

'Burfi? Who's Burfi?' Kunal asked.

The owl pointed at the dog.

'You have got to be kidding me!'

CHAPTER 3
LANDLORD OF CHAOS

KUNAL TRIED TO TUNE OUT all of the animals' voices. Why bother with the imaginary, right? That was the only explanation he could think of for what he had witnessed. Something must've triggered some unresolved past trauma in his mind, prompting it to conjure delusions to protect his feelings. But, even in his fantastic hallucinations, he was just a side character.

Kunal decided he needed a lot more serious therapy. Maybe even a psychiatrist.

And a hot chocolate. Definitely a hot chocolate.

Kunal was determined to fix everything. He had to take a few days off work. Then he had to find another home for Burfi. *Damnit, that name's perfect!* After that, he would have to talk to someone and find a reliable psychiatrist who wouldn't scam him out of his hard-earned money.

Kunal hurried back home, Burfi trotting happily next to him.

Kunal approached his building, realising that the hyper-realistic figments of his imagination were still following him. He tried to ignore them despite their presence being very much unignorable due to Adira's constant complaining.

Kunal spotted the security guard still watching his C-grade film. Normally, Kunal would've felt anxious about walking in with all these animals.

But he wasn't feeling normal. So, he just walked in with a dog, a cat and an owl in tow. The security guard looked at him, looked at the animals, shrugged dispassionately and continued to laugh at the misogynistic jokes in his film.

Kunal felt a chill. He stopped and looked at the security guard. He pointed at Adira and Guru and asked him, '*Bhaiyya*, can you see them?'

Without pausing the loud video on his screen, the guard looked at Kunal, then at the animals, then back at Kunal. 'Yes, sir.'

'What do you see?'

'A dog, a cat and an owl. You planning on opening a zoo?', the guard laughed at his own joke and continued to watch his film.

Kunal nodded, sweat drenching his face and body. 'Okay. Good night. Love you.'

Love you? What the hell is wrong with me?

Luckily, the guard was too immersed in his film to care about Kunal's accidental proclamation.

Kunal rushed up the stairs and reached his apartment. He made sure none of the other neighbours were around, and quickly unlocked the door. 'Get in!'

The animals obeyed.

Once inside, Kunal ran into his bathroom to splash water on his face. Then he ran into the kitchen to drink water until his stomach exploded.

His body was alive from all the adrenaline his panicked brain had produced. But now, his mind was inching towards the other direction. Fatigue.

Burfi barked. He was breathing too heavily.

Kunal realised he needed water. He filled the feeding bowl and watched Burfi quickly run to him and drink the water with rapid laps of his tongue.

It was then that Kunal saw the cracked fish pendant. Similar to the pendant that the owl had wrapped around his neck. Similar to the ones around Guru and Adira's necks.

Kunal turned and found the owl perched on the fridge.

'Boy...' the owl said.

'My name's Kunal!' he snapped. *The owl isn't real. This has to be a nightmare.*

'I understand this must be too much to take in. But you have to trust—' Guru paused, then pointed at Burfi with their wing, 'Look at Burfi! You saw him getting attacked, right?'

Kunal paused. *That's right...*

'Why do you think he's unhurt?' Guru's voice was calm and soothing. It almost pacified Kunal's anxiety.

But that anxiety was slowly being replaced with fear. What if this were real? What if this were bigger than Kunal could handle?

'Burfi is...' Guru continued, '... in a matter of speaking... invulnerable. We can't hurt him. No one can. Except Snaitun.'

'NO!' Kunal shouted, refusing to believe them. 'You are NOT real!'

'But I am...'

'Prove it!'

Adira headbutted Kunal, throwing him on the floor. She licked her paw and wiped her face. 'Real enough for you?'

Kunal lay sprawled on the kitchen floor, not sure if he wanted to get up and face the absurdity of that night. But the mild soreness in his chest where Adira had hit him was real.

Or maybe it's just a symptom of my anxiety...

Kunal's anxiety had made him a sceptic. And in the modern world, scepticism is a more practical approach to situations like these. He was very much right to question the actuality of everything.

Unfortunately, reality didn't wait for mortal minds to process it completely. It flowed forward like a river, with apathy towards swimmers and drowners alike.

It was all too much to take in. Kunal wanted to shut down. But he couldn't.

Because his doorbell rang.

Kunal shot up. The panic he felt, surprisingly, was lethargic. He treaded slowly towards the door and opened it.

A portly man with a patch of baldness and a walrus moustache stood at the door glaring at Kunal. He wore a white linen shirt, with gold chains hanging around his neck and arms. It was his landlord.

Kunal hoped this wasn't about the dog.

Mr Tambe asked rather rudely, 'Did you buy a dog?'

The panic wasn't lethargic anymore. It wasn't even sharp and roaring. It was in a dampened middle ground, like cooling lava or the soggy crust of an otherwise perfect toast.

'Mr Tambe... hi...'

'Answer the bloody question, boy! Did you buy a dog?'

Burfi woofed and rushed forward, sniffing at Mr Tambe's feet.

Mr Tambe frowned and crossed his arms. 'No dogs allowed in the building.'

That wasn't true at all. Kunal had seen the neighbours with pets, which made him wonder why he was worried in the first place. With feigned confidence, he said, 'But your broker said they're allowed. Even the neighbours have pets.'

'Fish and birds. No dogs,' Mr Tambe snapped and walked into the house. He was a short man, barely coming up to Kunal's chest. But he owned the house and the air around him exuded it. He sniffed in the air and covered his mouth in disgust, 'Bloody animals. You're dirtying my house. Get this filthy thing out of here!'

Kunal held his ground, resisting the urge to kick Mr

Tambe. 'I asked you specifically when signing the contract. You said yes.' Kunal always dreamed of adopting a dog, so he wanted to keep the possibility open.

'You never asked me,' his portly landlord lied.

Kunal hadn't realised his panic had turned to rage. Without thinking, he shouted, 'Liar! Don't lie to me you...' his rage suddenly subsided, choking his words.

Mr Tambe uncrossed his arms, fists clenching on the side. In a threateningly soft voice, he said, 'Don't shout at me, boy. I'm your elder.'

I'm your elder. You should respect your elders—This one idea had been at the foundation of Kunal's trauma. Hearing those words sent a jolt deep within Kunal's heart that fumed out in a flurry of insults. Kunal didn't so much say, as he piercingly screamed some very nasty things unfitting for a decent man.

As Kunal verbally vomited his rage onto Mr Tambe, he felt better. The horrible uncle deserved it. Now that Kunal felt light and empty, his mind welcomed reason back. Kunal saw from his landlord's face that he had probably made a huge mistake. Mr Tambe was fuming with rage, eyes red and nostrils flared, spit foaming at the corners of his walrus moustache.

Mr Tambe raised an accusatory finger at him, '*Tujhya nanachi taang!*' *Your maternal grandfather's leg.*

Kunal never understood that insult. He slapped the doorframe and shouted, '*Tujhya aichi g...*'

Mr Tambe sprayed spittle, shouting, 'Get out of my house! Bloody youngsters these days have no manners. God knows what gutter your family's crawled out of. I hope you die poor and suffering!'

Kunal's courage had left with his rage. The urge to beg for forgiveness was strong. After all, that's how all disagreements—major and minor—went down with his parents.

Kunal opened his mouth to say something. But Mr Tambe continued to rant—this time choosing to insult

Kunal and Kunal's parentage—vile things that a functional grown-up shouldn't even think about unless they have some deep-seated generational trauma that has left them emotionally stunted.

You might have heard the saying – fight fire with fire. For staunch believers of that ideology, everyone ends up getting burnt. No winners, only losers with ugly burns that'll always remind them about how they carelessly played with fire.

Mr Tambe's words had triggered Kunal's trauma. Kunal's retaliation had triggered Mr Tambe's trauma, which in turn attacked Kunal's trauma again. Before they knew it, they were engaged in a fierce battle of insults that woke up the entire building. A crowd gathered outside Kunal's door, crowding the passage like a Mumbai-local compartment.

Kunal's neighbours thought this was the best opportunity to complain about Kunal's habits, particularly concerning Aisha's visits. Kunal never thought of her as Muslim or a spinster; apparently, it was really important for his neighbours. After all, the building was full of Maharashtrians, and not the liberal kind.

One wobbly old uncle accused him of playing loud music late in the night, which was preposterous given that Kunal didn't even like music. Another aunty claimed Kunal and Aisha made vulgar sounds that disturbed her kids while studying.

The complaints piled up. Mr Tambe looked at Kunal with an evil grin.

He wasn't Kunal's friend. He wasn't Kunal's family. He was just a man looking to make money by renting out his overpriced apartment. And now he had an opportunity to kick out his tenant and get a new one who could pay more.

As the mob started losing energy (it was way past the old folks' bedtime), Mr Tambe gave Kunal a final warning. 'I will send you a written notice. I want you out of here by next Tuesday.'

Kunal started to protest, but Mr Tambe yelled at him and stormed out. The rest of the audience also muttered curses and passive-aggressive taunts before returning to their own homes. They would gossip about this for months to come.

Kunal defeatedly closed his door, the gravity of the situation still sinking in. And as he turned, he saw the three animals huddled together.

His rage, confusion and fright had a subject now. He stormed towards them, 'You! Get the hell out of my apartment!'

Adira bared her teeth and slapped her front paw on the floor, 'Shut up, boy.'

'His name is Kunal, Adira,' Guru corrected.

'No, you shut up!' Kunal shouted, fists clenched and ready to punch. 'I'm going to be homeless now! Because of you three!'

'I don't care!' Adira pushed, 'We have to leave before Snaitun finds us!'

'Why should I listen to you!?' Kunal yelled, 'How do I even know if you're real!?'

Guru hopped closer and gestured with their wing, 'I haven't yet figured out the weave of this reality's fabric. But...' they began moving their wings about. A glowing blue flare of light trailed behind the tip of Guru's grey wing. They continued to move their wing about, forming what looked like a rune.

Kunal couldn't identify what language the rune was in, nor did he have the time.

The rune flashed a blinding light at him, and all went black.

He wasn't knocked out; just that everything around him exploded into stars, which dissolved into black within a heartbeat. Kunal felt weightless, almost as if he didn't exist.

Am I having an out-of-body experience?

Kunal had tried to induce one when he was younger and was going through a spiritual phase. He was never successful, neither in inducing the experience nor in putting his mind into quietude.

But as he looked around this astral plane, he wondered if this was a spiritual experience or a nightmare.

The landscape stretching before him wasn't a star-filled haven. It was a miserably barren blackness extending to the ends of eternity. The sky was a void with endless depth, dark mountains cresting the horizon like menacing giants waiting to trample everything in sight. Massive rocks floated in the void sky, holding caves that were blocked by smaller boulders that shivered as unseen horrors shoved at them from inside, trying their best to escape.

There was something familiar about this void-scape. It smelled like Kunal's worst memories, muffled sounds of traumas buzzing in the distance.

Kunal held his breath, only to realise he wasn't really breathing. That made him breathe faster, panic faster.

'WHERE AM I!?' he screamed out loud.

'We're inside your mind... this is your mindscape,' Guru answered, flitting into view. They were still an owl.

'Why are you still an owl?' Kunal asked. That seemed like the appropriate low-stakes question to break the ice before unleashing his existential rapid fire.

'Because,' Guru replied patiently, 'You've only seen me as an owl. To you, I am still an owl. Right now, what you see of me is your mind's projection of my form, and I'm not adept enough to project my real form here.' They paused, then added, 'In this plain of existence, you are in absolute control.' The distant muffled groaning of cosmic terror nudged the air with dread. 'Save for... whatever those are,' Guru said, pointing to the void with their wing.

Kunal blinked in confusion, still reeling from the panic of his literal breathlessness. Finally, he asked, 'Why are we here?'

'You asked if I were real...' Guru said, 'I presumed you were experiencing a kind of existential crisis.' Guru chuckled, 'When you study the very fabric of reality and magic, you tend to encounter a lot of those crises.'

Kunal's legs gave in. He fell on his butt, still staring into the void of his mindscape. 'Why is...?'

Guru looked at the horizon, 'Ahh... my question too, honestly. I've seen many mindscapes but rarely was one this...' Guru turned their head a hundred and eighty degrees, their orange gaze piercing Kunal's. 'Are you into black magic?'

'No!' Kunal snapped instinctively. Wasn't the first time he was accused of that.

'Then why is your mindscape so... dark? It's...' Guru looked around with concern. 'I've peered into the mindscapes of warriors, mages, civilians... people from all walks of life... but I've never seen a mind this...'

'Dangerous?' Kunal asked, the edgelord in him puffing up with pride.

'Disturbed,' Guru said, turning their head, 'You need help, Kunal...'

Like I don't know that already...

'Can we trust you, Kunal?' Guru asked, 'We don't have the luxury of time.'

Kunal frowned. Guru's tone was grave.

'Kunal?'

Kunal nodded. He didn't have time to think of his response.

'You seem unsure,' Guru said.

'You expect me to answer with absolute certainty? Then give me enough time to think!' Kunal said.

'We unfortunately...'

'Then don't!' Kunal cut them short, raising a finger, 'Just tell me what you want.'

Guru continued to stare at him for a few seconds. Finally, they flew up and began explaining, 'We aren't really animals, Kunal. We're humans too. But we come from another world. Another reality.'

Kunal's jaw dropped. 'The multiverse exists?'

'That's… an oversimplification. But yes,' Guru said.

Now that caught Kunal's attention.

'As I was saying…' Guru continued, 'We come from a different world. Our world isn't as technologically advanced as yours. We still fight with swords and shields…'

As Guru narrated, Kunal's mindscape manifested vague shadow visuals before him. Soldiers that looked like they were from the Iron Age clustered behind Guru in the sky. They held spears and swords, storm clouds gathering just above them as they chanted their battle cries.

'But we have identified our world's weave… giving some of us access to magic.'

A mage stepped forward from among the soldiers casting light into the dark sky.

'And the strongest, most adept among all those mages and high mages was Snaitun.'

A monstrous shadow loomed above the army, eyes glowing red. The dark lord.

'Snaitun has one sole purpose: To become the most powerful being in the universe.'

The dark lord grew impossibly larger. A mountain looming over the skies.

'With the might of a thousand armies and the knowledge of a thousand arcane tomes, Snaitun conquered our world.'

The dark lord wielded a spear in one hand and a shining orb of light in the other. The armies below him were decimated until only the dark lord remained. The glowing orb in his hand transformed into planet Earth.

'And when he had no more nations left to conquer, he turned to lands outside our worlds.'

The earth turned to sand, slipping away from the dark lord's hand. He clenched his fist in anger. Screaming, he tore a rift into the air and pulled the fabric of reality apart, opening a view into another world.

'Snaitun now has come to your world,' Guru declared.

The dark lord looked straight at Kunal. Kunal imagined his heart skipping a beat.

'But he isn't at his full power, yet. We're here to stop him, but the only way to do that is to find the Dung Egg.'

'The Dung Egg?' Kunal asked dumbfounded. This was getting ridiculous. 'What in the world is the Dung Egg?'

Kunal felt a sharp pain across his face. When he opened his eyes, he was back in his apartment. Adira stood above him. Had she just slapped him?

But Guru wasn't even done telling Snaitun's story. They hadn't explained why they were here, or why they were in the bodies of animals. And what the hell was the Dung Egg?

'Guru!' Kunal shouted, but Adira cut him short.

'We're out of time…' she said. Kunal wasn't the only one panicking.

Burfi had climbed up on the couch, growling with his teeth bared. He barked threateningly at the window. Guru flew up to look outside. A gaunt shadow fell on the owl's face.

Kunal hesitantly walked over to see what was happening. What he saw made him go pale. He could get answers to his questions later. Right now, he had other things to worry about.

The entire neighbourhood was crowded. With animals.

Stray cats. Dogs. Crows.

And they were all looking at him.

CHAPTER 4
A STORM OF STRAYS

KUNAL FEARED ANIMALS just as much as he feared unsolicited socialising. Seeing countless strays swarming outside his building sent shivers down his spine. Kunal wasn't sure if he'd rather socialise with a hundred wedding guests, or flee from a hundred stray animals.

They were waiting for the right moment to attack. Their silence was unsettling. Kunal longed for Mumbai's traffic and construction noises, even his neighbours' loud TV or their quarrels. But everything was deathly silent. The street lamps cast menacingly long shadows of the dogs and cats that crowded the street outside his building.

The horror of the situation had Kunal's adrenaline pumping, and not in a good way. He wasn't sure what he was supposed to say or do, and it was impossible to note any social cues from his furry companions (not that he was adept at human cues).

Gulping, Kunal tried to break the silence, 'How many are there?'

'I don't know,' Guru replied, 'We need to get away from here.'

Burfi barked, then licked his snout.

Kunal's mind wasn't ready to deal with this crisis. To be honest, no human in their right state of mind would be.

Panic was justifiable. But panicking was second nature to Kunal, which always made him wonder if he was just overreacting.

It didn't matter. They were running out of time. Restlessly, Kunal began looking for a solution. He just blurted out the first thing that he came up with, 'Maybe we can negotiate with them.' That was better than trying to fight them. Kunal didn't like the thought of hurting animals. Hell, even seeing Burfi being attacked by those stray cats was enough to turn his stomach.

'Negotiate?' Adira scoffed, 'There's no negotiating with Snaitun, boy.'

'There's always a negotiation,' Kunal defended, trying to hide the hurt in Adira's heartless dismissal, 'I'm sure we can offer him something. What does he want?'

'Burfi,' Adira said, pointing with her paw.

Of course, he wants Burfi. 'Why does he want Burfi? And why are you animals?'

Burfi woofed and sniffed at Adira's paw. His ears flopped, disappointed at the lack of treats in them. Kunal made a mental note to ask why he was a stupid animal while Guru and Adira were so intelligent.

'It's a long story…' Guru said, 'I wish I could tell you, but we really need to leave… Snaitun's animals have found us. It's only a matter of time before they break into this place.'

Kunal sighed and looked at Burfi, once again searching for scratches or marks. His fur was dirty, but there was nothing that suggested he was attacked. That had to mean something. Maybe he really was the chosen one? *Am I really buying this?*

Burfi growled, restlessly shifting his weight on his legs. Kunal was worried Burfi was done with his idiocy.

But then something slammed into the window, startling everyone. It was a fruit bat.

'Not bats again…' Kunal muttered.

Another bat slammed into the window. Kunal

flinched. Adira remained unmoved. The bat slid down, knocking the other bat as they both tumbled away.

Below, the security guard had stopped watching his movie. He was ineffectually trying to shoo the animals away with his *lathi*. A rickshaw had stopped nearby. The driver filmed the strays on his phone. More people had come to their windows, observing the unusual scene.

Kunal was too focused on the bat. If the animals had started attacking, they didn't have time anymore. In a panic, he screamed, 'We need to run!'

'I already said we shouldn't have come here. It was a stupid idea,' Adira snapped.

'I'm sorry!' Kunal yelled, 'But we need to leave!' he ran inside, trying to grab whatever he could to pack.

'What are you doing, Kunal?' Guru asked.

'Packing!' Kunal shouted, grabbing a bottle of water, some snacks, Burfi's water bowl, a Swiss knife and his phone's charger. He dumped everything into a bag. That's when he noticed his laptop, realising he hadn't logged back into work. It was still on. He probably had messages to reply to. Did he have the time?

Another bat kamikazed on Kunal's window. Kunal flinched again.

He ran back to the window. A larger crowd had gathered. What a night for his neighbours! First, they got to shame a tenant, now they might get to witness a potential slaughter. Some of the men from his building had come out with sticks and cricket bats, trying to shoo the animals away. Some made noises and clapped loudly. Nothing seemed to deter the animals.

Another bat slammed into the window.

'Put out all the lights!' Adira yelled, perching on the sofa.

'What?'

The bats still continued to slam against the windows. *Bats use echolocation...* 'The bats can track us anyway...' Kunal said, 'They can see in the dark!'

'Doesn't matter,' Guru said, 'They think the only way in is through that window.'

'Why?'

'Because they're dumb animals,' Adira said.

Another bat slammed into the window. The glass cracked slightly.

Adira continued, ignoring the crack, 'Snaitun is controlling them. Their only purpose is to catch us… to catch Burfi.'

This made just as much sense as talking animals. Kunal decided not to probe further. 'Fine!'

'The lights! We'll escape through the shadows…'

Right. Kunal rushed inside. Burfi followed him as he started switching off all the lights in his apartment. In a matter of seconds, the whole place went dark. Only the warm light of the street lamps spilt in from the outside. That, and his pulsing laptop indicator.

Cursing himself, Kunal rushed and opened the laptop. He saw a bunch of unread messages, but time wasn't on his side. He closed all his applications and shut down the laptop.

Another bat slammed into the window. The crack grew wider.

'Now what…?' Kunal shouted, putting his laptop back in its sleeve. He really needed to rethink his priorities.

'You live here!' Guru said, 'Do you have a secret exit by any chance?'

Secret exit? This was an old building in Mumbai. They didn't even have a fire exit.

Kunal strapped on the backpack.

Focus, Kunal. Kunal visualised a map of the building in his mind. He always took the front exit because those annoying kids would be playing near the back exit. Also, because the one time he had taken that route, the kids had thrown water balloons at him, which had made him really angry.

FOCUS! 'We can go through the back, where they park

the cars and jump off the compound wall.'

'Lead the way,' Guru ordered.

Kunal was surprised to see how quickly they trusted him. Moreover, he was surprised by how calmly he was behaving. Normal people probably felt like this all the time, minus the racing heart and rapid breathing.

'Kunal,' Guru said, landing on his shoulder, 'Please hurry.'

'Sorry…'

'This boy isn't right in the head,' Adira said, looking out of the window. The bats continued their kamikaze attacks. A sliver of the glass dislodged from the web of cracks.

The window wouldn't stay for too long. Kunal barely even thought of what Mr Tambe would say about the damage.

'NOW!' Adira screamed.

Kunal ran to the door and unlocked it, only to realise something. 'Wait…' He ran back inside and grabbed Burfi's leash. Burfi obediently knelt before him and let him buckle it in.

'Are you serious, boy!?' Adira hissed.

'I don't want to lose him, okay?' Kunal screamed at her. He turned to Burfi and said in an almost parental voice, 'Okay, let's go!'

Burfi wagged his tail. He looked genuinely excited to go for another walk.

If he's a human like me, why is he acting like a dog?

Another crack. More glass shards crashed onto the tiled floor. Crows cawed. Dogs howled. The night was full of ominous cries from the strays. The echoes of the wild drowned even the concerned mutterings of petty humans.

Kunal ran out. In the passage, some of his neighbours were discussing how the apocalypse had arrived. Given what he knew about Snaitun, that could be a probability.

Kunal embraced it. He didn't care if this was a nightmare or reality. It was less mentally exhausting to just go with it. Worst case scenario, he'd end up strapped to a hospital bed. Best case scenario, he'd end up with awards and applause for saving humanity.

You're not the chosen one, idiot. Your dog is.

Not a dog.

Kunal ignored his neighbours. Especially when they called out to him. He didn't have the patience to explain why he was running out of his apartment with a dog, a cat and an owl while there was a horde of other strays crowding the front of their building.

They reached the ground floor. Kunal turned right and led the animals to the back entrance, which opened into the building's compound.

The night was dim. It's never really dark in Mumbai.

Kunal would've preferred the dark. At least they could hide in the shadows.

Adira shouted, 'Why does your city have so much light?'

'I don't know!' Kunal shouted back.

'Where do we head to?' Guru asked urgently, 'We must make haste.'

Kunal nodded and stepped out into the open. He looked around to verify that no animals were spying on them. Surprisingly, Burfi didn't tug and pull. He walked calmly beside Kunal, occasionally looking up to make sure Kunal hadn't vanished.

This was the kind of attention and affection Kunal had longed for all his life. But, obviously, now that he had it, life had to throw a world-ending threat his way to balance it out.

Kunal nodded and walked to the edge of the compound. Beyond the compound was a disputed piece of abandoned land, fortified by a four-foot-tall concrete wall, above which they had erected a wire fence to prevent intruders from entering the building. Everybody knew that it was supposed to remain unused until the court's next order. What they didn't know was that some neighbourhood kids had managed to cut a makeshift opening in the fence and would occasionally sneak in to play cricket. Who could blame them? Building compounds weren't spacious enough and space in Mumbai was harder to find than mental peace. In fact, Kunal remembered how they had used that opening to escape after assaulting him with water balloons last Holi.

In the distance, he could hear screams. It sounded like the humans and animals had finally clashed.

They didn't have much time.

Kunal located the spot and helped Burfi through. Adira and Guru didn't need help to cross the fence. Kunal started crawling through awkwardly.

That's when he heard a wild growl. He turned and found three stray dogs running out of the back entrance. They looked just like Burfi, lean and arguably cute, with the minor difference of foaming mouths and murderous looks.

Of course, they'd find them just when Kunal was in an awkwardly susceptible position. He couldn't afford to get bitten or scratched by any of them. He didn't want a rabies shot.

Kunal scrambled through the fence, its metal wires scratching his jeans. He felt the metal scrape through his flesh.

The panic returned.

What if the metal's rusted? He didn't want a tetanus shot either. How many shots did he need? He had lost count, and that only made his fears worse.

Kunal fell face-first onto the ground. Just in time, because the stray dogs rammed into the metal fence. It'd only be a matter of moments before they found the opening.

Kunal clambered to his feet and ran. Burfi ran beside him, leash dragging between his legs. They were free. It felt glorious.

Kunal remembered the few moments of freedom from

his childhood when he ran like this in the open. Though this wasn't a clean or beautiful field, it was empty. It was easy to ignore the discarded *gutka* packets, given that strays were chasing them like predators.

Guru glided next to them, 'Shadows. Hide. We need to hide!'

Kunal swerved to the side. Burfi tripped and fell, wailing for help.

Kunal skidded to a stop. Burfi's leash had gotten stuck in something lodged in the ground. In the distance, he saw the stray dogs rip the wire fence apart.

Adira dashed forward, freeing Burfi's leash. Burfi ran straight to Kunal as the stray dogs pounced on Adira.

Indian pariahs are larger than cats. That should give them an advantage, especially when they outnumber one, but no. Cats can generally hold their own.

Besides, this was Adira. She pounced forward, claws drawn for maximum damage. She scratched the dog in front straight on the face. She lodged onto his head, biting and scratching with all fours. The dog shook itself free, whimpering but not submitting.

Adira dashed forward again, attacking the dogs. Her fighting style was a fusion of wild feline attacks and human-like martial arts. It was absurdly beautiful. Kunal couldn't take his eyes off her.

'What are you doing!?' Guru shouted, 'Adira can handle herself. We need to run!'

Howls and barks filled the ground. Another stray had found its way through the fence. This one was a huge grey dog with a red collar. Much larger than a regular Indian Pariah.

It looked like a security dog trained, well-fed, and bred for ferocity.

Kunal stared wide-eyed. There was no way Adira could hold her ground if that red-collared monstrosity joined in the fight.

Burfi had the exact same thought. Which was probably

why he darted forward barking at the grey dog.

The grey dog accepted the challenge.

Time slowed down for Kunal as the two mutts advanced towards each other like battle hounds ready for bloodshed. Razor-sharp fangs bared, claws out, hackles raised... Kunal's memory showed him a flash from his childhood. The one where the neighbour's kid had thrown a stone at a street dog, prompting the poor mutt to aggressively attack the kid.

His friends laughed as the dog chased the poor kid, but Kunal had been scared stiff.

Burfi and the grey dog clashed. Their fierce battle growls rumbled through the air.

'No!' Guru shouted, flying towards Burfi. 'Kunal, help me! We have to get Burfi away from here!'

HOW? Kunal looked around him. He couldn't fight with his fists. Hell, if he had a gun, he'd probably miss his target point blank.

Kunal spotted a discarded iron rod.

The grey dog grabbed Burfi by the neck and tossed him aside. Burfi squealed. Protective instinct wrung Kunal's gut. He needed to save his dog.

'KUNAL!' Guru shouted as they clawed at the grey dog's head, trying to bait him away from Burfi.

Burfi, unfortunately, hadn't gotten the memo. He regained his footing and snapped his jaw shut on the grey dog's tail.

The grey dog whimpered, returning his attention to Burfi.

'Kunal!' Guru shouted, gliding back towards the dogs, 'Help me!'

Without thinking further, Kunal grabbed the iron rod. Kunal always ran away from fights. For the first time in twenty-five years, he ran towards it.

Kunal looked on as his puppy—the one he'd known for less than five hours, but whom he was willing to sacrifice his life for—was in danger.

Kunal closed in. He raised the rod high up and screamed, 'SHOO! SHOO!'

He was the only individual in that barbaric battle not striking his enemy. Even his battle cry sounded pathetic.

But Kunal hated violence. Violence against animals was a whole different level of horror that made him furious. Which was why he couldn't bring himself to act beyond empty threats.

The animals probably recognised that because everyone ignored him. All around Kunal, animals fought for their lives. They attacked and defended with nails, flesh and blood.

'Hit him, Kunal!' Guru screamed just as they clawed at the dog's face.

'But—I don't want to hurt him!' Kunal cried.

Guru swung again. 'Just hit him!'

Kunal hesitated. Once. Twice.

The grey dog pounced on top of Burfi. Burfi squealed in fright.

'BURFI!' Kunal screamed. He had to save Burfi. Without thinking, he whacked the grey dog. Surprisingly, the rod struck him straight on its head.

The grey dog whimpered and fell to the ground. Burfi pushed him off and freed himself. He barked excitedly and growled at the grey dog lying still.

Burfi trotted up to Kunal. He was unscathed yet again. But Kunal was too occupied with the sight of the unconscious dog to care. His heart started racing again. A mild pain was building in his chest. 'Did I...' horror choked his voice. He couldn't even say it.

'Run!' Guru commanded.

Kunal looked at Adira, who had knocked out one dog and was fighting the other two.

At the fence, Kunal noticed birds gathering.

'We have to go. Now!' Guru slapped Kunal's face with their wings, bringing him back to the moment.

Kunal grabbed Burfi's leash and ran for his life. This

time, in the shadows.
'What about Adira?'
'She'll find us. She's a warrior.'
Not questioning further, Kunal fled the scene.

CHAPTER 5
LEVIATHAN SHAKES

BATS AND CROWS FLEW OVERHEAD, as did a police helicopter. Those were rare in Mumbai, at least in the localities where Kunal had grown up. The helicopter's blades rattled loudly enough to drown out Mumbai's traffic.

Kunal had led Guru and Burfi through a confusing maze of narrow back alleys and unlit slums, managing to exit on an empty corner road. His flight instinct was burning to the point that he kicked a rat and continued to run without a second thought.

But, now that Kunal had found a spot to sit and catch his breath, he found himself apologising to the unfortunate rodent, wherever it was. He hoped he hadn't caught the plague; he was wearing shoes, but his mind kept conjuring the feeling of the rat's dirty fur brushing against his exposed skin.

Kunal shoved that thought out of his head. There were more pressing matters at hand. He looked around his environment with suspicion. He sat on the pavement next to a broken bench, uncaring of the filth on the road. Parked cars and warm street lights were his only companions, not counting the animals. Despite the lights, the street felt darker than usual. Kunal reasoned that it could be because of the old residential buildings around them which didn't cast any light. Were the buildings ever occupied, or had they been abandoned? Both scenarios were unsettling to him. But it was only a temporary respite. They'd have to find a better place to hide. After some time, when he was certain that there was not a soul nearby, Kunal let out a sigh of relief.

Suddenly, Kunal felt conscious of his parched throat. His lungs were on fire. Hands trembling, insides roiling, Kunal hadn't felt like this in a long time.

He was having an actual panic attack.

No no no no no… not now… not now… why now!?

'Kunal?' Guru said, hopping over next to him.

'I can't do this…' Hyperventilating, he held his chest and tried to do the breathing exercises that his therapist had taught him.

Guru and Burfi both looked puzzled. Guru, at least. Burfi just stared with concern.

The breathing exercises worked just enough to calm Kunal down, but his insides blared alarms like an unstable nuclear reactor ready to explode. Worse, he wasn't even sure what the explosion would look like.

His mental to-do list flooded his mind. His skull felt like it was ready to cave. He held his head trying to hold everything in.

Four seconds inhale, seven hold, eight exhale.

I need to look for a new apartment…

Would Mr Tambe even allow him to retrieve his stuff? Was it a crime scene now?

My job… My laptop… Did I launch those creatives…?

Why was he thinking about work? There was a literal dark lord who had sent mind-controlled strays to capture him.

Did I kill that dog?

Of all the many voices screaming at him, that thought finally cracked the dam holding the flood of his anxieties.

'Kunal, boy, what are you doing?'

'I'm having a panic attack,' Kunal replied in a shaky voice. His eyes were beginning to well up.

'Something is attacking you?' Guru asked.

'Yes…' Kunal thought about it, 'No… my… I'm…'

'Is it something to do with your troubled mindscape?'

Kunal looked up, unable to hold back the tears.

Burfi barked, trying to scare away the enemy. But the enemy was Kunal's own mindscape.

The dark desolate plains of Kunal's mindscape resurrected emotional traumas from every conflicting event of his life, petrifying and shaking him simultaneously. The void in his mind made its presence felt, the darkness, the traumas… If only he could weaponise all of this to take on Snaitun.

Kunal continued, managing to form words from memory, 'I just… I have trouble… my mind constantly tells me there are threats around, making me nervous and jittery.' The thoughts were numbing his words, but he needed someone to listen. If only he were braver, stronger… maybe he would've been more of use. Why *did I have to be this pathetic?*

Kunal was a nobody. He had the wit and intelligence to participate in a roleplaying adventure but didn't have the mental and emotional strength to do the same when reality called for it.

Why me….? It took all his strength to hold back every emotional cramp his mind shot his way.

'What is bothering you, Kunal?' Guru asked.

'A lot of things…' Kunal blurted, eyes squeezed shut.

Burfi tried to calm him down by licking his hand. Kunal had the urge to wipe away the sticky saliva but was too occupied containing his breakdown. Another surge of anxiety rose up in his chest.

'Maybe I can help…' Guru suggested kindly.

Kunal clutched his hair, almost pulling it. As the pangs of pain passed, he whispered, 'How?'

'I… I'm a high mage. Only the most learned

individuals from our societies are invited to study as mages. Perhaps I can ease some of your sufferings.'

Kunal considered it. If he had agreed to adventure with a talking owl, what was the harm in opening up to them about his feelings?

Kunal remembered his first therapy session. He wondered what his therapist thought of him when he told her he didn't trust her. Not the best way to start a relationship, no matter how transactional it is. But, over time, he had learned to trust her and open up about his deepest issues. And while she hadn't resolved any of them for him, she had equipped him with enough coping techniques to deal with his issues in a significantly healthier way.

One of the biggest things he had learned in the past year was to trust strangers. Not blindly, of course; Kunal was still a sceptic. But his slightly more trusting attitude had gotten him a well-paying job, a loving girlfriend and an annoyingly nosy landlord. Two wins out of three, the odds were in his favour.

Kunal cleared his throat and wiped away the tears. Boys cry. Even men cry. But Kunal had grown up believing otherwise and still found it hard to shatter that belief.

Kunal began grounding himself. The road, the dirty pavement with blades of grass growing next to it, he began placing each element around him until he was back to reality. His mindscape had retreated to the back of his head again, far enough to be harmless. Kunal then focused on the light under which they sat, the warm yellow light, strangely cold and uncaring, just like the past hour.

Some time passed. The slowly pain faded, leaving Kunal's chest feeling empty and light.

He wiped his face and looked at his companions. Guru and Burfi were still next to him, Burfi resting his head on Kunal's feet.

'I'm here if you need me,' Guru said. Normally, those orange saucer eyes would've freaked Kunal out, but what he saw in them was unfiltered kindness.

Kunal knew in his heart that he could trust Guru. So, he said, 'I don't know where to start. But right now, I'm worried I killed that dog.'

Burfi whimpered, lifting his head. Kunal pet him, which seemed to calm them both down.

'No,' Guru shook their feathery head, 'You just knocked it out.'

'I was violent. That's not me.' Kunal said, holding back memories of animal cruelty. No, Kunal wasn't the one being cruel. But he might as well have been with his inaction. That poor turtle in the park's pond, that puppy with the broken leg... Kunal hit the brakes on that train of thought. It would only make him sag deeper.

Guru nodded, orange eyes piercing Kunal's soul. They finally said, 'You're a noble who's never had to face the real world. Correct?'

Kunal bit his lip. 'I'm not rich... but I have a lot of privilege compared to a lot of people out there.' Kunal became aware of the slums they had crossed to get here. The shantytown was empty and quiet, but who knew what its inhabitants had to deal with every day? Before his mind could spiral into a series of what-ifs of life in the slums, he reined it in.

Guru was still looking at him. Burfi had curled up on the ground, head once again resting on Kunal's feet. His warmth made Kunal feel nice. He didn't even mind the slobber.

Kunal's mind was still a flurry of thoughts. 'I'm not a warrior. I'm not a hero. I always choose the path of least resistance. Least conflict.' Was he even worthy of being on this adventure? He paused to sigh. 'I just want to be left alone. No conflicts, no problems. Just an ordinary, peaceful life.'

'But that's impossible,' Guru said, 'No matter how

peaceful you want your life to be, it isn't entirely up to you.' Guru flapped their wings, landing on Kunal's thigh. 'I once knew a hermit who lived on an island, away from all civilisation. He lived a peaceful twenty years secluded in his paradise.' Guru paused, then asked, 'Can you guess what happened to him?'

Kunal wasn't in the mood to guess. Normally, he would've said something funny to seem more likeable or racked his brains to find the right answer. But, right then, he simply shook his head, although he knew what the answer might have been.

'Snaitun learned of the hermit's paradise. He invaded that small island, upturning every single grain of sand hoping to find some buried treasure or forgotten lore.' Guru shook their head, 'A life of peace, ended violently because someone else chose it.'

The lesson was clear. 'You're saying I can live peacefully, but I must learn to fight when life demands it?'

'Fight, or flee,' Guru said, 'You can't avoid them forever. Given that the very fabric of reality depends on us, we might be compelled to commit violent acts occasionally.' Guru raised their wing and gently brushed Kunal's face. 'I wish we could have parted ways, but Snaitun knows about you. He will find you, one way or another.'

Kunal cursed his luck. Rarely did his worst-case scenarios come true. But the one time it did, it had to be the absolute worst. Kunal sighed.

Burfi sighed too. Kunal looked at Burfi, remembering that the fate of the universe depended on this adorable little dog.

'I can't believe he's the chosen one...' Kunal said. He reached out for the baby-pink backpack next to him and flinched.

Adira was perched on top of it.

'When did you get here?' Kunal asked, clutching his chest and hoping his heart didn't explode.

Adira shrugged, her tail swaying behind her. 'When you were crying.' She turned to Guru, 'You really want this boy to come with us? He cries like a baby.'

Guru hopped over to Adira, 'He has a mental affliction... be nice.'

'I told you he's not right in the head.'

'I can hear you, you know,' Kunal said. He normally didn't confront people, but he also normally didn't have mind-controlled animals chasing him on the orders of an extra-dimensional dark lord either.

'Sorry...' Adira said, crossing her forelegs a little too humanly, 'Are you going to cry?'

Kunal wanted to punch her but resisted the urge. 'I hate you,' he said and stuck his tongue out.

Adira cringed. 'Very mature.'

Guru stepped between them with their wings spread wide. 'Enough!'

Burfi barked too, nudging at Kunal's hand. He grumbled and whined, trying to tell Kunal something.

'What is it, boy?'

Burfi continued to grumble.

Kunal pulled the pink backpack close and pulled out some treats. Burfi's tail wagged rapidly. He'd have swallowed the plastic packet if Kunal hadn't been quick enough. Kunal looked inside and was surprised that he had managed to pack Burfi's feeding bowl too.

He poured some food into the bowl and watched Burfi gobble it up in seconds. After he was done, Kunal poured some water into it.

Only after Burfi was done did Kunal quench his own thirst. He guessed this was what it meant to be a parent. He couldn't believe it took him this little time to make Burfi an important part of his life.

He's going to leave... don't get too attached.

'Can I have some water too?' Guru asked.

'Of course,' Kunal said, pouring water into the bowl.

He saw Adira waiting for them. She was too proud to

ask.

After Guru was done, Kunal simply pushed the bowl closer to her and poured the last of their water into it.

She looked at him and nodded thanks before drinking.

Once everyone was done, Kunal put everything back into the backpack.

'We need to go,' Guru said, 'It's only a matter of time before they find us again.'

'Should we start looking for the Dung Egg?' Adira suggested, licking her paw.

Burfi barked, as if in agreement. His tail wagged excitedly.

Did he even understand what was happening? Why was he acting like that? And what the hell was the Dung Egg?

Kunal was about to ask, when his phone suddenly started ringing. Smartphones had penetrated human lives so deeply that Kunal hadn't even realised when he had his phone in his pocket this entire time.

He pulled it out. The screen read: *'Mom Calling'*.

Another bout of anxiety assaulted his heart. He wasn't sure if he had the mental energy to deal with her.

Then, an idea clicked.

*

Aisha wanted to hide away from everyone.

Not because she felt insignificant or unworthy of being there amongst the country's finest scientific minds, no. It was because of that insufferable General Shah.

Aisha believed in peace and harmony; she also believed that General Shah was the kind of person who deserved to be slapped across the face with a sledgehammer. Imagine one of those old uncles in societies who complain about the kids playing in the compound, who refuse to return cricket balls when they accidentally enter their homes, the very antisocial kind of geriatric who reminisce about the good old days of patriarchy and casteism. Now add a military uniform decorated with medals and pins, and that's General Shah.

'Why is he in charge?' Aisha asked under her breath. She wasn't one to hold her tongue, which made working with General Shah a nightmare.

'Because,' Abbu replied, matching her whisper, 'this could devolve into a matter of national security.'

'It's just a relic...'

'... of unknown origin,' Abbu said, helping her put on the protective suit. 'With radioactivity, unlike anything we've seen before. Do I really need to spell this out for you?'

Aisha had been airlifted to this secure facility outside of Mumbai. When they arrived at this location, she was disappointed upon seeing a gated community with the desi-western hybrid name of Shri Tranquillity. She was mesmerised by the sprawling lush residential complex that would probably only be affordable to the richest of Indian society. Then she was led into a mediocre-looking conference room to be briefed about her assignment.

It was then that she was made aware of Abbu's deep involvement with RAW and their secret projects.

An hour in the air, almost two hours of security clearance, complete isolation from the outside and now so many precautions, just to see the relic—if this wasn't an alien artefact, Aisha would be really upset. Either way, she couldn't wait to tell Kunal about all this. She didn't mind breaking some rules.

Thinking about Kunal and that rescued dog made her feel a little better. The whole facility was as cold as a politician's soul and just as apathetic. Even Abbu had been too occupied with his work to even greet her properly.

Maybe that's why Abbu had taken the onus of briefing her and getting her ready for the observation himself. He handed over her helmet and instructed her on how the comms worked, including commands and responses.

Aisha put on the massive helmet and switched on the comms. 'Am I audible?'

Abbu just showed her a thumbs-up.

Aisha wasn't a fan of helmets. They made her feel a little claustrophobic. Although the faceplate was huge enough to give her a good view, it still felt like a cage. The more precautions she had to take, the more convinced she was that India had finally made some form of contact with aliens. That, or it had found an ancient weapon of mass destruction.

'Come on now. Don't waste our time!' General Shah barked over comms.

Aisha wanted to yell back, 'Can you not rush me? This is bloody stressful already!' Instead, she just said, 'I'm on it. Please be patient.'

Abbu blinked, then said over comms, *'You need to click on the channel before you say anything. He didn't hear a word you said.'*

Aisha held back a groan and clicked on the channel with Abbu. 'Copy that.'

'What's taking so long!?'

'Is he always this annoying!?' Aisha asked Abbu.

Abbu nodded forlornly, *'Through there...'* he gestured. *'You'll have one lab assistant in there to guide you.'*

Aisha nodded and walked through the door into another cleaning draft of air before stepping into the laboratory.

Aisha wondered if the builders of Shri Tranquillity had run out of budget by the time they came inside the facility because the inside had zero aesthetic value. To their credit, though, Shri Tranquillity's interiors did have a 100 per cent functionality.

The laboratory wasn't clinically white as was a staple to sci-fi shows in the West; this was just an empty room painted ivory with cheap-looking tiles. For a room so basic in its build, the equipment was impressively advanced and looked appropriately out of place. There was just one massive glass box in the middle with handling gloves. All around it, there was monitoring equipment with dangling wires that connected to screens on the walls and then proceeded outside.

The first thing Aisha noticed when entering the lab was the smell. Foul like faeces, it smelled like Mumbai on a bad day. Aisha had to stop herself from gagging. The lab assistant—wearing a similar protective suit as Aisha—guided her towards the glass box and explained how to use the equipment. The closer she got to the box, the sharper the stench grew. *It's okay. You can do this!*

Aisha felt sweat on her forehead. This was more stressful than any other job she had undertaken in the past year. Slowly, she put her hands into the black gloves. The assistant adjusted the eyepiece and put it on Aisha's face. *Is this a VR headset?*

Through the eyepiece, she could see inside the box. The visual was focused on the subject, a brownish rock. Looking at the relic through the headset with readings on the screen made her feel like she was playing a hyper-realistic video game.

Aisha slowly and gently grabbed the relic and began rotating it in her gloved hands. It was about the size of a coffee mug, weighing about the same if it were ceramic.

Is this a fossilised egg? It sure smelled like rotting eggs, though its shape was more of an oblong sphere. The texture of its shell was rough as if it were covered in dirt. Was it covered in dirt, or was it made of dirt? For a brief moment, Aisha's mind made her think of faeces and her stomach turned.

Focus, Aisha.

Aisha noticed a uniform slit on the top of the thing, making her wonder if this were an ancient piggybank. It was possible, except that the slit didn't seem hollow. And, by the weight and feel of it, neither did the relic feel hollow.

Though the shape was undoubtedly egg-like, the surface didn't exactly look fossilised. There were strange patterns on the grainy surface that didn't look like anything Aisha had seen before. She remembered reading 'unidentified script' in one of the reports, thinking that was probably it.

Oh my god... is this an alien egg?

Now she was really sweating. What if it decided to hatch at that moment? What if this was an alien parasite? *No. Focus.*

Shoving back memories of popular films, Aisha studied the relic, running through every test she remembered. Sometime in the middle of her observation, the egg pulsated. A faintly orange-red glow made Aisha almost drop the egg.

The egg-like shape. The pulsing radiation glows. It had to be other-worldly. Her gut told her it was alien.

When the pulsating stopped, she continued with her tests. Luckily, it didn't glow again. Finally, she returned the relic to its stand, pulled out her hands and breathed a sigh of relief, having secured some distance between herself and the egg.

Aisha said over comms, 'If this is an egg, you need a palaeontologist. I'm an archaeologist.'

'Brilliant!' General Shah exclaimed sardonically.

'Aisha, please come to the observation room,' Abbu ordered.

Aisha acknowledged the message and walked out. On her way, she thanked the lab assistant, knowing full well that such courtesies were probably non-existent under General Shah's regime.

As she entered the room, she heard General Shah's revolting voice. He was screaming, 'A bloody waste of time! This is your expert, Raza?'

Abbu—Aisha always found this fascinating—wasn't like a stereotypical scientist; he spent a healthy amount of time in the gym, enough to intimidate men younger and sturdier than him. He was even bulkier and taller than General Shah; he could easily knock the old man out with one punch.

However, Abbu preferred not to get physical. He just screamed back, 'You rushed me!' Abbu spotted Aisha and gestured towards her, 'And I trust my daughter. Just like your father-in-law trusted you.'

'Bah!' General Shah threw up his arms.

Aisha had guessed that General Shah's high rank wasn't entirely merit-based. The confirmation only made her more furious. Why did she have to answer to an incompetent twat like him?

The observation room had only General Shah, his assistant, Abbu, two more scientists and Aisha.

Abbu asked, 'Your report?'

'I don't think this is from any Indian civilisation. There are no discernible marks or patterns. I... the thing was glowing.'

Abbu nodded. General Shah grumbled and gestured for her to continue.

Abbu claimed he found the object lying on the ground near his regular office building, the spot where he would smoke. The unusual nature of the object, coupled with the highly unusual nature of its radiation, had prompted him to flag it. How that single flag led to them in the secret facility was a story Aisha would dig out of Abbu another time.

Right now, it was important to know what the object even was. She finished giving her report, which in short was, 'I don't know what that thing is.' It was just a preliminary observation. Of course, she'd need to run some more tests to be sure. 'If you could give me some time...'

'Time!?' General Shah snapped, 'That bloody thing has pulsed radiation a few times already! God knows what's happening that's making it do that! I have ZERO

ANSWERS, Raza. ZERO!'

Aisha looked at the glass wall separating them from the lab. The egg was there, and the stench. The root of this crisis.

Whenever Aisha had to figure something out, she thought of the problem as a puzzle. The moment her mind perceived something as a game, it became easier. In this case, observing everything through a microscope wasn't giving them the right answers. Maybe it was time to look at the bigger picture.

And the most obvious question popped into her mind, 'What time did it pulse?'

'Shut up, girl!'

Aisha clenched her fist. She wanted to slap the man so hard. But she knew it was better to stay silent. She grabbed Abbu's arm and looked at his watch. 'The egg pulsed when I was there, at roughly 22:12. What other times did the thing pulse? If we can match the pulses with any other event around the world, we can…'

Abbu crossed his arms, looking annoyed. Aisha stopped speaking. Was she wrong? Abbu turned to General Shah, pointed at Aisha and barked, 'THAT'S EXACTLY WHAT I SUGGESTED, YOU OLD FART!'

General Shah muttered a curse under his breath, then said, 'I know that. I sent out the orders, and guess what we found? NOTHING!' He crossed his arms and added, 'I know I'm a difficult man, but I trust my associates. Especially when they've proven their mettle.'

Speechless, Abbu muttered under his breath. He had always been an openly communicative father, which had made adjusting to society a little tough for Aisha. Like General Shah, most Indian men didn't bother to voice their thoughts or intentions clearly.

General Shah, at that moment, reminded Aisha of a particular species of social being in Indian society – the male patriarch who made innumerable sacrifices to give their family a happy life, but in making those sacrifices they'd neglect their families, have a highly toxic relationship with them, making them resent the patriarch and invalidate the sacrifices in the first place. Why couldn't life be easier?

No, don't be like that. He's probably had a difficult life. You don't have to stoop down to his level. Aisha almost felt sympathetic towards the General.

That's when he barked, 'Get this little girl out of here. Bloody waste of time.'

Aisha's sympathy died; she wished General Shah would too. *Calm down.*

An assistant knocked on the door and let herself in. 'General Shah, you asked me to inform you if something came up in the readings.' She had a laptop in her hand.

'Finally! What is it?'

'Radiation spike.'

'Where?'

'Andheri, Mumbai.'

Aisha felt a pit in her stomach. *That's where Kunal lives...*

Abbu had a vindicated expression, contrary to General Shah's worry. General Shah asked, 'Anything in the news?'

The assistant turned her laptop around and showed them an online news article. 'Yes...'

CHAPTER 6
THE BLAME ITSELF

KUNAL SAW HIS PARENT'S CAR approaching the bus stop half an hour later. It was a decade-old Maruti 800 that even the manufacturer had discontinued a few years back. Despite the regular maintenance costs, his father refused to sell it. It was the first car he'd bought with his own money. Its on-road price was nothing compared to its sentimental value, but when talking to others, Dad's excuses alternated between the price of modern cars and the quality of their make.

Adira stood up and assumed a defensive pose. Guru and Burfi too looked at the car in the distance. Kunal gulped, feeling his parents' presence so close by. He hadn't seen them in over two months, which, in a desi household, is criminally long.

Kunal almost started up. Expectedly, all his reasons for moving out of his parents' home started flooding his mind. He had spent the past hour convincing himself that this was the right thing to do, but now that he spotted them, he froze. He didn't want to deal with his parents, didn't want to dig up unresolved issues. But they didn't have enough time. Snaitun's strays were still looking for them.

Kunal started up. He took a deep breath to ready himself, then said, 'That's them.'

Burfi rose to his feet, wagging his tail, excited for no reason.

'Those are your parents, yes?' Guru asked.

Kunal nodded, wiping away sweat from his forehead. He wasn't scared of his parents, so much as he was of his reaction to their ramblings and complaints.

'Why do you seem unhappy?' Guru prodded.

'Because he's not right in the head,' Adira said.

Kunal looked at the white shorthair and said threateningly, 'If you want to live to see the dawn, you'll keep your feline mouth shut.'

Adira smirked. Was she enjoying this?

'Kunal!' Guru gasped, surprised at Kunal's reaction. 'Is this more of your…?' Guru hesitated, then pointed to their owl head with their wing.

Adira scoffed. Kunal held back the urge to kick her. Given her size, he was sure he'd be able to throw her off by a few feet at least.

Then he remembered that she was a warrior. *She'll probably still beat me up.*

'Kunal?' Guru called.

Burfi sniffed at Kunal's hand, gently licking it. Kunal looked at his beady eyes, his golden-brown fur almost glowing under the street lamp. The white spots were dirty, but no wounds. Kunal pet him and felt the warmth of Burfi's affection slowly melt away his anxieties.

'I just…' Kunal started scratching Burfi's ears, remembering Guru's question. 'I don't get along with my parents. I left their home so I could become a better person. I don't call or text as often as I used to before, which is good for me. But, in doing that, I know I'm hurting them.'

'Is leaving your parent's home not common here?' Guru asked.

Kunal shook his head, 'Children… boys… never grow up. And parents don't accept it even if they do grow up.'

'That's…'

'Messed up?'

Guru frowned, feathers shifting. 'No. It's incredibly sad. An entire nation full of immature old men.'

'Run by them too.'

Adira scowled in disgust. 'I hate old people. Especially the ones who cling onto the past as if everything were better then...' she shook her head, 'I don't want to bicker.'

Kunal smiled at her. 'I can understand. I...' his phone buzzed with a message.

Mom:
We are here.

Kunal took another deep breath and led the way. Actually, Burfi led the way, dragging Kunal behind him.

Mom got out of the car as they approached. Burfi, seeing a new person to play with, started running.

Mom whelped and locked herself back in the car.

'Burfi! No!' Kunal scolded, 'No! Down, boy!'

Burfi looked up at him, then shook himself and sat down obediently. Guru and Adira marvelled at how obedient Burfi was being.

This is really the chosen one...

Mom lowered her window, 'Is he going to bite?'

'No, he just wants to sniff you.'

Burfi jumped up to the window, craning his neck to get a better view. Although Mom seemed frightened, she tried to pet him. Another hand reached out and started playing with Burfi's ears.

'Kunal,' Dad nodded.

'Dad,' Kunal nodded.

'Why do you have a pink backpack?'

Kunal clenched his teeth, feeling his cheeks redden. He had forgotten about the backpack entirely. As if Dad didn't judge him enough. Ignoring his question, Kunal pointed to Burfi, 'This is Burfi.'

'Hi, Burfi...' Mom said awkwardly.

Dad didn't talk to the dog. But he had a smile on his face. A genuine smile that rarely graced other people with its presence.

Kunal opened the back door and gestured for Adira and Guru to enter.

'Oi! What is that!' Dad shouted.

Burfi dropped down from the window. Dad got out of the car, proceeding to clap his hands and shoo the owl and cat away.

'Wait! They're my friends!'

'Friends!?' Dad repeated with suspicion and shock. There was also disappointment, but that was perpetual at this point in his life.

'I meant pets!' Kunal corrected, suddenly realising that they were making noise.

Even Dad became aware of the silent night. His anxieties also kicked in. He whispered, 'What are you doing with all these animals?'

Mom asked quietly and sincerely, 'Are you on drugs?'

Kunal looked at his soiled clothes, his beat-up self, covered in dirt and blood, the animals he was with—he might as well have been.

Kunal shook his head, 'No. I'm just… can we drive? I'll explain on the way.'

'I'm not letting the animals in!' Dad declared. The whispering weakened it.

Kunal ignored him and turned to Mom and did something he was utterly ashamed of. Something he hadn't done in a very long time, but something that was a proven strategy working every single time.

Kunal pouted like a puppy dog.

Burfi kept his head out of the window, tongue and ears flapping in the breeze. Kunal had seen a million videos of dogs looking outside car windows, but none of them matched the splendour of the real thing. He wished he could've done the same, lived a carefree life like Burfi.

He's the chosen one. He's supposed to kill Snaitun and save our world.

Kunal didn't hesitate to imagine fighting any dark lord who tried to harm Burfi. In the few hours that Burfi had come into his life, he'd quickly gone from being afraid of dogs to literally being ready to die for this dog. It was low-key concerning how quickly Burfi had made a place in Kunal's heart. Even Aisha hadn't fallen for Kunal this quickly (he guessed).

He checked his phone and the twenty-five unread messages in Aisha's chat. Single ticks, meaning she hadn't even received the messages. Had she at least seen the news? Maybe then she'd think of calling him.

At least Kunal's parents had seen the news. To their alarm, they immediately recognised Kunal's apartment building. Luckily, Kunal had answered his phone on the very first attempt.

Kunal lied to his parents that he had left his building even before the stray animal hordes had attacked it. Unwise, since Mom recognised the claw marks on Kunal's arms and clothes. As he kept defending that lie, the backburners of his mind were trying to cook up an explanation about the animals he had.

'And why are you with these three? Are you fostering them?' Mom asked, not giving him enough time.

Dad added, 'Did the animals attack your building because of…' he pointed to the animals sitting around Kunal.

He was right, but Kunal couldn't tell them that. It was a huge miracle that they were able to evade the strays. So, he lied, 'No, of course not!'

Dad shook his head, 'I don't believe you. There's something very bad happening in Mumbai. Strays are going wild. Some people are predicting it might be an enemy testing some kind of mind control device. I think that makes sense.'

Kunal pursed his lips. Although the source of that

information was a fake news outlet—fake news had sadly been the most common form of news reporting in the past decade—they weren't entirely wrong this time. 'That sounds probable.'

'Kunal,' Guru called, 'You have to tell them.'

Kunal looked at them and gently jerked his head up to sign, *What?*

Adira growled and ripped the string around her neck. She grabbed it with her paw and handed it over to Kunal.

'Give it to your mother,' Guru instructed.

Kunal looked from Adira to Guru, then to Burfi. Burfi was too mesmerised by the moving outside world to care. There was a blissful daze in his beady eyes.

Kunal sighed and took the fish pendant. 'Mom, can you please wear this?'

Mom turned to look at him. 'What is that?'

'Just trust me,' Kunal pushed his hand forward.

'But…'

'Mom, please,' he insisted, more firmly this time.

Mom took the pendant and began tying it around her hand. Kunal waited, looking at the empty roads. Where was the traffic when he needed it? They'd reach his parents' apartment sooner than he'd like.

'Now what?' Mom asked.

'Please don't freak out,' Kunal said, 'Guru…'

'Hello, ma'am,' Guru said.

Mom freaked out. Not just that, she screamed until even Burfi turned his head inside to inspect the commotion.

'Ma'am… please…'

'AAAARGH!!'

'What is the matter!?' Dad shouted, not slowing down the car.

'The owl is talking!'

'The owl is hooting!' Dad yelled, annoyed.

'Kunal?' Guru asked, at a loss for words.

Kunal sighed, 'Dad, can you stop the car for a bit?'

Dad obliged. He parked it next to a bus stand. Luckily, there were no pedestrians or beggars around who'd come to bother them. Even the shops lining that road had their shutters down.

Dad turned the engine off, then turned to look at Kunal. 'What in god's name is happening?'

Mom was clawing at the pendant, but Kunal had tied it a little too tightly.

'Dad,' Kunal removed his own pendant and gave it to him, 'Please wear this.'

'No! Don't!' Mom shouted, 'It's black magic.' Typical Mom.

Guru hooted, and Kunal realised he couldn't understand them. *Wow.*

'Dad, trust me.'

Dad puffed his cheeks, then tied the pendant.

Guru hooted. Dad's expression turned gaunt. He repeated, this time in an exasperated low tone, 'What the f—?' he held his tongue, not wanting to curse in front of his son.

Guru hooted again. They continued to make noises, inviting further panicked reactions from his parents.

Seeing how his parents reacted to the owl's hoots, Kunal was able to make sense of his own anxieties. He had already identified it in therapy, but seeing it in practice after so long was fascinating to say the least.

Mom and Dad asked questions, and the owl hooted in response. Essentially, his parents seemed to have the same conversation with Guru as Kunal had earlier. Even their behaviour and reactions were eerily similar to Kunal's own.

Finally, Dad undid the pendant and handed it over to Kunal. 'This is ridiculous!'

'I know…' Kunal proceeded to tie it around his hand. He should've just done this earlier.

'We're going to Igatpuri,' Dad announced, starting the car. 'Your dark lord will be searching for you in Mumbai.

Better to add distance between us.'

Mom gave Kunal her hand, 'Can you take this off, please?'

Kunal proceeded to untie the pendant. 'What happened?'

Mom had tears in her eyes. 'So, the stray attack *was* your fault!'

'My fault!?' Kunal asked, surprised, 'How is it my fault?'

'If you hadn't adopted that damn dog, the strays would've left you alone.'

Mom's inability to accept the raw truth had always stunned Kunal. But to blame him?

'Mom…' the pendant came off.

'Five people ended up in the hospital. A lot more got bitten and clawed! Even you got hurt! Do you know how many injections you're going to need to take!?'

Kunal felt paralysed. Why did she have to mention injections? 'Mom… it is what it is…'

Adira jumped up to Kunal, offering her neck. He began tying the pendant around it.

'This is all your fault! God is punishing you. When did you last go to the temple? At least, you could've kept a small photo of Ganpati in your apartment!'

Not this again… Kunal ignored his thoughts, focusing on tying the pendant.

'You have forgotten our culture, Kunal. Our heritage! Our identity…'

Finally, the pendant was tied, and Kunal had nothing to do. Nothing to distract him.

His parent's flurry of blames didn't stop. Kunal didn't have any patience left in him. He had lost all his tolerance for them years ago when he started picking fights unreasonably. And just as he had done countless times before, he shouted, 'SHUT UP! JUST SHUT UP! Either help me when I ask for help or say no!'

'We should've never let you leave the house,' Dad

grumbled, 'Alcohol we can tolerate. Maybe even *Ganja*. But black magic?'

Kunal looked to Guru, 'What did you tell them?'

'Everything.'

'That *Shaitan* is after your damn dog!' Mom shouted, wiping tears. 'After us, now!'

Burfi barked, happy to be a part of the conversation. Kunal scratched his neck to calm down.

'His name is Snaitun,' Kunal said, 'And, like it or not, I'm a part of this mess.' It took effort not to curse in front of them. He felt his heart rate rise, but it wasn't the bad kind. He was excited. He decided to stand up to his parents, not yell at them. For once, he wanted to reason with them. Like the few rare moments in his life, he was speaking his mind. 'I'm scared, but I have to do this. I *choose* to do this. You can help me, or let me do this on my own.'

'Let you choose death over safety?' Mom asked sarcastically.

Kunal took in a deep breath. *I'm not letting them win.* 'Mom, Dad, throughout my life, I kept blaming you two for ruining my childhood.' Mom stiffened. 'But that's wrong. You two had no idea what you were doing. And here you are, blaming me for making bad decisions when your own life decisions haven't been the best. You're the reason I need therapy, why I was in—' he held his tongue, 'I don't care what you think. I know what I'm doing.'

Surprisingly, they didn't retort.

'I love you guys, and I'm done blaming you. And I hope you can find it in your hearts to stop blaming me. I'm an adult now, so stop treating me like a kid.' He leaned forward, his head between the two of them, 'Please, trust me.'

Mom was still weeping, but she ruffled his hair. Dad just grunted in agreement. He started the car and began driving.

That was their peculiar way of supporting him. He

accepted it.

Once he leaned back, he felt an emptiness in his chest.

No, not emptiness. It was quietude. Peace. He'd finally done it.

He had faced many problems growing up, and a single burst of confidence and frank speech wouldn't come close to resolving them.

But it was a start. And he was happy.

He couldn't wait to tell his therapist.

Igatpuri was a three-hour drive, and he was exhausted after everything that had happened. He wondered what would happen to his laptop and apartment. He had spent a lot of money building that independent life of his.

Kunal should have been anxious about his stuff. But, at that late hour, after everything he had been through, he found it hard to care. All he wanted to do was rest.

The world sped by quickly. No traffic, barely any cars on the road, this was the Mumbai he preferred. Quiet, peaceful, yet strangely alive. His eyes grew tired looking at the running roads.

Burfi yawned widely and rested his furry head on Kunal's lap. Within a few heartbeats, he was dozing soundly, his breath warm against Kunal's leg.

Kunal smiled, fighting the urge to pet Burfi. He didn't want to wake him up. *Sleep tight, Burfi. I'll protect you.*

Mom took out a neck pillow from the glove box and handed it to Kunal.

Kunal nodded. 'Thanks.' He put it around his neck and leaned back. Sleep came rather easily to him. In his dreams, he dreamt of Aisha. He dreamt of a picnic somewhere in the mountains. Aisha and him sitting on a picnic table because Kunal hated sitting on the ground. In front of them was a large spread of fruits, meats and other delicious-looking food. In front of the picnic table was a large sheet that projected one of Kunal's favourite movies.

It was a good dream. Kunal's mind drifted into a comfortable daze, granting him some much-needed rest.

*

About two streets away from Kunal's apartment building stood an abandoned bungalow from the British era. The owner of the bungalow had died without making his will, leaving his nine children to fight among themselves for prime real estate in a major part of Mumbai. Those nine children spent their entire lives suing each other. Some died without seeing the final verdict of the case, others depended on their progenies to continue the fight.

Mr Tambe was well aware of the property dispute; one of his closest friends was one of thirty-four grandchildren who were currently embroiled in a legal battle for its possession. As a child, Mr Tambe would often break into the bungalow's dilapidated garden with his friend, mostly for the thrill. As an adult, he was wholeheartedly jealous of his friend for even having a chance at owning such a place. Mr Tambe couldn't afford the down payment for this bungalow even if he sold both his apartments.

Mr Tambe's childhood escapades flashed before his eyes along with the rest of his life as he recognised where he was. He just wasn't sure how he had ended up here. His memory was a little hazy. He'd never admit it to anyone, but he had been feeling a mid-life crisis scratching at his mind for a while now. Maybe this was another symptom of ageing.

Mr Tambe remembered arguing with his stupid tenant Kunal. How dare he bring a filthy street dog into Mr Tambe's sacred apartment? Irresponsible boy with no understanding of how the world worked! Dogs, cats, animals didn't belong in homes. It was a problem with his whole generation.

Mr Tambe remembered threatening to evict him. He had even called his lawyer to check if Kunal's actions violated their rent agreement in any way. And then he was attacked by the street dogs. Dogs, cats, even filthy rats. It had looked like a scene from a horror movie, the kind that Mr Tambe avoided.

He claimed they were boring, but really he was just scared.

Maybe Kunal was behind this abduction. After all, he was the only person Mr Tambe knew who would mingle with these filthy street dogs. He was half convinced that Kunal had drugged him and brought him here. It had to be the boy.

That boy represented everything that was wrong with the younger generation.

Kunal, you filthy animal!

Mr Tambe heard a sound. From under a cupboard covered by dirty white bedsheets, a rat scurried forward sniffing at the air. A dozen more followed behind him.

Mr Tambe froze.

The rats gathered in a stretched square of moonlight beaming in from the dusty windows. As Mr Tambe's eyes followed the beam of light, he saw a pair of golden eyes staring straight at him.

It walked into the light to reveal its feline form and let out a menacing meow that clawed at Mr Tambe's heart. Another joined in. And another, and another, until the room reverberated with haunting mewls.

Mr Tambe's innards turned. He felt lighter than before. Then he felt dampness in his pants. A full-grown man forced to relieve himself out of fright, the world was being unjust to him.

Panduranga! Why is this happening to me? I've never even hurt a fly. Why me?

Mr Tambe cursed Kunal. Wished the worst upon that boy for doing this to him. He swore unto the gods that he would ruin that boy's life if he were set free.

Then some dogs started growling. They stepped into the room as well. Darkly lit, the room and its horrors surrounded Mr Tambe. These weren't shadows of cats and dogs and rats; these were rakshasas. Demons from hell summoned up by some black magic ritual.

Panduranga... protect me...

Above, bats fluttered in place. Crows even. As if all of Mumbai's stray animals had gathered in that room to discuss the end of humanity.

Mr Tambe was outnumbered, countless to one. Even with his hands-free, it would've been impossible to fight through them all.

Panduranga... protect me...

No matter how brave a man was, he was bound to surrender when faced with the power of raw nature. After all, man was powered by human will, but nature—even animals—was blessed by the gods themselves.

At that moment, Mr Tambe was made to face one of his worst traits. He had never liked animals. Dogs, cats, didn't matter. As a kid, even as an adult, he had thrown stones at stray dogs. Only his wife knew this, but he had even run over a dog in his native place. He hadn't even considered slowing down and checking up on the animal.

Who cared about animals anyway?

The gods... Mr Tambe realised to his horror. This wasn't Kunal's evil doing. He wasn't at fault here. Mr Tambe's immoral actions towards animals had brought bad karma upon him.

At that moment, Mr Tambe blamed himself for his poor judgement.

Panduranga... forgive me...

That realisation was his cue to let it go. This was the end. The world was a cruel place and it had chosen this night for him to die. He wept and whimpered like a damsel in distress, chanting hymns to protect his soul. He wondered if the gods would save him at all.

The animals and birds continued to look at him with dazed eyes. Every single wild gaze in that room was fixed on him. Those red rakshas eyes glowed ominously, stabbing his very soul, making him feel like a baby at the mercy of a pack of wolves.

Panduranga… forgive me…

And he wept. Louder. Wetter.

Panduranga… please forgive me…

How had the strays even managed to bind him and drag him all the way here?

'*Who is this man…?*'

That voice didn't belong to this world. That voice didn't come from this world. It thundered inside Mr Tambe's head. Mr Tambe began chanting out loud, 'Panduranga… Panduranga… Panduranga…'

The animals made their noise and filled the dark room with nightmarish cries.

'*Is that so…*'

The nightmare continued until the animals suddenly fell silent.

Only Mr Tambe's chants echoed, 'Panduranga… Panduranga… Panduranga…'

He paused, conscious of the dead silence. This was it. His time had come.

A presence made itself felt. The moment Mr Tambe was aware of it, he felt empty and drained. His mind felt like it had just finished studying for the board exams for seventy-two hours nonstop. His body went cold and he wanted to run as far away from there as possible.

'*You know where Burfi is…?*'

'Burfi?'

'*Speak, you pathetic man!*'

Was this the king of the rakshasas? Why was he asking about burfis?

'*SPEAK!*'

'What do you want!?' Mr Tambe screeched. 'Please, I don't know anything,

'*Where is Burfi?*'

Thinking on his feet, Mr Tambe replied, 'My cousin owns a sweetshop. I'll get you all the burfis you want. Even the expensive ones with the dry fruits!'

'*YOU DARE JEST?*'

'S-sorry, my lord, p-please forgive this insignificant s-soul... I-I d-don't understand what you w-want...' he stammered.

In response, the animals began creating their ruckus. The cats drew their claws. The dogs readied themselves to pounce on him. The rats were already at Mr Tambe's feet, debating on which part to nibble on first.

'They smell Burfi on you. Where is Burfi?'

'What... who is Burfi?'

The rakshas appeared before him. Under normal circumstances, Mr Tambe wouldn't have looked twice. But right there, surrounded by bloodthirsty stray animals, every single movement contributed to his fear of getting mauled to death.

'Panduranga... Panduranga... Panduranga...'

'You will answer me. Or you will die.'

And with that, the animals pounced on him. The panic knocked Mr Tambe out. Unfortunately, for him, even his unconscious mindscape was filled with nightmares.

*

Mom woke Kunal up when they arrived at their Igatpuri farmhouse. It was a few hundred metres away from the NH 160, but you could see it in the distance if you looked past the under-construction resorts and homestays that corporations had erected around these lands with the hopes of attracting tourists. Kunal hated the fact that even so far away from Mumbai, construction still obstructed his view.

Kunal's parents' farmhouse was a cosy single-storey bungalow with a moderate-sized front and backyard. Such spacious accommodations were rare in Mumbai, which is why they had to come so far out. The building was faded blue, its yards unkempt and barren owing to a lack of care. His parents had invested in this place a few years back. It was meant to be their vacation home, but

Mom and Dad never had the time to visit. The neighbouring bungalows all looked just as abandoned. Probably their owners didn't have the time either.

Kunal had asked for the keys to the house a few months back. He had wanted to spend a romantic weekend here with Aisha. Unfortunately, he made the mistake of expressly telling his mother that, permanently making it impossible for him to get the keys without *adult* supervision.

Kunal led the animals to the first-floor bedroom. He had picked this room the first time they came here because it was the only one where you could see the sunset in all its glory.

When he entered the room, he expected nostalgia to assault him. What hit him instead was the dust. The room had been unoccupied for years. Even the blue paint on the wall was fading. He opened the window overlooking the main road that connected to the NH 160. Cars and trucks still drove past at this late hour. Above, the sky was bursting with stars.

Once settled in, Kunal fed the animals whatever pet food his parents had bought on the way. He took a quick shower and cleaned his wounds. Luckily, none of the cuts were too deep, and the shower made him feel fresher than ever before.

After he was done, he sat on his bed and munched on a cold takeaway burger, realising he had skipped dinner that night. He began craving a nice cup of lavender mint hot chocolate; it was his comfort food in times of crisis. He had all the ingredients back in his apartment, provided Mr Tambe hadn't emptied the place already.

Kunal wondered what was even happening back home. Or with his office. He hadn't informed anyone and wasn't sure what he should even tell anyone at this point.

Where was Aisha?

He tried her number, but her phone was switched off. Was she still working on her secret project?

Trying to distract himself, he looked at Burfi eating his food happily. As his tongue lapped, he noticed the fish pendant again.

'Guru?'

'Hmmm?'

'Is Burfi's pendant broken?'

Burfi looked up at Kunal, curious to see why his name was mentioned. He didn't stop chewing though.

'Unfortunately, yes.' Guru replied, 'But it doesn't matter. Burfi wouldn't have spoken to us anyway.'

'Why not?'

Guru and Adira exchanged looks.

'Kunal, there's something you should know about Burfi.' Guru said. They shook and flapped their wings, fidgeting around while finding a way to reveal something.

Kunal would've normally grown restless at such moments. However, he had learned to be patient that night. Exhaustion does that to folks.

'Kunal, I'm over a hundred years old,' Guru said, then pointed with their wing to Adira and added, 'Adira is about thirty.'

'Twenty-eight,' Adira hissed.

Kunal chuckled. Guess women being sensitive about their ages was common across all dimensions and species. *Wait, is that sexist?*

'Burfi, however, is just two years old.'

That information didn't land as easily as he would have expected. But when it registered, Kunal exclaimed, 'He's a baby!'

'Yes.'

Burfi barked and stuck out his tongue, almost beaming. He looked at Kunal with his innocent affectionate eyes. *That makes so much sense...*

'But it should work in our favour,' Guru said, 'This dog's body is much more agile and dextrous than Burfi's original baby body. This gives him a fighting chance against Snaitun.'

Kunal nodded. 'Is Burfi going to remain a dog forever?'

'Let's hope there aren't any long-lasting effects,' Guru said without much confidence.

Kunal sighed and plopped back onto his bed. 'You were telling me about Snaitun earlier. Why is he trying to invade our world?' He paused, then asked the more important question, 'Why are you guys in animal bodies?'

'It's a long story,' Guru said.

'I'm too roiled up to sleep tonight.' And he'd slept in the car as well.

'Well, I'm taking a nap,' Adira said, curling up on the pillow in Kunal's bed. She declared, 'We leave at the break of dawn.'

Kunal nodded.

'She was there through it all,' Guru said, 'She doesn't need to hear it again.'

Adira purred in response. Burfi hopped onto the bed and curled up next to Adira. Adira didn't seem to mind. Almost immediately, the two started snoring.

'You don't want to rest, Guru?'

'I'm okay,' Guru said, then asked, 'You want to know the story of Snaitun?'

'Yes.'

'So listen...'

CHAPTER 7
THE COLOUR OF TRAGIC

Not so very long ago, in a reality that's both right next to this one yet impossibly far away, a baby was born in a poor farmer's home. This would be the first and the only baby that the farmer would father. Unfortunately, the farmer wouldn't even have the luxury of being present to hold his only son because he had been summoned by his king to join the war.

The baby grew up without the shadow of a father, no man to look up to for guidance. Despite everything, his mother raised him to hold his head up with pride. After all, honour and pride were the only things those poor folk could cherish in those days.

He was small, powerless and alone. But he was happy. As happy as a baby could be.

The baby grew up to become a healthy boy. Living in a war-torn kingdom, his only solace was the local temple where he would devoutly pray to appease the gods. He never forgot to thank his absent father for granting him life and never forgot to ask the gods to protect his father and help him find his way back home.

The war that stole the boy's father ended, but his father didn't return. All that came back was a letter thanking the family for their sacrifice and a sack of coins that would feed them for a month.

The other families in their village raised their voices, demanding more for their losses, but the king who sat on the throne didn't bother to respond. A few years later, he was dethroned by a foreign king.

This new king worshipped different gods from a different land.

A month into this new regime, the temple gathered the villagers to speak of their concerns. The new religion with its strange gods was seen as a threat to their way of life.

What had been peaceful assemblies to discuss their welfare slowly degraded into hateful conferences of fear and loathing. The boy attended all of these, becoming a sharp student of hate early on in his life.

He hadn't realised it yet, but he had started to forget what happiness actually meant. As much as the wars and losses had affected his mind, the hate speeches of his elders had corrupted it beyond redemption.

As he grew older, he watched his family wither away from lack of care. Only the king was able to provide aid, and the temple had rejected any and all help from this invader. *How could they accept help from a sinful king? What if their souls were tainted, never to enter heaven for being touched by foreign gods?*

The more injustice he saw around him, the more hateful he became.

The boy's mother died when he was twelve. With no direction and no family, he chose the life of a pilgrim and began travelling the kingdom. He saw how widely the foreign invaders had established their stronghold over his motherland. He also discovered that priests and religious warriors of his own faith had been secretly training to wage a holy war against the invaders.

The boy's hatred already had a target in these foreigners. Now it had become his mission to stop them for good.

To dethrone them.

To destroy them.

To erase their very existence.

From a sharp student to an able warrior, the boy rose to the higher ranks to fight in this holy war. He trained under veteran soldiers all day, and wise magicians all night. By the time they waged war, he had already gained prominence in their holy army.

A white flag with a pink flower was their symbol, and that symbol painted the whole kingdom red. The boy had started out as a mere foot soldier. By the time they had reclaimed half the kingdom, he was a man. A general and a mage, he became the only living man to hold both titles.

The people loved him. They found him charming. They accepted him. Looked up to him. He was just like them, a commoner, a farmer, who had fought his way up the ranks. Even the gods seemed to have blessed him with skills, making him the perfect leader of and for the people.

All this led the leaders of holy warriors to appoint him as the face of their cause. Where most mages were expected to shed their identities, they decided he should retain his.

This was the first time in his life that he had received so much love and affection. But, more importantly, this was the first time in his life that he felt powerful.

It was intoxicating. He wanted more.

Within a matter of years, he dethroned his superiors, becoming the sole leader of the cause. With the support of the masses and the might of the holy warriors, he rid the land of the invaders. He would bring back the golden age of the past when foreigners and strange religions didn't plague their lands.

But, in truth, it was no longer about justice or doing the right thing for him. It didn't matter what he told the people.

For him, it was all about power. It was all about feeling bigger.

The entire kingdom celebrated his victory over the enemy. They saw this moment of history as their liberation. What they failed to see was that the man's holy and righteous cause was fuelled by hate and loathing.

And if anyone knows anything about humanity, hate and loathing bring only more hate and loathing.

The man—now the crowned king—had no cause to fight for. He had no experience in ruling a kingdom and, naturally, the kingdom suffered. The only thing he knew was to rile people up for more war.

And so, he did.

From being the invaded to becoming invader, he rapidly ravaged the rest of the world. He united the world but under the mighty fist of tyranny. From king, he became a god emperor.

But now there was no one else left to conquer. No enemy, no cause.

Now that the wars were over, the people started turning their attention towards their own lives. This was a golden age for them, but a dark hour for the god emperor.

With nowhere else to go, the god-emperor looked beyond his world. He employed magicians to scout enemies for him.

Unfortunately, they found the perfect enemies.

The Dung Dimension.

With no rhyme or reason, the god-emperor prepared his armies to wage war against the Dung Dimension. What he wasn't prepared for was the might of these extra-dimensional enemies. Their magic was superior to his.

All their efforts went into basic defence and survival. With his world withering away, the god-emperor decided it didn't matter whether his world survived or not. All he wanted was to feel more powerful.

The god-emperor started dabbling in black magic. Where before he only tapped into nature's potential, he now attempted to gain power from the celestial beings themselves.

After much prayer and pleading, the god-emperor managed to gain an audience with one of the gods of the Dung Dimension.

The Dung Master.

They found in him a worthy warrior. His blind hunger for power was unlike anything they had seen before. They offered him a boon of unlimited power, but to gain it, he would have to sacrifice his world.

The god-emperor would have readily sacrificed billions for more power. But there was a catch. That billion would have to start with his own flesh and blood—his son.

The god-emperor hesitated. He was so close to gaining more power. Finally, his intoxication triumphed over everything; he commanded the infant prince to be brought before him.

Unfortunately, for him, he had this audience with the Dung Master before his trusted council. His council had stood by him at every milestone. But, at this crucial juncture, the high mage challenged him. They questioned his motives and his sanity. And as the high mage voiced their accusations, the council too showed their true colours.

They had decided to betray the god-emperor.

What started as a heated debate ended up in a clash of magic and might. One god-emperor against twelve of the world's strongest warriors and sharpest mages.

Their confrontation lasted a full night. The night sky was illuminated with the sparks of magical attacks. By the time the sun peeked from the horizon, the traitor council was reduced to just two members. The god-emperor still held his ground, ready to take on a whole battalion by himself.

In a desperate attempt, the high mage summoned the Dung Master. The soldiers had managed to draw just a few drops of the god-emperor's blood. The high mage offered that blood to the Dung Master in exchange for a boon.

They asked for the Dung Master to give them an even ground for battle. They asked for the Dung Master to send them somewhere where they weren't so overpowered by the god-emperor.

After a complicated bout of bargaining, the Dung Master accepted the high mage's proposition, on the condition that the Dung Master would set up the pieces to make a game out of it.

The Dung Master sent the god-emperor and the last surviving members of the traitor council into a distant dimension.

When the remainder of the traitor council awoke, they found themselves in the bodies of stray animals. Why? Because the Dung Master found it amusing. The fate of two worlds and more rested on the entertainment of an eldritch god.

Without any options, they agreed to this ridiculous situation. At least here, they stood a fighting chance. They had all their memories, but none of their magical or physical prowess. Not yet, at least.

A single foreign thought had inexplicably entered their minds. The Dung Egg.

What it was, why they had to find it, they didn't know. All they knew was that they had to do it before the god-emperor.

Boon or curse, the traitor council wouldn't be able to return to their homeland as long as the god-emperor lived. The same was true for him as well.

*

As Guru finished narrating the whole story, Kunal felt goosebumps all over his hands. Kunal's mindscape dissolved the shadows that danced to Guru's descriptions. Slowly, they returned to the real world.

A million questions stormed his mind, and he gathered himself to ask them all.

Guru obliged without complaint.

'Firstly,' Kunal cleared his throat, 'Are you the high mage?'

'Yes,' Guru said.

'And Snaitun is the god-emperor.'

'Correct again.'

'Adira's...'

'...a berserker,' Guru said, 'The only other survivor of our council.'

Kunal nodded, 'And... Snaitun isn't the only evil we're fighting. There's also the Dung Master...?'

Guru's feathers slumped more. 'I didn't want to bring them up, but since we had time, I thought I'd paint the full picture.' They looked outside the window at the quiet night. Who knew how long that peace would last? Probably not for long. They added, 'If we can stop Snaitun, your world doesn't have to ever face the Dung Master. But if we fail...'

'The Dung Master will be the *real* danger. Yes?'

Guru nodded.

Kunal sighed and clutched his knees tightly. The situation was much more complicated than he had imagined. And all of this depended on Burfi?

Kunal pointed to the string with the fish pendant around his hand, 'What about this? Whom does this belong to?'

Guru shuffled in place, avoiding Kunal's gaze. They finally replied, 'When we awoke, Snaitun had already located us. He couldn't use any magic yet, but he could attack us. In the scuffle, Adira managed to snatch his pendant away from him.'

Kunal's eyes threatened to bulge out of his head. He immediately thought of the worst. *Don't tell me it belongs to Snaitun.*

'It belonged to Snaitun.'

The pendant suddenly became too heavy to hold. Kunal clawed at it, trying to untie it. 'You gave me Snaitun's pendant! What if he's spying on us? What if…'

'No,' Guru said, 'The pendant is the Dung Master's doing. Snaitun can't use it to do his bidding. It's an aid for us, not a weapon against us.'

Kunal ripped the pendant off and threw it on the floor. 'Why wouldn't you tell me the truth?'

Guru hooted in response.

God damnit! Kunal picked up the pendant again and tied it around his wrist.

Guru waited patiently before replying, 'We didn't want to worry you. If you knew it belonged to Snaitun, you might not have agreed to wear it.'

'That's fair,' Kunal replied, looking at the pendant. The pendant that belonged to Snaitun. Kunal gulped, letting that settle in. After some time, he asked, 'You said Burfi's the chosen one?'

'In a manner of speaking, yes…' Guru said, again sounding cryptic, 'He's the key to this.'

Kunal's mind had already connected most of the dots. He hesitated before saying, 'You mean Snaitun's blood is the key…?'

Guru paused, a reluctant shadow on the face. Finally, they asked, 'So, you understand?'

'You were transported here using Snaitun's blood. That means the Dung Master's magic works on blood, and you'll need Snaitun's blood again. But the blood doesn't have to come from Snaitun himself, does it?'

Once again, Guru nodded. 'The journey to this world was Snaitun's blood. The journey back…'

Kunal looked at Burfi and said, 'has to be his son's.'

CHAPTER 8
THE PIGEON AT THE END OF THE LANE

MR TAMBE AWOKE with his drool pooling beneath his face. He spat and got up, trying to wipe the grogginess from his eyes. He felt intoxicated, but couldn't remember drinking. He remembered dreaming about a luxurious apartment in Colaba. His dream home. His mindscape.

Then, he remembered everything.

Mr Tambe scrambled to his feet and stood up straight. The room was exactly as he remembered it. The darkness painted everything with non-existence, save for the dull moonlight beaming in from the dusty windows. But something was very different this time.

There were no animals around.

You will answer me. Or you will die.

The rakshas' voice echoed in Mr Tambe's mind. Flashes of horror returned to him. He could once again feel the rats' little feet crawling over him, the rabid dogs barking and snarling at him, their hairy warm bodies pinning him down as the rakshas pried into his mind.

Mr Tambe was no stranger to violence. Mr Tambe had seen his share of bloodshed and torture—on TV. But this... this was something else.

Mr Tambe thought back to his childhood, the time he had gotten lost in the woods outside his native home. He had managed to find a small temple of Panduranga and slept next to it. Panduranga had protected him then.

And now, his Panduranga had protected him again. The animals were nowhere to be seen. Mr Tambe joined his hands and prayed to his Panduranga. Prayed to Rukmini, to Ganpati, and all the gods he could think of at that moment. He was a good man and they had seen it.

Thank you, Panduranga.

Now it was a chance to prove it. *I need to get out of here. I need to stop this rakshas.*

Reluctantly, Mr Tambe began pacing the room. He checked the corners, and looked outside the windows, finding them all empty. There were spiders and cockroaches, maybe even ants, but no dogs or cats. No feral beasts controlled by that rakshas.

Good.

Mr Tambe braced himself, picked up a loose PVC pipe he found in a corner and wielded it like a sword. If any animal came near him, he'd whack it unconscious. He slowly reached the door and pulled it open. The abandoned bungalow was menacing enough, but without the horde of strays occupying it, it felt fairly homely.

If only he had the money to afford such a house!

Mr Tambe stepped into the hall. It was a little brighter, given it had so many large windows. In the centre of the hall, he spotted three stray dogs napping on the floor. Those were the only three he could see. Maybe there were more hiding behind the sofa, or in some other room. He didn't want to stir any trouble, but you can't make an omelette without breaking a few eggs.

Mr Tambe's stomach grumbled. He hadn't eaten dinner yet. He remembered an *anda pav* stall that was usually set up near this bungalow post-midnight. He checked to ensure his wallet was still in his pocket. He saw the main door was open too. He could escape.

One of the dogs stirred, its pointy ear flicking twice as it stretched and changed positions. Mr Tambe defensively raised his PVC pipe, but the dog continued to sleep soundly.

You can do this. Mr Tambe decided to make a run for it. *Panduranga, protect me!*

One… two… three!

Mr Tambe ran.

In his panic, he stepped on his own foot.

Mr Tambe fell. Face first, nose crunching on the tiled floor.

The loud thud woke the dogs, and they began barking like mad animals.

Growling, Mr Tambe swung the PVC pipe and scrambled to his feet.

The dogs all started up, barking wildly. Mr Tambe cursed and took a threatening step forward. He swung the PVC pipe at them.

The dogs flinched.

Mr Tambe saw their eyes. They weren't in a trance like before. They weren't under the rakshas' control anymore.

Thank you, Panduranga…

Mr Tambe felt his confidence return, and with it returned his stupid courage. He dashed forward, making loud noises and swinging the rod around.

That was more than enough to frighten those stupid dogs. He slapped the PVC pipe on the floor, and smacked it on the sofa and cupboard, uncaring of the damage it had caused. The loud noise alone was enough to make the dogs scamper into the other room.

His coast was clear. Mr Tambe ran out of the main door, breathing in the cool fresh air outside. He had never felt this free and relieved before.

His stomach growled again, and he instinctively walked towards the *anda pav* stall.

Food first. Revenge against the rakshas later.

*

Kunal watched Burfi sleep, his mind still digesting his backstory. First, he had to accept that the dog he was fostering was the chosen one from another dimension. Then he was made aware that the dog was really a two-year-old baby. Now this baby had turned out to be the offspring of the dark lord?

Yeah, that checked out.

He just wished he had read more fantasy books so he could anticipate the next approaching conflict.

Maybe I should call Aisha?

He pulled out his phone and was about to hit the call button when he saw the time—03:28.

It was past midnight. Aisha was probably asleep. So, he drafted a text for her.

Kunal:
Hey, text me when you get this. I need to talk about Burfi.

Kunal hit send before even proofreading it. *What am I doing?*

He read the text twice. Then added:

Kunal:
The dog's name is Burfi.
We're all safe, don't worry.

He reread the new texts thrice.

Would Aisha even freak out? Kunal knew he would if he got a text like that. Aisha was nothing like him, thankfully.

Still only single ticks. Where was Aisha?

'Kunal!' Mom barged into the room. Horror plastered her face.

'What's happening?' Kunal asked starting up. Adira

woke up too. Burfi stirred, but continued to sleep.

Mom showed Kunal her phone, where a news article had Kunal's face as the featured image. The headline read: *Stray Animals Attack Andheri Building. 14 Injured, 1 Missing. Sources Blame Unemployed Tenant.*

'What the hell!' Kunal exclaimed, 'I'm not unemployed!' He heard that immediately after blurting it, wondering what was wrong with him.

'You need to leave,' Mom said.

Just then, Kunal's phone started buzzing. It flashed *Mr Tambe Landlord.*

Suddenly, Kunal felt out of breath. His mind struggled to decide if Mr Tambe was calling because he was suing him for property damage, or calling him to get his location so he could send his goons to kidnap Kunal and teach him a lesson

'What are you doing?' Mom snapped, 'Don't answer the phone. He might be working with the cops.'

Kunal hadn't even thought of that. After all the insults he had hurled at Mr Tambe, he had probably filed a case against Kunal. With the fate of the world depending on them, he couldn't afford to waste time on bureaucracy.

Kunal panicked and tried to disconnect the call. In his panic, he accidentally answered the phone. *Curse me!*

'Hello... Kunal beta?'

Kunal went blank. What should he do? Just disconnect? Or talk and throw him off course?

'Hello! KUNAL!?' Mr Tambe shouted.

Instinctively, Kunal replied with, 'H-hello? Mr Tambe?'

'Beta, are you... kay?' Mr Tambe's voice sounded choppy.

'Y-yes, Mr Tambe. Why are you calling?'

'Beta, the animals...'

Kunal's heart skipped a beat. Mom leaned in to listen. Adira and Guru were looking at him. Burfi was stirring in his sleep, his little legs running. He was dreaming. Kunal felt like recording a video of the pup but remembered he was on call. Also, he was in the middle of a world-ending crisis, but the call was the more immediate threat. He shook his head to focus and replied, 'What about the animals?'

'They're... looking for you. They kidnapped me and... are now looking for you.'

'Kidnapped!?'

'Don't go to your parents' house. They know where they live.'

Kunal felt a pit in his stomach. They were coming? *Snaitun is coming...*

'I don't know how to explain, but their leader is a rakshas. A real rakshas...' Mr Tambe sounded like he was eating something. *'I'm sorry for everything, beta. I didn't mean to... hurt you or say those bad things...'*

'Mr Tambe, where are you right now?'

'Right now? I'm eating anda pav. *I missed dinner because...'* he paused to swallow, then continued, *'They held me captive in this old bungalow. He... he entered my mind, beta. I don't know how, but he used black magic to enter my mind, and he trapped me there and tortured me. It was a beautiful sea-facing apartment, but he wrecked it while torturing me.'* His voice turned sombre. *'We have to stop that rakshas.'*

Kunal cleared his throat. 'Why are you calling me?'

Mr Tambe sniffled, then said, *'To warn you, beta. I don't know what mess you've gotten yourself into, but no one deserves to be treated like that. Not even good people like me.'*

'Mr Tambe...'

'Just stay away from your parents' house, okay?' he cleared his throat, his broken voice becoming firm, *'I'll talk to my cousin. He has connections. We'll find this rakshas and get rid of him before noon.'*

Kunal clenched his teeth, wondering what a regular landlord from Mumbai could do in this case. Then he asked, 'Mr Tambe, you're not with the police are you?'

'Police? No, beta, *the police are useless. This is a matter we have to handle ourselves. Okay? I'll go to the temple after this, need*

to cleanse myself of that rakshas.'

'Uh... isn't it a sin to go to the temple after eating non-veg?'

Mr Tambe swallowed. *'You're right, absolutely right. I'll take a shower first. I'll call you later, okay? Bye,* beta.*'*

'Mr Tambe, one last thing...' Kunal hesitated before asking, 'When did Sna... when did the animals kidnap you?'

Mr Tambe thought about it. *'About two–three hours ago. But then they knocked me out again. I only woke up ten minutes ago.'*

Two–three hours. That was enough time for Snaitun to go to his parents' apartment, identify Kunal wasn't there, find another hapless soul who could direct him to this Igatpuri farmhouse, and set out for here.

Goddamnit... 'Thanks, Mr Tambe. I have to go. Take care.' He disconnected the call and ran to his backpack.

'Kunal, what happened?' Mom asked. Guru and Adira glared for answers.

Burfi was stretching awake, eyes groggy. Kunal would give anything to be as ignorant and naïve as this pup.

'We have to leave,' Kunal said panicking, 'But we can't just keep running about. We have to find a way to solve this once and for all.'

'We solve this by killing Snaitun,' Adira said matter-of-factly.

'And how do you plan on doing that?' Kunal asked, 'You've already fought him and lost, right?'

Adira sulked, then growled. 'He's invincible! I didn't expect that. Damn Dung Mas...' she paused, turning to Guru, 'I mean...'

'I told him about the Dung Master.'

'Great! Damn Dung Master!' Adira shouted, shaking her paw.

But Kunal was more focused on what Adira said earlier. 'Back up! Did you say Snaitun is invincible?'

Adira nodded.

'Like Burfi?'

Adira opened her mouth, then turned to Guru.

'Yes, we made that connection already,' Guru said, 'But he's just a puppy now. There's no…'

'Burfi, up!'

Burfi stood up.

Kunal thought about it, then knelt and gave him his hand, 'Paw.' Burfi placed his paw in Kunal's hand and shook it. 'Sit!' Burfi sat. He turned to the others, 'He listens to me.'

'Making him sit isn't the same as making him attack,' Adira said.

Kunal frowned and looked around the room. He spotted an old pillow. Pointing at it, he commanded, 'Burfi! Attack!'

Burfi blinked at Kunal, then dashed forward, chomping down on the pillow and shaking it violently.

Vindicated, Kunal turned to Adira.

Adira crossed her paws, 'And you think you can stand your ground against Snaitun? You ran away from mere cats!'

'But—'

'Adira,' Guru cut in, 'Kunal might be on to something. If Burfi listens to him, we can use that. We just… we need to figure out how.'

Kunal nodded, 'Thank you!'

Adira scowled. She didn't seem happy about including Kunal, but she nodded. 'Okay, how do we proceed?'

Guru looked at Kunal. Kunal felt powerful, knowing at least one of them had confidence in him. And that one happened to be a high mage. He cleared his throat and said, 'We start looking for the Dung Egg. If we're going to defeat Snaitun, we need a plan! We can't just react to everything that comes our way. We need to make a move ourselves. And the only thing I can think of right now is the Dung Egg.'

Guru nodded. 'Me too. Except, there's one small problem… we don't know what we should do with the

Dung Egg. Even if we find it, we'll need time to figure out a solution.'

'Curse the Dung Master!' Adira said, 'I hate whatever game they're playing.'

Kunal frowned, thinking of the puzzle games that he had on his phone. Half of the puzzles didn't even explicitly give out clues. However, everything they needed was on the screen. 'So, Dung Egg... fish pendants... Snaitun... You three...' Kunal replayed the events of the day in his mind. 'And Burfi too is invulnerable, and so is Snaitun. But you two?' He didn't have to ask. He could already see the wounds on Adira's body.

'I'm lucky I haven't been mortally wounded,' she said.

'Right... And why is Snaitun after you guys? Isn't he looking for the Dung Egg?'

Adira shook her head, 'My guess is that he wants to get rid of us. Once we're out of the way, no one can stop Snaitun.'

Kunal nodded. 'That, or he needs Burfi to find the Egg.' *Of course!* 'Burfi's a dog! He can sniff and find the egg! Right?'

Adira shrugged.

Kunal felt hopeful for the first time since meeting these animals. He just needed time to figure this out. He loved solving puzzles.

I just wish I were as good as Aisha. 'We need to find Aisha!' Kunal exclaimed.

Burfi started barking excitedly. Guru flew up to him, trying to calm him down.

'Who?' Adira asked.

'The girl who found Burfi!' Kunal said, 'She's...' he paused, feeling himself blush. 'She's my girlfriend, and she's an expert archaeologist. She's also the best at solving these kinds of puzzles. I bet she can figure this out.'

'Great!' Adira said, looking hopeful and responsive for the first time, 'Where is this... Aisha?'

Kunal frowned. 'I don't know. But if we wait, I'm sure

she'll return my calls.' He had already sent her a hundred messages asking for her to call back.

Kunal checked his phone again. Still only single ticks.

'KUNAL!'

Everyone jumped.

'KUNAL!' It was Mom.

Kunal ran to the door, 'What happened?'

Mom showed him her phone. Another article: *Strays Attack Another Building, This Time In Goregaon. Ransack Only One Apartment*

'They got to your house...' Kunal said, 'Mr Tambe...' He turned to the animals, 'We need to leave.'

'Take the car,' Dad said, standing in the passage outside his door. 'The cops are probably going to be here any minute.'

As if they were waiting for his cue, police sirens announced themselves in the distance. They probably had a window of a few minutes.

Kunal didn't think twice. He grabbed the keys, thanked Dad with a nod and ran down the stairs. Kunal hated doing things without extensive planning. In this case, he didn't have a choice. It was like playing a video game without any walkthrough or hidden treasures guide.

He'd just have to wing it.

Kunal ran out of the main door and hurriedly got the animals inside the car. He dumped the backpack into the back and sat in the driver's seat.

Kunal stole a glance at Mom and Dad standing at the main door. Finally, he shoved the key into the ignition and started the car. One try, then a second. At the third, the engine revved to life.

Kunal looked at his parents and waved goodbye.

Mom, teary-eyed, waved back.

Dad nodded and said, 'Don't trash the car.'

Kunal didn't know how to respond. He simply reversed the car.

Now, Kunal was a terrible driver. To be very fair, Dad

was 100 per cent right in not trusting him. Because, as he reversed, he crashed straight into a tree.

Kunal fumbled with the gear shift as Dad advanced to him shouting. The police sirens weren't that distant anymore.

Kunal quickly shoved the stick into first gear. He slammed the accelerator and the Maruti 800 screeched out. The side of the car scraped against the open gate, but Kunal didn't have time to worry about Dad's reaction. He just drove straight into the road and kept his foot pressed down for maximum speed.

In the rear-view mirror, he saw some cars with lights approaching his parents' farmhouse. He had to keep driving. He couldn't let the cops catch up to him.

But the cars stopped at the bungalow. None of them were following him. And he was speeding forward as fast as the Maruti 800 would allow.

'WHOOOOO!!!' Kunal screamed out in excitement. He hadn't felt this wild in ages. For once, he understood why characters in movies felt alive when they did something rebellious and stupid.

This isn't a movie, idiot!

Flashes of jail made him lift his foot slowly. The car stopped accelerating.

'Are we safe?' Guru asked.

'I don't know...' Kunal lied. Of course, they weren't safe. Now the entire police force, maybe even the military would be after them. 'But it doesn't matter. We need to find the Dung Egg, and we can't do it with the police or anyone else interfering.'

'Why?' Guru asked, 'Are they not trustworthy?'

Kunal tried to explain himself as best he could, 'The Indian army and the Indian police force are actually great at their jobs. Which is exactly why we need to avoid them. If they catch us, they'll spend way too much time questioning us, giving Snaitun enough time to—'

'Fine,' Adira cut in, 'Where are we headed?'

Kunal refused to answer. Moments passed.

'You don't know, do you?' Adira asked angrily.

He did not. Kunal refused to admit it.

'You're taking the lead on this hunt for the Dung Egg, and you don't even have a plan! At least discuss it with us!' Adira yelled at him.

'I'm trying!' Kunal yelled back. 'I haven't had the time to strategise, okay? We've been on the run ever since you two assaulted me!'

'Assaulted?' Adira jumped up on the dashboard, 'I saved you!'

'GET OFF!' Kunal cut, swiping the white shorthair away so he could keep looking at the road, 'Don't ever do that! We could've crashed!'

The road before him was empty. Even the street lamps weren't on, the car's headlights were their only source of light. The road suddenly switched to a dirt road, making the car rumble and shake. The sudden change made Kunal hit the brakes in a panic.

The car skidded to a halt, throwing the animals off their feet. Adira and Guru bumped onto the windscreen. Burfi, who was sprawled in the back knocked into Kunal's seat. Kunal luckily had his seatbelt on. He only felt a sharp pain in his abdomen where the seatbelt prevented him from flying out.

'Sorry...' Kunal said. He turned the key and the engine revved back to life. The lights came on, illuminating a figure at the edge of the light.

A tiny, silver figure with glowing red eyes. Kunal felt those eyes puncture his soul.

Kunal shook his head, shoving all negative thoughts into the back. He couldn't afford to freeze now.

Kunal gripped the steering wheel tightly. Ignoring Adira's complaints, Kunal hit the accelerator. The car shot forward.

The figure before them flapped away in a panic.

'God, I hate pigeons,' Kunal complained, relieved that

he hadn't hurt an innocent animal or bird. He would never admit it, but if there were one animal he could push into extinction, it would be pigeons. He had a deep-seated hatred for those filthy rats with wings, almost as much as he hated mosquitoes or cockroaches.

'What is the matter with you!' Adira complained, regaining her footing.

'You don't know anything about driving,' Kunal said, 'If I hadn't stopped, the car would've gotten damaged.' He wasn't entirely sure that was true, but he hoped it was enough to pacify the warrior shorthair. He had said that he could take her on, but deep down he knew he couldn't. Adira was a trained warrior. She was more fatal in a cat's body than Kunal could hope to be in a lion's.

'Did anyone see that bird?' Guru asked.

'The pigeon?' Kunal asked, avoiding further interactions with Adira. He started the car and drove forward.

'Yes,' Guru said, flying over to the backseat. Burfi sniffed them.

'Pigeon!?' Adira asked in a panic.

Guru looked out the rear window, and Burfi joined him. Immediately, Burfi started barking loudly.

'What the...' Adira gasped, hopping into the back.

'The pigeon...' Guru gasped, orange eyes full of dread.

Kunal saw the bird hurtling towards them, red eyes glowing murderously.

'Faster!' Adira commanded, 'We need to lose him!'

The Maruti 800 was already running at maximum speed. It couldn't run any faster.

'He's closing in!' Guru shouted.

Burfi barked. He attempted to lunge at the pigeon but thumped against the rear window.

Bloody pigeon! Kunal slammed the brakes again. This time, he hit the clutch so the engine didn't die. The animals still slid off the back seat though.

The pigeon thudded into the rear window and slid

down.

Kunal quickly shifted to reverse gear and slammed the accelerator.

The pigeon cooed and fluttered before the car ran over him. Then the pigeon appeared lying on the ground before the car, completely unharmed.

It flapped its wings loudly and rose to the air.

Kunal rapidly switched to first gear and slammed the accelerator. This time the pigeon whacked onto the windscreen, lying pinned there with its wings spread wide.

Its eyes still glowed red, an inviting presence that held a world of terror. Kunal was transfixed by its glare.

'YOU DARE INTERFERE!'

'Did you hear that voice!?' Kunal shouted in a panic. That voice had echoed inside his skull. It sounded like something out of his nightmarish mindscape.

'Kunal!' Guru shouted from behind, 'That's…'

'One of Snaitun's birds?'

The pigeon opened its beak, a glow emanating from its open throat.

'No…' Guru began.

Flames burst to life from within the void of the pigeon's throat.

'The pigeon IS Snaitun!'

The pigeon's beak spewed flames onto the windscreen, engulfing the glass. Heat penetrated the car, thickening the air within. The glass began to melt, the view before them distorting with each wave of fresh flames.

Even the steering wheel's rubber cover sizzled. Kunal took his hands off the steering wheel as it began to smoke. He felt sweat dripping from his face. He was struggling to breathe.

With no hand on the steering wheel, the car lost direction. It raced out of the path, ran over a stray rock and flew into the air. Kunal watched as the flames died away. The pigeon—Snaitun—too lost his footing. Guru and Adira floated next to Kunal as his hands crossed before his face, bracing for impact.

The car arced downwards, the bonnet crashing loudly into the ground. The car fell with a thud on its four wheels, smoke rising from the dented bonnet. The car had filled with thick air and white smoke, making it hard to breathe.

Dad's going to kill me…

Kunal fumbled before finally unlocking his door to let the smoke out. The night air filled his lungs, relief spreading through his body. Kunal became more conscious of where they were. He undid his seatbelt and turned to the animals.

Adira stumbled to her feet. Burfi jumped onto his lap and out of the car, shaking and barking into the night sky.

Guru lay on the floor, the edge of their left wing black and sooty.

Kunal reached for them, 'Guru!'

Adira jumped over Kunal's shoulder to exit the car in a rush. Kunal carefully held Guru in his arms and exited the vehicle himself. Guru coughed, smoke rising from their burnt feathers, a charred stench disrupting the fresh air.

'Guru…' Kunal began.

'MY SON…'

Burfi barked aggressively at the pigeon. He feigned an advance, but his tail between his legs gave away his reluctance.

'Burfi, back!' Kunal shouted as he watched the cat and the dog stand off against the lone fire-breathing pigeon.

Burfi obeyed. Adira took a step forward. 'Snaitun…'

'Adira, you traitor! Do you think you can stand against me?' Only one of the front lights of the car had survived the crash, and it shone on Snaitun.

Snaitun flapped his wings, flames engulfing him, making him look like a phoenix. The smoke curled and glided over to Adira as Snaitun took flight.

'Snaitun…' Guru called weakly, jumping from Kunal's hands to his shoulder.

'SHUT UP, GURU!' There was disgust in his voice as he said the name. '***You traitor!***'

Snaitun breathed fire at Kunal's direction.

Guru spread their wings and blocked it. Surprisingly, the flames didn't touch them.

'Aah, so you have identified the weave of this world.'

'You didn't expect me to sit idly, did you?' Guru retorted. Their burnt feathers slowly lost their sootiness. Smoking feathers floated down around them. Guru was badly hurt, but the blue flames and shadows made them look mighty.

'What's the point, Guru? You're no match for me!'

'You might be my superior in magic,' Guru said, 'But you're still just a pigeon!' Guru took flight, claws drawn to attack Snaitun.

Snaitun let out another lance of fire, but Guru evaded it. Guru spat their own volley of magical attacks.

'RUN!' Adira shouted, scratching at Burfi's leg. Snaitun's fire and Guru's magic clashed in a blinding mix of red-blue light.

Burfi refused to move, astounded by the scene. Even Kunal wanted to see how it would pan out. But, he couldn't wait. He began running, 'BURFI, COME!'

For a brief moment, Kunal met Adira's gaze, and she nodded.

Adira ran, leading them away from the magical battle. Kunal peeked over his shoulder, catching a glimpse of sparks and flames exploding against the Guru's shadow. Guru's outspread wings took in most of the impact. The pigeon's coos and the owl's hoots rose in a cacophony of fierce offences. They might as well have been dragons locked in battle.

Kunal ran with all his might, but his limbs ached with exhaustion. His muscles felt like they were sizzling. Even his bones felt sore and spent. He hadn't had so much physical exercise in years.

'Adira,' he huffed, 'I don't know if I can keep up…'

Adira was already a couple of metres ahead of him. She slowed down and turned, 'Are you kidding me, boy!?'

Another loud explosion punctuated the urgency in her words.

Kunal looked back and found his father's car—the Maruti 800 that his father loved more than anything else in the world—go up in flames. Dark smoke rose to the skies as an amber glow lit the avian battlefield.

The owl was nowhere to be seen.

Suddenly, the pigeon flew towards Kunal and attacked his face, its sharp talons cutting through his flesh.

Kunal screamed and fell to the ground. He didn't have time to think of injections.

'Puny mortal!'

He felt Snaitun attack his head, claws and feathers beating violently at him. An intense heat was building up in a small source before Kunal.

This is it…

Burfi tackled Snaitun. Kunal opened his eyes to see the pigeon in Burfi's mouth. It fluttered, but Burfi's grip was strong.

'Good work, Burfi!' Adira cheered, preparing to attack.

Burfi shook his head violently, disorienting Snaitun.

A sudden burst of flames illuminated the ground. Burfi spat the pigeon away, smoke billowing from his puppy mouth. Snaitun flopped to the ground. The moment he saw Adira rush towards him, he sent a lance of flames her way.

Adira dodged just in time, rolling to a halt. She quickly recovered, ready to strike.

Snaitun had already flown away into the darkness.

'You will never win, you pathetic worms!'

Suddenly, Snaitun swept down towards Burfi.

No…

Kunal leapt forward and grabbed Snaitun. He clenched his fist, feeling the dirty grey feathers in his palm. As disgusted as he felt holding that rat with wings, he couldn't let go.

This was his chance. This was just a delicate little pigeon. He could feel the pigeon's insides, its bones within his grasp. If he just clenched his fist further, he could crush it. But, could he do something so vile? Even to a dark lord?

Snaitun spewed flames straight at Kunal's leg. His jeans singed. Instinctively, Kunal jerked, loosening his grip on the pigeon.

The pigeon, now free, shot another volley of flames in Kunal's direction. Kunal leaned back, losing balance. The flames shot overhead. Kunal fell on his butt.

No... no... no...

Burfi leapt into view, standing between Kunal and the pigeon.

'BURFI, NO!'

Snaitun took flight, claws raised, eyes glowing red.

Burfi barked agitatedly. His tail was between his legs.

Snaitun swept forward. Burfi retreated, whelping.

'NO!' Kunal screamed.

Adira leapt towards Snaitun. Claws drawn, murder in her eyes.

She missed.

Kunal helplessly watched Snaitun grab Burfi by the scruff of his neck. In an impossible sight, the tiny pigeon lifted Burfi into the air. Burfi cried in terror, but couldn't reach the pigeon with his claws.

Adira tried to jump, but the pigeon was too high up in the air. Kunal braved his fears and ran to the pigeon.

Snaitun foiled his rush with another burst of flames.

'You will never defeat me!' Snaitun declared and flew away into the darkness. As Snaitun's form disappeared into the black, so did Kunal's hopes.

They could still hear Burfi's whimpering for a while before it dissolved into the roaring flames of the car.

Guru...

Kunal turned and found Adira already rushing towards the flames. Kunal followed, ignoring the burning pain in his legs.

'GURU!' Adira found the owl lying on the ground. They were covered in dirt and soot, many feathers and parts of their face burnt black.

Guru croaked weakly, 'I'm... sorry...

'No!' Adira cried, her little shorthair body shivering, 'Guru, what can we do...?'

'Nothing...' they coughed.

Kunal felt tears roll down his face. His heart had opened floodgates of pain for the second time that night. 'The Dung Egg... we can still...'

'No...' Guru coughed violently, struggling to make words. 'Burfi...' They paused to breathe weakly. 'Without him...'

'But the Dung Egg...' Kunal sniffled, frantically clutching onto the one thread of hope he had, 'The Dung Egg can...' He stopped talking. Guru had stopped moving.

Adira slumped in her place. 'It's over...'

'No!' Kunal shouted, 'NO!'

'Kunal, it's over.'

'But...'

Adira sniffled.

'We can try!' Kunal pushed, 'If you know what it looks like, or what it does...'

Adira looked up at him, whiskers slumped in defeat.

'You know what it looks like, yes!?' Kunal didn't want to let it go. If they failed, it would be his fault. His fault for not acting and reacting on time. His fault for failing Burfi. His fault for...

'Snaitun has Burfi. It's only a matter of time before he finds the Dung Egg. It's over.'

No... no... no...

Kunal heard distant sirens. The police. Someone

must've reported the explosion.

That was the moment he decided he wouldn't give up. No matter what. He wiped the tears away from his face and said to Adira, 'We can't give up now. Your world and mine both depend on us not failing.'

'Boy,' Adira snarled, 'You don't even have the courage to stand up against three stray cats. How do you expect to fight a god-emperor?'

'I don't know,' Kunal said. The sirens had almost reached them. 'But I know we have to try. I will try, however, I can.'

The police cars, fire trucks, ambulances, even some SUVs with black-tinted windows stopped before them. The firefighters rushed out to extinguish the flames. The amber glow died away, leaving behind only the cold LED lights from the cars.

Kunal braced himself, not sure how he would go about explaining everything. But he had to.

Then a familiar voice called out to him, 'KUNAL!'

Kunal turned in search of the voice. She couldn't be here.

'KUNAL! Over here!'

Kunal looked at one of the black-tinted SUVs. There was a RAW logo on the side. Walking towards him from that SUV was the last person he expected to see, but the only person he actually wanted to meet.

'AISHA!'

CHAPTER 9
CHAIDRINKERS

AFTER HE HAD HIS FILL of *anda pav*, Mr Tambe took a shower and visited the temple, as promised. He even made a generous donation of ₹1,001, hoping it would be enough to atone for his sins.

All spiritual matters settled, Mr Tambe was ready for vengeance. He rang the temple bell, asked Panduranga for strength and headed straight to his cousin Dilip's house.

Tambe Nivas was a three-story house that their grandfather had built with the intention of keeping the family together. And, despite all the brothers and siblings moving onto different businesses and jobs, they would convene here every weekend to celebrate the smallest of successes. Unlike his friend's abandoned bungalow, no one fought over the possession of Tambe Nivas. It belonged to the whole family, and anyone attempting to seize it would be ostracised beyond redemption.

However, at any given point, there was always one patriarch of the family. That patriarch would end up being the de facto owner of the house. And the current patriarch was Mr Tambe's younger cousin, Dilip.

Everyone knew that to run a business you needed manpower. To run operations beyond legal grounds required even more. And Dilip, the social butterfly that he was, had managed to do both, bringing together their entire community to form a massive empire. Officially, he employed over five hundred people for his work. Unofficially, that number was incalculable. Dilip's hard work and community support had helped him build a reputation.

With such a strong force backing you, you could easily strongarm your enemies. He was even approached by local politicians to join their parties, a power move that he had happily accepted years ago.

Dilip's influence was exactly why Mr Tambe thought it appropriate to ask for his cousin's help. The only problem was, Dilip loved to annoy Mr Tambe.

'*Rakshas?*' Dilip said, adjusting his sunglasses. He was larger than Mr Tambe in every manner. He had two thick gold chains around his neck, a silver cap on one of his front teeth and sunglasses that he never took off. Mr Tambe used to tease him when they were younger but stopped when Dilip built his unofficial army with their community's youth.

Mr Tambe nodded, 'Yes, Dilip. I wouldn't lie...'

Dilip leaned forward and sniffed Mr Tambe's breath. 'Pakya, have you...?'

'No! Not today,' Mr Tambe replied, brushing his walrus moustache. He hated being called Pakya. 'Dagya, I just came from the temple. I'm sober and am seeking revenge.' Mr Tambe used his pet name, but Dilip didn't seem to mind.

Dilip raised a hand and pretended to inject something into his arm. 'What about...?'

Just beyond where he sat, Mr Tambe could see a calendar with Lord Vishnu and Goddess Lakshmi looking straight at him. 'NO! You know I don't do that!'

'Mushrooms?'

Mr Tambe could see his reflection in Dilip's ridiculous sunglasses. And he was visibly out of patience. 'The only mushroom I had was the Mushroom Kolhapuri my missus made for lunch yesterday!' Mr Tambe groaned with annoyance, 'You have to believe me. I wouldn't come to you if it weren't serious, Dilip Tambe.' Maybe using his full name would highlight the seriousness of the situation.

Dilip chuckled mockingly, 'Pakya, let's face it. You're not the bravest of us cousins. Hell, you couldn't even kill the sacrificial rooster for Ganpati when it was your turn.'

A lanky youngster came in and whispered something in Dilip's ear. Dilip nodded and ordered him something in code language.

After he left, Mr Tambe said, 'I agree, I'm not the best fighter. But I'm not a liar either!'

'Didn't you lie about the square footage of your apartments to overcharge your tenants?' Dilip grinned, knowing what ticked Mr Tambe off.

But Mr Tambe wasn't going to fall for that. 'Yes... but that's business... you understand, right?'

Dilip shrugged and popped a spoonful of *mukhwas* into his mouth. Chewing, he said, 'Look, Pakya, I can forgive all your lies, but you also skimped out on donations for this year's *palki*. Cheat other people, fine. Cheat your family, and you get punished. But to cheat god himself?'

'I didn't skimp out! I asked Avi to pay for me. I can't help it if he...'

'Pakya, stop it. I don't have time for your nonsense. Rakshas controlling your gully dogs and cats? That's just...' Dilip shook his head and whistled.

A young girl came in with a tray full of hot masala chai and cheap biscuits. She placed it on the teapoy before them.

Mr Tambe shook his hands, 'No thank you... I...'

'You never send guests without at least a cup of chai, Pakya. Have it.'

Mr Tambe nodded and picked up a biscuit. How was he going to convince his cousin? There had to be some way. This wasn't just about a local bully. This was a *rakshas*, and Mr Tambe needed vengeance. If he failed, the whole world could be at stake. Really, he was doing the world a favour.

If only he could show Dilip some evidence.

Dilip grabbed the remote and switched on the television. Even in the age of OTT, Dilip preferred his old-school cable TV. As he flipped through the channels, Mr Tambe saw a shot of his apartment building.

'Dilip! Go back!' he shouted.

Clicking his tongue, Dilip said, 'You're a real leech, you know.' He switched the channel. A Bhojpuri song with a half-naked girl dancing amidst old men played rather loudly. Dilip was already placing the remote down, ready to enjoy the visuals.

'Not this! The news!'

Dilip looked at Mr Tambe with an annoyed expression, then said, 'Which one?'

Mr Tambe snatched the remote and began changing channels until he found his apartment building.

The headline read: *Stray Animals Attack Building. Is This The Apocalypse?*

'That's my building!'

Dilip looked at the news report, then snatched the remote back and increased the TV's volume.

One of the residents spoke, '... *as if their minds were under someone' control. This has to be the work of a rakshas. There's no explanation. Why else would all these animals work together?*'

They cut back to the reporter, '*As you just heard... a rakshas controlling stray animals. That's right, you heard it first from us. A rakshas has begun terrorising Mumbai and is using stray animals as his weapon. Is this the gods' way of punishing us for AI-generated art? Find out after this short break...*'

Dilip switched off the TV. '*Aichi ga...*'

'I told you,' Mr Tambe said, 'Those stray animals... it has something to do with my tenant, Kunal Chitre.'

'Kunal Chitre?'

'He adopted a stray dog, and that's when all this started. The rakshas... it kidnapped me and...'

'And?'

Mr Tambe gulped. 'I don't know what he did. He cast a spell or what.' He tapped the side of his head, 'He infiltrated my mind.' Visions of his mindscape flashed before his eyes. The beautiful 10-BHK bungalow in Colaba with a sea view from every room. His precious mindscape, and that rakshas had defiled it, searching for information. 'Thieves rob your homes when you're out, dacoits rob you at gunpoint... but this rakshas? He...' Mr Tambe paused, knowing it was enough to roil his cousin. 'I'm asking as your brother, Dilip. This rakshas needs to be stopped!'

Dilip had grown angry at that point. Any attack on one family member was an attack on the family itself. And Dilip would burn the world if anyone dared to harm his family.

He called in three of his boys and asked them to scour the internet. It took them less than a minute to locate a report on the strays attacking an apartment building in Goregaon. Kunal's parents' apartment. Footage of the attacks, the aftermath, Dilip scoured all of it. And, with every passing piece of evidence, Dilip grew angrier.

Mr Tambe felt vindicated.

Dilip took off his sunglasses. 'So, there really is a rakshas?'

'Yes.'

'And you...?'

'... bravely escaped his clutches,' Mr Tambe said, hoping Dilip wouldn't ask too many questions. 'The rakshas is on his way to find Kunal. If we can find him first, we can ambush him and save the world!'

Dilip nodded. 'If we kill this rakshas, I can use it to win the local elections.'

Mr Tambe smiled. 'Of course. I'll even contribute to your funds. I promise.'

'No, brother. This isn't about money. This is about revenge.' Dilip shook his head. He rubbed his eyes and put his sunglasses back on. He barked orders at his unofficial army to assemble.

'Let's go!' Mr Tambe said starting up.

'They'll need time to prepare. We still have to find this Kunal too.'

Mr Tambe nodded and sat down. 'What do we do while we wait?'

Dilip pointed to the teapoy, 'Have your chai. It's getting cold.'

*

Kunal sipped on hot masala chai, wishing it were hot chocolate. He didn't complain though. After the night he'd had, this was a luxury for him.

He stood with Aisha, nervously looking at his parents talking to Dr Raza.

'I didn't expect them to meet this way,' he told Aisha.

'I didn't expect them to meet this early,' Aisha said, then chuckled to mute the awkwardness between them.

But there was no denying it. A lifetime's worth of changes had happened since Aisha had dropped Burfi at Kunal's place. Kunal almost longed for his overpriced apartment where he had bid Aisha farewell, basket in hand containing a sleeping Burfi.

Now, they stood in a secret facility just outside Igatpuri. Kunal couldn't believe how close Aisha was. It was almost like fate. Or plot convenience. He decided to go with fate.

Unlike futuristic secret facilities from various popular shows and films, this one was just a redeveloped apartment complex called Shri Tranquillity. Kunal hated when desi builders tried to merge random desi and English words to make such ridiculous hybrids. However, whoever this builder was had done a fantastic job—the complex was full of luxurious amenities, a massive garden, three jogger's paths, gyms, pools, a beautiful view of the mountains and everything else that Mumbai's apartments refused to offer unless you were filthy rich.

Kunal cursed himself for even thinking of such things. It was one of the indicators that he was growing old.

'How much do you think the rent is in this place?' he wondered out loud. Shri Tranquillity seemed like it could offer him a lot of silence and mental peace. And just like actual silence and mental peace in Mumbai, it was probably out of his budget.

'Seriously?' Aisha asked, holding back her laughter, 'The world is about to end and you're thinking of that?'

'No, but I'd rather not think of the end…'

Aisha's amusement faded away. A look of genuine concern painted her face. 'I'm sorry, Kunal… I can't even imagine what you must be going through.'

Kunal shrugged, 'I'm all right.'

'No, you're not,' Aisha said, taking a step closer, 'You must be freaking out right now. And I know, you feel the need to put on a brave face for your parents, and for everyone around you.' Aisha held his hand, 'But you really don't have to. There are professionals here who can take over.'

Kunal was tempted to let go. Just give up and let the *adults* handle it.

I've been an adult for eight years now.

Kunal shook his head, 'No, I can't give up now.'

'Why not?' Aisha asked, gripping his hand tighter, 'You're not a hero or a soldier or…' she took in a deep breath, 'Please don't do something stupid.'

'I won't,' Kunal said, 'Not anymore. I've been acting stupid since this whole mess started. I just…'

'If talking animals approached me to save the world, I'd freak out thinking I'd consumed the wrong mushrooms!'

Kunal chuckled.

'I'm serious. You acted like any human would in your situation.'

Kunal nodded, not wanting to exert himself with the conversation. Besides, Aisha was right, no matter what his mind told him. He had been stupid, but that's just how humans act.

But his stupidity might cost the world its very existence. Snaitun was a dangerous enemy. Even in the body of a pigeon, he had wreaked so much havoc. Kunal couldn't even begin to fathom the carnage he would unleash if he were permitted to regain his full potential.

He tried to think of Burfi, but that only made his mood worse. What condition was he in? He'd be so scared, that tiny pup. Kunal's stomach lurched knowing Burfi was in Snaitun's clutches. And it was all Kunal's fault.

'I can't give up now,' Kunal said again, this time making sure that the conviction in his voice was loud and clear. 'Snaitun knows who I am... he even kidnapped Mr Tambe to try and find me. I don't think I have a choice.'

Aisha frowned, but didn't let go of his arm, 'Then I'm going to be by your side. I promise.'

Kunal rested his free hand on hers, and smiled, 'I love you, Aisha.'

'I love you too,' she smiled back.

Kunal looked at her, she looked at him lovingly with her large anime-like eyes. Finally, he asked, 'Why didn't you answer my texts?'

Aisha frowned and looked away. 'When I saw the news, I was 90 per cent sure you were involved. But gut feelings don't count for anything. At least not with General Shah,' she said the name with disgust, as if she had eaten a spoonful of chocolate powder without realising it was unsweetened.

'You could've at least checked your phone.'

Aisha looked at him, a million thoughts making themselves seen in her eyes. Kunal realised he was being inconsiderate. But he deserved to know, right?

Aisha sighed. 'I'm sorry...'

Kunal flinched. Why? Because he was expecting Aisha to burst out with anger at how inconsiderate he was being. But this was Aisha. She was the most understanding person he'd met in his life. He wisely decided to keep quiet and let her speak.

'I tried to get my phone, but General Shah didn't allow me to. And he has absolute control here.' Aisha sipped some of her chai. 'After the attack on your parents' apartment, I was certain it was you. That's when he agreed to look into you. But even then, he didn't let me switch on my phone because he wanted to make sure you weren't an enemy.'

'But...' Kunal thought back to his escape with the car. If those police vehicles had been part of this secret service convoy... 'Oh boy, was that you at my parents' farmhouse?'

'We tracked Snaitun's radiation to Igatpuri, and I remembered your parents' farmhouse.' Aisha blushed.

Kunal remembered the plans they had made, and how Mom had spoiled them by refusing to give him the keys. 'I can't believe you were this close.' Shri Tranquillity was less than an hour's drive away from his parent's farmhouse.

'If only there wasn't so much red tape...'

'I know...'

They sipped their chai quietly. Kunal was certain Aisha would want to know about the animals, but she had the patience to ask at an appropriate time. Kunal was still recovering from multiple attacks. The paramedics had given him a single shot—which he took bravely, crying only on the inside—and bandaged the scratches. That was his adventure. Aisha's on the other hand was boring research work. Guess she still had the emotional capacity to answer more questions.

Kunal decided against it. He wasn't sure he had the mental capacity to even ask the right questions. He needed to sleep and rest.

But not until we find Burfi…

Sadness clutched him like Snaitun's claws had clutched Burfi. He was feeling anxious again. But he had an idea.

Kunal asked, 'So... your father does work for the secret services?'

Aisha snorted and burst out laughing. He wanted to cover her mouth, but that wouldn't be right. Besides, everyone was already looking at them, including Dr Raza. He crossed his beefy arms and looked straight at Kunal.

Aisha's laughter was infectious. Kunal couldn't help but laugh with her, feeling the tension in his chest unwind. He realised this was the first time he had laughed and enjoyed the moment in ages. He had spent almost half a day's worth of time in a perpetual state of worry.

The laughter was a healthy change. The perfect distraction he needed. Without a care for who was looking, Kunal hugged Aisha tightly, 'Thank you... thank you so much.'

Aisha rested her hand on his head and stroked his hair, 'Sorry, I couldn't call earlier.'

Kunal let go and cleared his throat. 'It's okay. Secret project and whatnot.'

Aisha shrugged, 'Exactly.' She shuffled her feet before adding, 'I really can't believe Abbu's actually working with the secret services.'

Kunal playfully punched her, 'Guess you owe me a hot chocolate.'

'Umm, we never bet on it.'

'Don't lie!'

'I can't seem to recollect us having any such agreement whatsoever, Mr Kunal Chitre.'

Kunal crossed his arms and nodded. 'Okay... then how about a counteroffer?'

Aisha cocked her head, 'I'm listening…'

'Tell me everything. Whatever you know.' Kunal

smiled with his teeth. *Was that smooth? Am I crossing a line? But... she might know something that can help me save Burfi.*

Help us *save Burfi.*

Aisha hesitated, 'Umm... I don't know if I can...'

'Why not?' Kunal threw his hands up, 'I'm neck-deep in this mess! The least you can do is paint me the full picture.'

Aisha bit her lip, 'I don't know if I'm authorised to do that. Sorry, Kunal...'

Kunal frowned, 'Seriously?'

'Yeah,' Aisha said, 'This isn't a movie, love. There's a command structure, clearance and not everyone...'

A passing clerk handed over a docket each to them, 'Case docket. Briefing in five minutes,' she said and walked away.

Kunal eyed the docket, then turned to Aisha with a vindicated look.

'Fine!' Aisha groaned.

'That's two wins for me. Hot chocolate and *khrwa-sow*.'

Aisha chuckled, then flipped through the docket. 'Okay, look here.'

Kunal looked at what she was pointing at. It was an image of a spherical object covered in dirt.

'Abbu found this outside his office this morning. The office in Trombay, you know?' Aisha paused, recounting the time. 'Sorry, yesterday morning. Almost twenty-four hours ago.' She cleared her throat, 'His team was alerted because of the strange nature of radioactivity this thing was emanating. He called me in because they needed an archaeological expert to help identify it.

'The geologists involved couldn't identify the substance. It's been emanating radiation every other hour. When we got reports of the attack on your building and your parent's building, we compared the approximate time of the events and realised that they matched. This...'

'... is the Dung Egg...' Kunal's eyes were threatening

to pop out. The very thing they had been looking for! 'Where is it?'

'Here, underground for safekeeping. The scientists are doing their…'

'We need to warn them!' Kunal said, his body shuddering with excitement, 'This is the Dung Egg!'

'Yes, we also considered the material to be…'

'It's from the Dung Dimension! Where's Adira!?' Kunal was shouting now. 'She needs to know we have it!'

'Kunal, slow down,' Aisha said, trying to hold him, 'I can't understand what you're saying…'

'The Dung Egg…' Kunal repeated mindlessly with frustration. He kicked the ground, realising Aisha didn't know everything about his own adventure. 'Aisha, please trust me!'

'Listen up, everyone,' General Shah called out. His voice was deep, sounding otherworldly almost. Everyone turned to him with anticipation. He looked around, then declared, 'We've located the threat's whereabouts.'

'Sir…' Kunal shouted at him, waving the docket overhead, 'You have the Dung Egg…'

'In the briefing,' General Shah said with finality.

'The Dung Egg!' Kunal shouted at the top of his voice, 'It's key to defeating Snaitun!'

General Shah glared at him. Just one look at his expression made it clear why Aisha hated him. Through clenched teeth, he repeated, 'In the briefing.'

Shri Tranquillity's conference room didn't look modern enough for a corporate or government office; its ivory walls and minimal furnishing made it barely suitable for a society office. A boring square of a room with plastic chairs arranged haphazardly for quick discussions. In the centre of the chairs, however, a futuristic projector shone an azure light onto a screen. Kunal sat next to Aisha as the rest of the executives gathered on time, quite uncharacteristic for government officials.

Kunal, unwilling to socialise, decided to focus on all the key points of the case listed on the screen. Seeing Burfi's image from a security camera footage made Kunal feel sad. He wondered if the puppy was all right.

He's kidnapped by a dark lord who's going to sacrifice him to gain unimaginable powers. What do you think, genius?

Kunal spotted an attendant place two thermoses and a platter of snacks on a nearby table. Grateful for the distraction, Kunal walked over to the table and poured himself another cup of chai. It wasn't masala chai, but it was enough to help him avoid eye contact. The lukewarm samosas sitting abandoned next to the plastic thermos were another welcome treat. Samosas were Kunal's second favourite way of packaging potatoes.

The mini snack combo made Kunal nostalgic. It also made him question the efficiency of the team that was handling this—*Case? Project? What the hell is happening here? And why can't they have hot samosas?*

Kunal picked two samosas and walked back to his seat.

'No, thank you,' Aisha smiled.

Kunal blinked, unaware that he was supposed to share.

Aisha bit her lip at the realisation and stifled a laugh.

General Shah walked into the room. Adira prowled after him and jumped onto the chair next to Kunal.

'Are you all right?' he asked her.

Adira ignored him.

Kunal frowned and bit into his sad samosa. He had thought Adira was warming up to him.

'I'll get straight to the point,' General Shah said, 'The threat identified as Snaitun the pigeon has been located. For those of you who weren't on this mission from the get-go, your docket contains all the information. Thank you, Dr Raza, for the quick work.'

'My daughter helped me,' he replied, gesturing to Aisha. A proud father's smile flashed to reveal his teeth.

Aisha blushed but maintained her composure.

Kunal's leg shook incessantly. He was too anxious to reveal his findings. The one thing Guru had said could help them, help Burfi and defeat Snaitun was now within reach.

Guru... if only you were here...

Kunal swallowed the now-cold morsel of samosa, expecting to have to interrupt the meeting at any point to correct them.

'Now...'

'Sir!' Kunal shot his hand up, 'Please! If you could hear me out...' He didn't even care about the spilt glass of hot chai over his jeans.

'The Dung Egg, I know boy! For god's sake, shut up or I'll have you thrown out!'

Kunal's hand slunk down, the hot patch of chai growing cold now. He already knew? Kunal had been proud of himself for being vocal, but they didn't seem to need him at all. Kunal looked to Adira for support but found her ignoring him.

Kunal looked to Aisha, who just put a finger to her lips.

'The Dung Egg is an essential part of this mission,' General Shah stated, 'But its highly unclear nature makes it as much a threat to use as the actual threat himself. Our scientists are still running tests on it.'

Slinking further, Kunal stuffed the remaining samosa into his mouth, careful not to chew loudly. It wasn't just an essential part, it was *the key* to this whole mess. *That, and Burfi...*

'Using the Dung Egg's unique radioactivity, we've developed a method to track Snaitun. Once again, courtesy Dr Raza,' General Shah nodded to him.

'This one was entirely my idea,' Dr Raza said proudly, showing his toothy smile again.

General Shah continued, 'We've discovered that Snaitun has taken shelter very close to this place, an abandoned warehouse. Perhaps because it's only a matter of time before he locates the Dung Egg. If that is the case, there's no stopping him.'

'We're constantly surveying this warehouse, and reports suggest that he is attempting to use... *his magic...*' there was disgust in his voice when using those words, 'for unknown purposes. Our extradimensional ally—warrior Adira,' he pointed to the white shorthair, 'Suggests that he might be attempting to return to his original form. I'm inclined to agree with her. Which is why, as we speak, one of our elite black ops team—the Silent Langurs—is en route to neutralise the threat.'

Kunal shot up again, 'Sir! Snaitun is a highly potent mage. A literal dark lord! It's stupid to approach him like that!'

General Shah looked annoyed. 'You're really getting on my nerves, boy.' He sighed from the effort to deal with Kunal. 'While the threat is a *mage*, he is also confined to the body of a pigeon. That factor might just give us an edge.'

Kunal turned to Adira, demanding, 'You didn't tell him Snaitun's invulnerable?'

Adira scoffed. 'Like that old fart would listen.'

Hearing those words sent relief down Kunal's throat. So, Adira wasn't mad at him; she was just annoyed after talking to General Shah.

'Once the threat is apprehended or neutralised,' the General continued, 'We will proceed with phase two of this mission, which is to establish contact with the extradimensional reality in hopes of peaceful exchange. Any questions?'

'Do we get to watch this pigeon's encounter?' a voice said from the back.

'Yes,' General Shah clicked on the screen and moved to a separate window that displayed bodycam footage overlooking a warehouse. 'Looks like our strike team has reached their location.'

CHAPTER 10
THE RAGE OF THE PIGEONS

BARDS HAVE GLORIFIED WARRIORS since the dawn of storytelling. From valiant soldiers to heroic kings, you've most likely heard tales of impossible deeds made real by lionhearted men. But glorifying these dangerous individuals with unrequited praises tends to ignore that these aren't gods or demigods, but just humans.

Captain Mangesh always reminded his squad of that every time they were sent on a dangerous mission.

'Forget about glory. Forget about honour. What we do is none of that. The point of our existence is to carry out missions that no one will hear of except our superiors and the enemy's superiors. Don't fight expecting reward or merit. Fight, because it is the right thing to do, and we're the only goddamned soldiers brave enough to do it.'

Captain Mangesh had first heard those words from his squad leader on his first mission. Ever since, he had abided by those words. The firm grip on reality helped him maintain his composure and make split-second decisions with logic and practicality.

'Silent Langurs in position. Over.' Captain Mangesh announced over comms. He always found their squad's name ridiculous. Langurs were some of the loudest nuisances he had ever come across in Delhi and other parts of the country.

'Copy that. Over,' General Shah said.

Captain Mangesh switched to night vision and looked at the abandoned warehouse. It appeared to be in stasis. The clouds above didn't seem to drift. No crickets or insects sang their nocturnal ballads. Even the blades of grass stood frozen in time.

Captain Mangesh gave his report, 'Sitrep: Target location in sight. 300 meters. Clear skies, no wind. No identified threats or traps. Four entry points located. Entry from staging area preferred. Please advise. Over.'

Finally, General Shah commanded, *'Silent Langurs, you're cleared for breach. Over.'*

'Copy that. Over.' Captain Mangesh took in a deep breath and relayed their orders. His team readied themselves and began their slow approach. They were a strike team of seven soldiers, two for backup, the rest for execution. However, Captain Mangesh wasn't sure if that would be enough.

'Proceed with caution,' Captain Mangesh said, taking a step forward.

The enemy was reportedly mind-controlling stray animals. The enemy itself was a fire-breathing pigeon. Whether or not it was true didn't matter. As a soldier, he had to take the threat seriously. And taking it seriously meant being prepared for a supernatural assault, whatever that meant.

A flash of something struck Captain Mangesh. Dark eyes like black holes sucking the life force out of him. He stopped in position, raising his submachine gun.

'Captain?' Lt Ana asked. His second-in-command.

Captain Mangesh swallowed his fear. He couldn't believe he had almost pulled the trigger. Loosening his grip slightly, he said, 'All clear. Keep walking.'

Captain Mangesh noted the absence of vehicles in the docking area. The shutters on the shipping area were down, but the staging area was open. It looked like there were crates stacked haphazardly, but no movements or lifeforms were visible from their position.

Another flash of fear assaulted Captain Mangesh. Slithering tendrils of smoke wrapped around his naked body, entering every orifice available to them. Captain Mangesh felt his legs refuse him. *Why?*

'Did anyone else see that? Over.' Surya asked from their tail. He was the youngest of their group, also their freshest, which is why he was left to cover them in the rear. Even Captain Mangesh had been afraid on his first mission as a Silent Langur; it was part of the job, and Surya would learn to keep a check on it.

'Affirmative,' Lt Ana responded, *'Target is capable of psychological assault. Over.'*

'Brilliant,' Surya said shakily, *'Over.'*

Captain Mangesh pushed his tongue into his cheek. 'Target has supernatural powers. Ignore and keep moving. Over.'

The closer they got to the warehouse, the more vivid the flashes of horror became. Captain Mangesh shook his head and focused on his breathing. *None of these are real. None of this is real.* 'Lt Ana, report. Over.'

Lt Ana was at the lead. She had reached the staging area and was ready to breach. *'Warehouse empty. No lifeforms detected. What's our move, Captain? Over.'*

'Thermal vision check. Over.'

'No signs of any lifeforms detected. Over.'

Surya called over comms, *'Report. I can hear rustling around. Potential threats—rats, snakes… God, I hate snakes…'*

'Stay put, Surya,' Captain Mangesh said, 'Do not fire until provoked. Over.' Something ran over Captain Mangesh's foot. Maybe it was a rat. He surveyed the area but found nothing.

After a moment, he heard Surya's shaky voice say, *'Copy that.'*

Captain Mangesh strode over to Lt Ana and switched to thermal vision. The only heat signatures were from his team. The warehouse was colder than a morgue. 'Come in Control. No lifeforms detected. Please advise. Over.'

There was just static from the other line.

'Please advise,' Captain Mangesh replied, 'Over.'

Finally, General Shah ordered, *'Perform a thorough sweep of the location. For all you know, they've cast a force field around the place that negates our surveillance gear.'*

'Copy that. Over.' Captain Mangesh signalled for Lt Ana to enter the staging area.

Lt Ana jumped onto the platform and immediately paused. *'Captain... run!'*

Before Captain Mangesh could react, a swarm of pigeons appeared out of nowhere, all rushing for him. Their loud fluttering filled their comms like static distortion. Captain Mangesh switched it off and focused on what he saw.

Pigeons can't harm me. Captain Mangesh held his ground, made sure his submachine gun was pointed away from Lt Ana and pulled the trigger. The spray of bullets cleared the swarm, and he rushed over to Lt Ana. The others followed behind him.

The moment they crossed the force field, their visuals changed. Inside was a swarm of pigeons, rats and other stray animals cooped up. They all stared at the Langurs with glowing red, rabid eyes.

'Open fire!' Captain Mangesh ordered, shooting at the horde of strays. His Langurs followed suit. The air rattled with the sound of miniature explosions propelling lethal rounds at the swarm.

When the smoke cleared, the animals were nowhere to be seen.

Then they were everywhere.

A sea of rats appeared out of nowhere, climbing onto the Langurs' legs. The pigeons and crows swooped and pecked at them from above. Chaos assaulted the human soldiers, sweeping them off their feet.

Captain Mangesh put on his gas mask, pulled out tear gas grenades and threw them at the strays. His soldiers followed suit, filling the warehouse with smoke, causing the animals to flee from the soldiers.

'Come in Control,' Captain Mangesh said, pulling out the magazine and reloading his gun, 'Threat is in large numbers. Rats, crows, pigeons... we have an opening. Request to retreat. Over.' The magazine clicked into place.

'Denied, Captain Mangesh!' General Shah screamed, *'Find me that damned pigeon.'*

Grunting, Captain Mangesh fired at the fleeing animals. There was no arguing with General Shah. 'Copy that.'

'Is that wise?'

Captain Mangesh turned, searching for the speaker. Sweat trickled down the side of his head.

The strays formed a defensive perimeter around the Silent Langurs, trapping them in. Captain Mangesh ordered his Langurs to hold.

'Retreat now, and I'll let you live.'

Captain Mangesh clicked on comms and said, 'Psychological warfare confirmed. Op...'

'Snakes... there are snakes here...' Surya shouted into comms, followed by loud gunfire. Surya's communication cut off abruptly.

There was a sudden silence in the warehouse. Residual smoke drifted over the floor like an alien miasma. The strays continued to stare. Their bodies were on the brink of collapse, but their eyes were rabid with murder.

'I'm warning you...'

Captain Mangesh considered the threat. If they retreated, they would be court marshalled. If they didn't, their fate was uncertain. If Captain Mangesh believed in glory, he would've fought on.

'Fall back!' he shouted, 'Retreat.'

'CAPTAIN MANGESH!' General Shah shouted over comms, *'That is a breach of o—'*

Captain Mangesh cut off communication. He turned

and started walking out of the warehouse, 'I'm going to get Surya...'

'Wise decision.'

Surya screamed in the distance. He was lying on the ground, his gun and knife lying out of reach. Snakes slithered over his body, strangling and suffocating him with their slimy bodies. *'Help!'* he shouted, doing his best to maintain composure.

The rest of the Langurs looked puzzled. Lt Ana voiced their concern, *'Isn't it just a pigeon, Captain?'*

'Target allegedly breathes fire. I'm not stupid enough to...'

'Help!' Surya cried. *'Please!'*

Cursing, Captain Mangesh raised his submachine gun and began firing around Surya.

The snakes didn't seem bothered by it.

'Weren't you fleeing?'

A cold fire burned within Captain Mangesh's gut. 'Let him go. We're fleeing.'

'No.'

'But...'

'Flee now, or you will all be my captives.' As if announcing himself, a pigeon fluttered into view, settling on top of the writhing snakes on Surya's body.

Captain Mangesh pulled out the magazine and clicked on a new one. He aimed at the pigeon.

'Final warning.'

Captain Mangesh felt sweat drip down his face. He held his breath and focused on the pigeon. Its eyes glowed red. It opened its beak, embers drifting out of it.

Captain Mangesh pulled the trigger.

Static crackled on the screen.

In the conference room, General Shah punched the wall in frustration. 'Bloody cowards!'

Kunal had blanched on seeing the bodycam footage. Although the footage was blurry, the pigeon shooting flames was impossible to miss. This night was turning out to be the worst of his life.

'You okay?' Aisha asked, grasping his hand.

Kunal nodded silently. He felt Aisha's fingers tangle with his. He looked at her and pursed his lips.

Aisha looked shaken too. 'That was Snaitun, wasn't it? You faced him…?' she asked softly.

Kunal nodded, still unable to speak. Trying to distract himself, he looked at the bodycam footage of the other soldiers still being broadcast over the projection.

The soldiers were running towards a black minibus. The footage was shaky, and there was no audio.

Out of nowhere, an orange glow engulfed the minibus. The soldiers stopped in their flight. The soldier, whose bodycam footage they watched, raised his gun to attack.

From the flames, a tiny figure emerged, cuing a shower of bullets. But none hit it. The pigeon flew straight at the bodycam.

One by one, all the soldiers met Captain Mangesh's fate. Their bodycams died, leaving the projection with seven frames of static.

Even General Shah looked flabbergasted. 'What the hell did we just see…?'

'Snaitun!' Kunal exclaimed, 'That's him!'

General Shah raised his hand to silence him. His other pressed on the earpiece, listening closely. He signalled to one of the techs, who changed the settings.

Snaitun's horrid voice echoed in the briefing room over the speakers.

'*… pathetic attempt. You really think you could get the best of me?*'

General Shah met Kunal's gaze. Kunal understood the question and nodded. General Shah gulped and ground his teeth.

'*Now, listen to me carefully,*'

The entire room fell silent, eagerly listening to Snaitun's demands.

'Your soldiers are alive. I will hand them over to you if you so request.'

Kunal exhaled in relief. General Shah, he saw, hadn't changed his expression one bit.

'In exchange, I want the warrior Adira, who is presently in the body of a white cat...

Kunal's relief was trampled by his racing heart. He looked at Adira, shock loud and clear in her feline eyes.

'... and the Dung Egg.'

Kunal's heart punched against his chest. He felt like he was having a heart attack.

'I know you have both in your possession. Bring them to me, and I will let your soldiers go.'

General Shah pushed back, 'Why should we submit to your demands? How do we know you won't use the cat and the egg to—'

'Refuse, and I will kill your soldiers.'

General Shah took a moment to breathe. 'Listen to me, Snaitun, we can negotiate...'

'No negotiation. Your submission is inevitable. The path is for you to decide.'

Adira scoffed.

'In the end, your entire world will bow down before me. It is your choice whether to bow peacefully or burn.'

'Wait...'

'You have one hour.'

The communication cut to static.

General Shah punched the wall again, this time with a flurry of curses. Finally, he set his hair back and looked at the room. 'We have fifteen minutes to decide how to proceed.' Then he looked at Adira, 'Any suggestions?'

'The Dung Egg,' Adira looked at Kunal. 'We need to see the Dung Egg.'

Kunal nodded, looking at General Shah with determination.

General Shah sighed, rubbed his eyes, and led the way.

CHAPTER 11
DUNGING EGG

'HERE IT IS,' General Shah said, 'filthy little thing.'

The Dung Egg was a majestically foul-smelling artefact. Kunal looked at its projection on the screen, noticing it was more of an oblong sphere than an egg. Covered in dirt—or perhaps dung—the grainy film of natural substance around the egg made it look like crystalised chocolate powder.

Kunal's mouth would've watered if he didn't know what it was, or if he had lost his sense of smell.

The Dung Egg lay inside a box made of five-inch-thick glass sealed with lead. There were two black gloves inside, which the lab assistants used to touch and examine the egg closely.

The room didn't look anything like Kunal had imagined. But that was expected, after seeing the state of the entire facility. It was modern enough by Indian standards, yet clung to its 90s roots. He hated the ivory walls and cheap tiles, but the monitors and devices made up for them. As a sci-fi nerd, he should've been more fascinated, but his mind was a little too preoccupied with the world-ending threat and whatnot.

Kunal imagined Burfi barking at the egg, out of threat or requesting a treat. He'd barely fostered Burfi for a few hours, yet he missed the doggo. His doggo.

His doggo was in danger. Kunal had to save his life, and with it their worlds.

'Smells like dung,' Kunal said, trying not to compare the smell to anything from memory.

'Imagine I had to hold it and study it up close,' Aisha said in a nasal voice, pinching her nose.

Kunal winced.

'The Dung Master likes to play games,' Adira said, 'Of course, they were going to make it hard for us to find or use this.'

'I don't think this is too hard to find,' Kunal said, holding back a gag.

'How do you think I located it?' Dr Raza said, reading reports on a tablet. 'I was out for some fresh air—'

'You mean smoke?' Aisha cut in.

Frowning at her, he continued, 'I was out for a *smoke* when an ungodly smell assaulted my nose.' He looked up at Kunal, 'I'm pretty sure some of the field workers couldn't stop retching.'

'Enough,' General Shah said interrupting their small talk. 'We have fifteen minutes to figure this out. Dr Raza, brief the others about this thing. Make it quick.'

Dr Raza sighed. He linked the tablet to the massive smart TV in the room.

Kunal was surprised how even in this state of emergency someone was asked to make a presentation. And this wasn't even a corporate office.

Dr Raza began explaining. 'Object DE9X0042, hereby referred to as the Egg, seemingly materialised in our research facility in Trombay. Early hypothesis states that it appeared due to the presence of the High-Temperature Reactor in our facility. The artefact was identified by its distinctive pungent odour. Without further delay, we contained the artefact and put it under observation. Our findings are as follows—' Dr Raza pointed and read them out one by one. Kunal read them in his mind again.

> **Observation 1:** the Egg is built of organic matter, possibly faeces. Strange unidentified patterns on its surface. A straight slit/crack on the top.
>
> **Observation 2:** the Egg is hollow, with some kind of unidentified matter trapped within it. Hypothesis: Gas, yet to be verified. Unclear why the matter hasn't slipped out of the slit/crack.
>
> **Observation 3:** the Egg is radioactive, but the radioactivity is incomparable to anything on our planet. Radioactivity uniformly spread on the Egg, even on the slit/crack.
>
> **Observation 4:** the Egg pulsed with radiation at certain time intervals that coincide with the stray animal incidents around Mumbai. Now identified as the doing of the extradimensional being—Snaitun.

'Any questions so far?' Dr Raza asked.

'What tests did you perform on the Egg?' Kunal asked.

'Kunal, this is a radioactive artefact of unknown origin. Those kinds of tests would require top-level clearance.' Dr Raza replied, then added, 'However, the Egg is unresponsive to light-to-medium forced taps. Mild temperature change and electric jolts resulted in no change or reaction from the Egg.' He sighed. 'Basically, none of the tests we performed were conclusive. We just didn't have enough time.'

Kunal reread the four observations, keeping in mind what Dr Raza had added about the tests. 'Can I see the slit?'

Dr Raza signalled for the lab assistants to move the Egg. They put their hands into the gloves and gently lifted the Egg.

Kunal and Aisha bent over to look at the slit.

Kunal narrowed his eyes, trying to find some kind of motif or symbol on it, but there was none. He scratched behind his ear, and something cold tickled his neck. He looked and found the fish pendant.

'What is that?' Aisha asked.

Kunal looked at her all puzzled. 'The translator pendant. This is how I can communicate with—'

Aisha didn't wait for him to finish. 'Abbu, how big is the slit?'

Dr Raza consulted his notes. 'About an inch long.'

Adira was looking at Aisha. 'What are you doing, girl?'

'I want to try something. Can I see the pendant?'

'Okay,' Kunal said. He lifted his hand, heart beginning to race. *I love you so much right now!*

Aisha measured the pendant. At its widest, it looked a little under an inch. 'Can we try sliding this in?'

Adira jumped onto the table, 'Girl...' but Aisha couldn't understand her. Only Kunal had a pendant.

'I trust her,' Kunal said to Adira. He was already untying the pendant. Aisha had figured it out! Probably.

'Boy!' Adira said, placing her paw on his hand. 'If you want to try this, use Guru's.' Her ears flopped as she mentioned Guru's name. She lifted her paw and sat straight. 'They won't be needing it.'

'Fine,' General Shah said, untying the pendant around his wrist. Kunal hadn't noticed it before. He was wearing Guru's pendant?

General Shah had already ordered two spare assistants to be dressed in containment suits, ready for such tasks. He had the pendant sent over to the assistants.

The assistants opened the glovebox and placed the Egg open on the table. Despite the thick glass separating the Egg from the observation room, Kunal could smell it.

The assistant announced, *'Testing effect of extra-dimensional pendant on the Egg.'*

They proceeded to slowly bring the pendant closer to

the Egg. As they did, there was nothing.

'Readings normal; no change,' the other assistant announced.

As the assistant brought the pendant closer to the slit, the slit emanated a soft glow.

'Luminescence detected from the slit upon bringing the pendant closer,' the assistant announced. The glow reacted to the pendant's proximity; the closer they put the pendant, the brighter it glowed.

General Shah turned to Aisha.

'Maybe you have to…' Aisha made a gesture.

General Shah ordered over the microphone, 'insert the pendant in.'

The assistant looked at them, then announced, *'Proceeding to insert the pendant into the slit.'* He slowly brought the pendant close to the slit. As the pendant touched the slit, the radiating light became almost blinding.

'Reading stable. Intensity of the luminescence from the slit increasing exponentially,' the other assistant announced.

'Pendant is inside,' the first assistant said. *'No change or reaction.'*

Aisha scratched her chin in thought. She grabbed the mic, 'Push it all the way in.'

The assistant looked at the observation window, confused.

'Do what she said, goddamnit!' General Shah barked.

Flinching, the assistant put his thumb on the pendant and gently pushed it all the way in.

The slit glowed blindingly for a second, then the glow died.

'Pendant fully inserted. The slit has returned to its former state.' The assistant announced. *'Unable to detect pendant.'*

The other assistant added, *'Readings stable. No change detected.'*

Nothing happened.

Kunal felt his hopes die.

'What happened? Did something happen?' General

Shah shouted frantically. 'We're running out of time!'

The door to the observation room opened with a thud. The arrival was a junior executive who looked like he didn't want to be there. 'General Shah... the morgue...'

The morgue was located underground, a level above the research centre. Once they entered, they found two researchers observing a body on the table. The body was a bald individual with greyish-yellow skin. Their robes were tattered brown and gold, unlike any religious attire Kunal could recognise. Their sides and face were singed and sooty.

'GURU!' Adira shouted, jumping onto the table despite the researchers' protests.

'Is that...?' General Shah asked.

'That's Guru!' Adira yelled back.

'What's she saying?' General Shah asked.

'That's Guru,' Kunal said. He realised not everyone might know the name, so he added, 'the owl.'

'The owl that... died?'

'That's their real form,' Adira said, looking sadly at the high mage. They looked at the ceiling with lifeless eyes. Adira gently pawed their eyes shut.

'What does this mean?' General Shah barked.

'Adira!' Kunal shouted, 'Give us your pendant!'

Adira still mourned for the mage. She shook herself then looked at Kunal, tail slumped down. She didn't want to leave.

Kunal took a step forward, 'You want to stop Snaitun? We need you at your best.' He extended his arm. 'Please.'

Back in the laboratory, the assistant pushed Adira's pendant into the Egg. The slit glowed blindingly, then died away.

Immediately, Adira fell to the ground and crouched awkwardly. She grunted in pain as her body started glowing. Her body convulsed as the glow crackled like wild flames, bright as the slit's but larger. Much larger.

When everything settled, a muscular woman knelt before them. Steam wafted from her body. Her skin glistening in sweat. She wore heavy iron armour. Her helmet was moulded in the shape of a tiger. On her breastplate, there was a floral insignia that was carelessly scratched off.

'Adira?' Kunal asked.

She looked at him with wide eyes, 'I'm back…'

'What's she saying?' General Shah asked, clutching Kunal's arm tightly.

'What's he saying?' Adira asked.

'Wait,' Dr Raza said, coming in with a briefcase. Inside were six earpieces. 'Experimental. We don't know if they work.' He winked at Kunal, 'We didn't have much time to make these.'

General Shah lifted one and placed it in his ear. Kunal picked one up and gave it to Adira.

The moment she put it in her ear, the piece buzzed.

'Say something,' Dr Raza said after activating his piece.

'I…' Adira began, '…can understand you!'

Kunal felt a rush of relief, his heart pounding with excitement. This was a major breakthrough. With the Dung Egg in their possession, and with Adira returning to her regular form, they actually stood a chance to stop Snaitun. He clapped and laughed, eyes welling up.

'Good job, Raza,' General Shah said, then turned to the warrior, 'We don't have much time. Have any plans?'

Adira lifted her helmet, revealing a shaved head. Her face was rugged, as would be expected of a battle-hardened warrior. 'Why don't you ask them?' she said, turning to Kunal and Aisha.

Kunal felt his heart flutter. *Adira's looking at me for advice!?* He fumbled. 'I don't know…'

'Kunal,' Aisha said, 'We don't have much time. I have a plan…'

'Then speak, girl!' General Shah pressed.

'We just need to find another white shorthair,' Aisha said. 'Snaitun doesn't know Adira is back. We can use that to our advantage.'

'Where are we going to find another white shorthair that looks exactly like her?'

'We don't need another shorthair,' Kunal said, thinking hard. He lifted his hand with the pendant, 'We can just give him this. Tell him Adira died in his attack. Or something…'

'That won't work, boy,' Adira said.

Kunal frowned. 'Why not?'

'Because,' Adira said, then sighed. 'I really wish Guru had told you.'

Kunal blinked in confusion, then realised something. Adira was asleep when Guru told him about the pendant. And the ensuing chaos had made him forget. *This is Snaitun's pendant…*

'Kunal?' Aisha asked with concern, 'Your eyes are twitching.'

He ignored her. His focus was on the pendant, and its effect. Adira had looked vulnerable for the few moments it took her to transform.

Kunal looked at Snaitun's pendant.

'Kunal?' Aisha grabbed his hand gently, 'What are you thinking?'

Kunal looked at Aisha. Then he looked at Adira. Then he looked at everyone around them. It was ridiculous, but it was something. 'I think I have a plan.'

CHAPTER 12
ATTACK ON SNAITUN

BURFI LAY CURLED UP in a wooden box, blanketed in darkness. The lid had been left slightly ajar, from which he could smell all kinds of bad things. Why were the other animals so mean to him? Cute, cuddly little critters—all of them baring their scary fangs, threatening to bite and scratch him. Finally, they had tossed him into this dark box and shut the lid.

Burfi understood they were not his friends. It made Burfi sad.

He tried to lick his wounds clean, but most of them were on his back and neck, out of reach.

Burfi wanted to cry, but couldn't. All he could do was whimper.

Burfi barked. First out of fear, then feigning threat and then again out of fright. He whimpered for pity and wailed for help, hoping someone would let him out. He did all that he could wordlessly, but it was of no use. He clawed at the wood but his little puppy paws weren't strong enough. He tried to bite at the wood, but the splinters in his mouth stung like bees.

Alone in the dark, finally, Burfi gave up. He was weak and he was scared. Worst of all, he was alone.

'My son...'

Burfi opened his eyes, dread filling every part of his little body. He shivered. Hackles raised, tail between his legs, he readied himself for defence. It was instinctive. He didn't even know he had assumed the position.

The lid came off, dousing the box in grey light. Burfi retreated to a corner, whelping.

'We will soon be away from this wretched place.'

The bad pigeon flew up to the edge of the crate, its eyes glowing a chilling grey. Normally, Burfi would've pounced on such a bird, but this one scared him stiff. He wanted to cry, wanted to run away. But the box was too small. There was nowhere to run.

'Do you not remember me?' The bad pigeon hopped into the box, stepping closer.

Burfi began to bark his warnings. Continued to bark incessantly until his throat went dry. He hoped it would scare the bad pigeon away.

It did not.

'My son... It is I...'

Finally, Burfi feigned an advance. The pigeon spread its wings wide and flapped them loudly. Burfi retreated into the corner again.

'Pathetic...'

Burfi whimpered. He hid his face with his paws, hoping it was good enough to trick the bad pigeon.

'I wish you weren't a pathetic weakling... I celebrated your birth, you know? I really did love you when you were born. But...'

Burfi removed one paw, looking at the pigeon out of concern.

The bad pigeon paused and turned to look at Burfi, the grey glow in its eyes fading. ***'You know I don't hate you, right?'***

Burfi removed both the paws and looked directly at the pigeon.

'I wish I had made you stronger... like me...'

Burfi raised his little head. The pigeon's tone had grown almost warm. Maybe he would let him go?

The pigeon hopped closer, raising one wing and caressing Burfi's head.

'I guess it's for the best.'

Burfi blinked hopefully. His tail started wagging.

'Your weakness makes it easier to sacrifice you.' The grey glow was back. The bad pigeon spread its wings again. *'Soon, I'll get what I want.'*

Burfi barked at the bad pigeon. But it was no use.

'As my son, you deserve a swift death. And I promise you that.'

Burfi felt a chill throughout his body. He cowered back into the corner and covered his face.

The bad pigeon sighed and fluttered away. The lid of the box came back on. Burfi was alone in the dark again, but it was better than being around that scary pigeon.

Burfi closed his eyes, remembering all the fun he had had with that boy, Kunal. And the cat. And the owl. He wished he could be with his friends once again.

Why had they abandoned him? Where were they? Burfi started shivering again, scared that he would be alone forever.

Burfi was too innocent to know that he was expected to be the saviour of the world. The burden was too heavy for that scared little pup waiting to be rescued.

*

'Are you sure about this, Kunal?' Aisha asked him just before his departure. Her voice was unemotionally dry. He knew she was trying really hard not to freak him out.

Kunal didn't reply, but the determination in his eyes was answer enough. Even he was surprised at how stoic he was being. His anxiety was beyond its peak, but, for some reason, it did not manifest physically. Maybe his situation had finally taught him to control it. Or at least cope with it.

Is this what it feels like to be brave?

Aisha, suddenly, hugged Kunal and kissed him. 'I'm not cleared to call the shots but know that I'll be watching. You better come back without a scratch. I'd hate to have to find a replacement.'

Kunal blushed and tried to hide it with an awkward smirk. Not wanting to miss the moment, he said the first thing that came to his mind, 'They broke the mould when they made me, baby!'

Aisha cringed. 'I liked you better when you were panicking.'

'I was being campy. Trying to be…'

'Whatever, never do that again.' Aisha's eyes peered into his soul. 'Good luck, love.'

Before Kunal could respond, General Shah howled, 'KUNAL! Time to leave.'

Kunal nodded to Aisha, then turned. General Shah and Dr Raza stood waiting for him next to the helicopter designated to take him. The blades whirred alive like a roaring dragon, ready for flight.

Kunal wished he'd receive something more hi-tech, but a helicopter wasn't too bad.

General Shah clasped Kunal's shoulder tightly and shouted over the blades' noise, 'No turning back now, son.'

Kunal considered his position once again. It had to be him. Burfi trusted him. Snaitun would trust him to be incompetent. His going with the Dung Egg would put Snaitun's guard down. It was risky, but the fate of their world rested on this.

'I know,' Kunal shouted back, accepting the noise-cancelling earpieces from the soldier inside.

General Shah nodded patted his hand. 'Good luck!'

Kunal put on the headphones and nodded to the General.

Kunal climbed aboard and clipped on the belts and

harnesses. He felt something stir within him. It reminded him of departing from his uncle's place during summer vacations, except this time he wasn't going back home to start a new school year.

Although, he'd much rather face literal death over going back to school.

No one waved at him, except Aisha. His parents had been taken to the guest quarters, forbidden from engaging in any of the ongoing activities. It was a miracle that General Shah allowed him to meet them once before departure.

Mom had slapped him across the face for volunteering for this suicide mission. Dad had simply shaken his head and said he hoped Kunal knew what he was doing. He wished his father could be less vague.

As the helicopter began ascending, Kunal ran through his kit one last time.

Briefcase with Dung Egg: check!
Snaitun's fish pendant: check!
Comms in left ear: check!
Bulletproof vest: check!
Knee pads: check!
Pistol in belt: check!
Swiss knife in pocket: check!
Treats for Burfi: check!

He could almost imagine Burfi's excited yelping and tail-wagging when he'd offer him the treats. The thought comforted him.

He kept picturing Burfi, trying not to focus too much on their altitude.

'Report, Garud 02,' General Shah asked calmly over comms.

'This is Garud 02. Skies clear. ETA ten minutes,' the pilot replied.

'Copy that.'

Radio silence followed that brief exchange. The silence stabbed at Kunal. His anxieties whispered themselves back to life, tickling his innards.

Kunal tried to distract himself by looking at the world drift by. He had sat in aeroplanes before, but never helicopters. There was something about being in a pressurised tube that always unsettled him, but it was incomparable to the doorless helicopter experience. Why hadn't they closed the doors? Speed? Aerodynamics? Had they just forgotten?

The only thing stopping Kunal from getting ripped out of the helicopter was the host of harnesses he had fastened. He kept checking to see if they worked.

No... not now! No... I overcame you! Not now!

Look at the pretty view! Bad idea.

Kunal's leg shivered, and his insides turned. His anxieties had reached his stomach acid and were pushing it up his throat.

Before he knew it, he leaned over the side of the helicopter and vomited his insides out. It burned in his throat, his lungs feeling like a squeezed sponge.

'*Sir?*' the soldier beside him asked out of concern.

Kunal continued to retch, feeling like his soul wanted to leave his body. Once he was dry heaving, he leaned back and closed his eyes. The helicopter vibrated around him, making the world spin.

I don't know if I can do this...

Panic gripped him once again. Like coming back to a downtrodden home after a luxurious vacation.

But I have to... I don't have a choice. I need to do this...

Four seconds inhale, seven hold, eight exhale.

It wasn't as easy in the helicopter, but Kunal still persevered. He reminded himself why he was doing this. Forced himself to think of Burfi, of what state the poor pup was in.

Kunal's mind fought for stability. He allowed himself this momentary lapse with the hope that he could stand his ground when the need arose.

You can do this... you can do this...

He felt something touch his hand. He opened his eyes and saw an energy drink proffered to him. The soldier beside him said, *'This should help.'*

Kunal mouthed a thanks, and gulped down the drink, relishing the sweet, mildly acidic liquid reenergizing him. How potent was this drink anyway? Was it even a consumer product, or one of RAW's many secrets that he was now privy to?

'ETA, five minutes,' the pilot announced.

He was panicking for five whole minutes!? Kunal swallowed his spit and took in a deep breath. He had to brace himself. *Just five minutes. That's not too bad.*

'Kunal, report status,' General Shah asked over comms.

He prepared his response in his mind, then replied, 'Freaking out, but ready to engage. Over.'

There was silence for a heartbeat. General Shah was probably cursing Kunal. Finally, he asked, *'You okay, beta?'*

'Just panicked for a moment,' Kunal replied honestly. 'I'm okay. I can handle it.'

Another pause and then came his voice, *'Good. Backup has departed and should be in position 120 seconds after your arrival.'*

Kunal's heart raced. Why couldn't they just say two minutes? A hundred and twenty sounded so much more intimidating than two.

He couldn't complain though. It was his plan, after all. Kunal hoped it would work. He prayed desperately to all the gods—including the Dung Master—that Snaitun would underestimate him.

'ETA, three minutes.'

'Copy that,' Kunal said. He emptied his mind and continued his breathing exercises.

I'm coming, Burfi. I'll save you.

'ETA, two minutes. Beginning descent.'

Kunal's mind suddenly focused on their target. He

could see the abandoned warehouse. Burfi was in there. And so was Snaitun.

This is how long it's going to take for backup to arrive. He tried to keep a mental count, but found it too distracting.

'*We've landed.*'

Kunal began unbuckling himself. Every loosening of a harness felt like cutting off a safety net. This was it.

He jumped off the helicopter with the soldier in tow. The soldier handed Kunal the briefcase that contained the Dung Egg.

The soldier showed him a thumbs-up and said, '*Good luck, sir.*'

Kunal nodded. He turned to look at the abandoned warehouse. They had landed just inside the compound. The warehouse building was a few hundred metres away.

He wondered where Snaitun was keeping the Silent Langurs captive.

They can handle themselves. General Shah is sending backup. You focus on Burfi.

He focused on the warehouse. He had only seen it as a pixelated image from the shaky bodycams. It had looked menacing enough in that poor-quality footage. He had even looked at it from a bird's-eye view, seeming small and approachable.

But now that he was on the ground, the building looked as menacing as a rabid dog. It was abnormally silent there. Then he remembered Snaitun's force field.

Damnit!

Kunal checked his watch. It was close to 5:15 in the morning. For some reason, he remembered his dead grandmother telling him how that was the hour of evil when the spirits were the most potent. Or was it between 3:00 and 4:00? Did it matter? It's not like Kunal believed in all that.

Kunal cursed his grandmother for ruining his childhood with ghost stories, among countless other things. Finally, he shook away all thoughts of ghosts and

Grandma.
Focus, Kunal. Focus!
Kunal had spent the entire helicopter ride just mentally preparing himself. He hadn't had time to run through his mission objectives.

He had run through them all thrice already before departure, but, as he looked at the abandoned warehouse, he decided a fourth run-through wouldn't be all that bad. The gods knew his mind needed the distraction.

Walking towards the warehouse, he mentally ran through his plan.

Step 1: Show Snaitun the Egg
Step 2: Shove Snaitun's pendant into the Egg
Step 3: Watch Snaitun suffer
Step 4: Let Adira and the soldiers capture Snaitun
Step 5: Find Burfi and give treats!

By the time Kunal reached the warehouse, he had run through the plan twice again. He hoped it would work.

Kunal walked in slowly, trying to delay his meeting with Snaitun as much as possible. Who wouldn't, if they were in his place?

Adira. Aisha. General Shah. Dr Raza. Maybe even Mom and Dad.
Focus, Kunal. Focus!

Kunal walked the same path as the Silent Langurs. He gulped and stared at the staging area, remembering the fate of the Langurs.

They're alive. They're held captive. Snaitun never showed us the bodies.
What if he was lying?
Damnit! Focus!

There was a force field around the place that distorted their vision. Inside, he knew, was a swarm of stray animals waiting to assault him.

He cleared his throat and shouted, 'SNAITUN! I've

come to bar—' *No, that's not it.* He cleared his throat again and shouted, 'I'm here with the Dung Egg!'

Suddenly, something slithered by his feet. A snake. Two snakes. They hissed at him, then slid towards the staging area.

As they crossed the barrier, the air rippled, revealing the force field's edge. Kunal clenched his teeth. *Burfi, I'm coming!*

He took a step inside, and the empty warehouse was suddenly full of birds and rats and cats and dogs. Phantoms that could hide in the shadows, flying overhead, scurrying below unseen.

Oh boy…

They all looked at him. Every single animal inside was looking at him with rabid glowing eyes. A hundred eyes? A thousand? It was too much to take in.

Kunal cleared his throat, trying his best to ignore the countless threats. He shouted, 'SNAI…'

'Where is Adira?'

The voice sent a chill through Kunal's spine. It froze his bones, rendering his muscles sore and immobile.

Snaitun…

'I asked you a question, boy.'

In response to the demand, the animals snarled and took a step forward, a shadowy wave of strays closing in. Kunal wondered how long it would take for them to devour him.

Would it be a painful death? Probably.

He shook his head. *Focus, Kunal. Focus!*

Kunal took in a deep breath and raised the fish pendant. 'Adira is dead. I have come in her stead.'

There was no response from Snaitun. The animals stopped but continued to stare at Kunal with their mindless glowing eyes.

'Liar. I can sense her life force—'

'I'm telling the truth!' Kunal shouted, panic tickling his throat. 'Adira—'

'—IS ALIVE!'

'Then I don't know where she is!' Kunal repeated the lies they had practised. 'I thought she died when you attacked us!'

'PATHETIC LIES!'

The pigeon flew into view, perching atop a crate. His eyes glowed red like the fires he commanded. Snaitun exuded an evil aura that could've sent a dragon scurrying.

'You would have me believe that my best warrior died in a mere fire? Guru, I can understand. They were a miserable old fool. But Adira?'

The animals growled threateningly. Snaitun raised his wing to silence them. He waited for Kunal to speak.

At least that's what Kunal assumed. So, he said, 'She was just a cat.' He looked around, anticipating the animals to attack him upon that gross insult.

Snaitun let out a volley of fire straight above. For a moment, the warehouse was illuminated in a warm light, showing Kunal the full extent of Snaitun's stray army. There were even some cattle in the back. Some of the animals left the warehouse.

He's sending them to reinforce the perimeter. Kunal wanted to inform Adira. He clenched his fist, fighting the instinct to touch the comms in his ear.

How long had it been? Had a hundred and twenty seconds passed already? They should have...

Snaitun flew over Kunal, landing just a step away from him. His menacingly small stature made Kunal insecure.

'Show me the Dung Egg.'

Kunal had to stall. 'Where's Burfi?'

Snaitun ignored him, continuing to stare him down with his red glowing eyes.

'Where's Burfi!?' Kunal demanded, louder this time.

'He is safe.'

'I want to see him.'

'You dare make demands about my own son?'

Kunal clenched the briefcase handle. *Just stay silent. It's better than any response you can give him.*

Snaitun shot a plume of fire into the air. Kunal silently did his breathing exercises. Finally, Snaitun pointed at a lone crate in the corner of the warehouse, next to a forklift.

'You may see him...'

Kunal took a step forward.

'... AFTER you show me the Dung Egg.'

Kunal jerked to a halt. That was good enough, he guessed.

'Fine,' he said, hoping it sounded firm enough, and knelt down. He placed the briefcase between them and clicked it open. The nasty smell of the Dung Egg assaulted his nose. He looked at the relic one last time. The slit was on top, within his reach.

This is it.

Step 1: Show Snaitun the Egg.

Kunal turned the briefcase and presented to Snaitun. Snaitun hopped over to the Dung Egg and began examining it. It was odd looking at the pigeon with his bobbing head prancing around the Egg to ensure it was the real thing. Kunal had the urge to grab the pigeon and twist its neck.

Then he reminded himself that this was no ordinary pigeon.

'Yes...'

Snaitun looked mesmerised by the Dung Egg. This was Kunal's chance. He held the fish pendant in his right hand, ready to go. He had to...

No... wait for the signal. Adira will make it.

Had it been two minutes since his arrival? General Shah had said—

An explosion shook the ground. Before the world could steady, rapid gunfire echoed in the warehouse compound.

'YOU FOOL...'

Step 2: Shove Snaitun's pendant into the Egg

Kunal's hand was already reaching for the Dung Egg. The pendant was almost touching the slit, a white glow emanating from it.

'*DIE!*' Snaitun shot a burst of flames outwards. The pendant slid a third of the way in before Kunal withdrew his hand. His flesh felt singed where the flames had licked him. It would begin to blister soon. Hopefully, RAW had an ointment for that. He couldn't survive another injection.

Around him, the animals howled and screeched, all of them waiting to pounce on Kunal.

Kunal didn't have time to react. He grabbed the pistol from its holster and shot straight at Snaitun.

The bullet ricocheted off the floor, hitting a crate in the distance.

The gun recoiled. Kunal's palms were sweatier than an old man in a sauna; the gun slipped back, slapped him on the side of the head and fell on his shoulder with a heavy thud.

Pain jolting through his side, Kunal staggered, kicking the briefcase.

'*YOU WILL DIE!*' Another jolt of flames emerged from the pigeon's beak. The kicked briefcase threw Snaitun off his feet.

From the corner of his eye, Kunal saw Adira leading soldiers into the warehouse. They opened fire at the strays that swarmed them. Adira had her sword raised.

Kunal turned to the briefcase. The Dung Egg slid from its holder. Kunal jumped forward and grabbed the Dung Egg. The surface felt oddly moist, and Kunal had to hold back a gag. The pendant was still sticking in the slit. Kunal advanced.

Snaitun spotted him. He shot flames straight at Kunal.

Instinctively, Kunal held the Dung Egg in front of him. The flames licked the Egg. And Kunal's fingers.

Kunal jerked and fell on his butt. The Egg slipped out of his hands, and he watched it fall to the ground in front of him. It fell on the pendant, pushing it deeper inside.

Snaitun's pigeon body jerked.

The strays' eyes stopped glowing. A moment of silence, followed by confused howling and screeching as the strays began scrambling to escape.

The soldiers now had the upper hand. The strays were no longer under Snaitun's control. They fled for their lives, leaving the soldiers—the uninjured ones at least—open to take on Snaitun.

Someone yelled, *'The strays are fleeing. Focus on the pigeon!'*

'What is the meaning of this!?'

He sounded angry. Kunal didn't have much time.

Kunal crawled towards the Dung Egg, but a wall of flame stopped him. He sat back, sweat tricking from his forehead. His heart threatened to burst out of his chest.

No...

The soldiers fired at Snaitun, but it was useless. Snaitun spat fire at the soldiers, forcing them to take cover.

Adira jumped in front of Kunal and raised her shield. 'Now, Kunal!'

Kunal nodded and followed her as she dashed forward.

Adira blocked Snaitun's flames as Kunal knelt before the Dung Egg. It looked completely unharmed, but the metallic pendant was sizzling. Without thinking, he grabbed the Dung Egg. Luckily, the flames hadn't heated it at all. *Strange.*

Kunal raised the Egg up high...

'HOW DARE YOU!?'

Snaitun flew into Adira's shield and spat fire from the edge. The flames licked past Adira's pauldron, racing towards Kunal. Instinctively, Kunal blocked the flames with the Dung Egg. The flames burnt the fish pendant red hot, almost liquefied.

Step 2! Step 2!

The flames licked Kunal's fingers, and he dropped the

Egg.

Adira knocked Snaitun away, grunting in pain.

Snaitun recovered mid-air and shot another volley at Kunal.

The flames hit Kunal in the chest this time. Luckily, the bulletproof vest was also fireproof. The heat made him sweat like never before, but at least he was alive.

He sat up and found the Dung Egg rolling towards him.

Snaitun launched himself, gliding towards Kunal.

'YEAH!' Kunal screamed in excitement. He grabbed the Egg and raised it once more.

Snaitun prepared to spit fire.

The soldiers shot at the pigeon to distract him. Adira stood between them, shield raised, sword ready to strike. Her pauldron was smouldering.

'NOW, KUNAL!' Adira shouted.

The pendant was too hot to hold. Kunal turned the Dung Egg and slammed it down.

The pendant sticking out of its slit was white hot. It was almost liquid.

When Kunal slammed the Egg down, the pendant broke off.

The molten half of the pendant fell onto the cold warehouse floor. The Dung Egg swallowed the other half.

Kunal watched the slit glow with blinding white light. Then nothing.

Before him, Snaitun's pigeon form glowed orange. It crashed to the ground, sliding past Adira and scratching to a halt next to Kunal.

Step 3: Watch Snaitun suffer.

Snaitun crackled like fire. The fiery glow engulfed him. When the flash faded, a hideous atrocity lay trembling on the ground. He turned to face Kunal, even the mere act looking painful.

Step 4: Let Adira and the soldiers capture Snaitun.

Before anyone could react, Adira leapt towards

Snaitun, falling straight to the ground. Her sword dug deep into Snaitun's chest.

A human chest.

But the monstrosity was only half human. The other half…

Adira screamed with her guts. Spittle flew out of her mouth as she bawled her fury at Snaitun's corpse.

With a jolt, the corpse's hand grabbed the sword and twisted it. With inhuman speed, the corpse rose to its feet and grabbed Adira by the neck.

'*Traitor.*'

Oh no…

Snaitun flung Adira away like she was a few grains of rice. She crashed through a few crates, stumbling to a halt at the far end of the warehouse.

She was within a few strides from Burfi's crate! Kunal tapped his comms. 'ADIRA! Burfi's right there! Next to the forklift!'

Adira grunted in response. Then added, *'What the hell is a forklift?'*

'He's getting up!'

Kunal turned instinctively, his mind conjuring the worst of his fears.

Snaitun stood up. He was slender and twisted. His lower half and torso were human, legs struggling to stand up straight. His left hand was human, flexing and stretching to get accustomed. But his right was a filthy grey wing, flapping incessantly. His neck was ringed, and above it… a pigeon's ugly bobbing head. An enlarged monstrosity of a head, proportional to the now tall, standing body of Snaitun.

It was hideous to look at. And just as terrifying.

'*You thought you could kill me that easily?*'

'Adira, the yellow vehicle! Burfi's inside that crate next to it!

'Okay!'

The soldiers emptied their magazines into Snaitun.

Every single bullet made contact. They, however, failed to penetrate. The bullets bounced off Snaitun's twisted form.

No... we're too late...

Snaitun shook his hand and wing. He leaned back, beak open and glowing orange.

Kunal shouted instinctively, 'TAKE COVER!'

Snaitun pushed forward, shooting a lance of flames at the soldiers. The soldiers scattered, evading the assault.

'YOU WILL PAY FOR THIS!'

The flames shot forward, flooding the warehouse with heat and smoke.

All hell broke loose.

Kunal located Burfi's crate again and dashed for it. Behind him, he heard screams and gunfire, punctuated with crackling flames. The smoke filling in the warehouse had made it hard to breathe. The warehouse wouldn't survive this fight.

We need to get out of here ASAP!

Kunal persevered. Adira reached the crate before him and ripped the lid out. From within, he heard Burfi's whelps and barks. Adira pulled him up by the scruff of his neck and cradled him in her arms. The moment she saw Kunal, she handed Burfi over. 'Get him to safety. I have to finish this.'

Burfi licked Kunal's face, his tail wagging wildly, slapping at Kunal's torso. 'Burfi! You're safe!' *Cough.* 'I'll get you out...'

An explosion in the distance made him flinch. He looked at the warehouse, now orange and red from all the flames.

Parts of the roof had collapsed, exploding into embers and debris as it crashed to the ground.

There was no exit in sight.

Adira had already found her sword and was running towards the twisted half-pigeon half-human monstrosity.

Kunal looked around him, seeing the flames closing in. Burfi shivered in his arms.

Kunal pet him gently, 'You're safe now, okay?'
'MY SON…'
Kunal looked up to see Snaitun staring straight at them.

Without thinking, Kunal ran left. He passed through the flames, jumped over a fallen steel beam and continued to run.

Snaitun swept above them, landing before him.
'You will not take him…'
Kunal dropped Burfi to the ground, 'RUN!' He gestured with his hands frantically.

Burfi looked at him confusedly.

'Go, boy!'

Snaitun laughed. A booming, horrid laugh that could make even the fires of hell freeze over. With a swipe of his twisted wing, he pushed Kunal off his feet.
'Come…'
Burfi barked at him, but Snaitun just grabbed him with his free arm and pecked at his neck.

Burfi wailed in pain, barking.

Kunal watched as a beam fell between them, sparks shooting in all directions. A wave of heat scorched Kunal's face.

Snaitun tossed Burfi towards Kunal, who quickly pulled him closer into an embrace. He saw the fresh cut on the pup's back, blood dripping out.

Snaitun roared with anger. ***'You brought this upon yourselves. Puny humans.'***

With that, he shot upwards, breaking out of the warehouse roof. Wood, sheets and debris crashed to the ground.

Once he verified that the coast was clear, Kunal got up on his feet and picked up Burfi. He covered his mouth and slowly, steadily made his way out.

The breath of fresh air outside was both welcome and painful. Kunal coughed violently, dropping to his knees. Burfi jumped off and began coughing too. Behind them was a wall of heat and smoke, ahead there was fresh air and darkness. His clothes were sooty, his skin felt raw. But Burfi was *unburnt*.

Even fire doesn't hurt him!

Through teary eyes, Kunal looked up, finding Snaitun airborne. He was suspended in the inky night sky. The moon had come out, making a black silhouette out of Snaitun's deformed body. His red eyes, though, still glowed menacingly. He held something in his hand, something that pulsed an ominous orange-red.

The Dung Egg...

Snaitun raised it above his head, facing the moon. The very fabric of reality began renting, a blood-red radiance emanating from them.

Burfi's blood...

Rents appeared in patterns around him, runes most likely. Larger runes began blooming into branches, giving rise to smaller runes that circled them.

Kunal looked in horror as the sky grew darker.

The runes formed a circle around Snaitun. The closer the circle got to completion, the brighter and more rapidly the Dung Egg pulsed. The orange and red pulses slowly began morphing into a pitch-black void.

Kunal watched dumbfounded.

What even is happening?

He heard some movements behind him. Adira pushed away a burning slab of wood and stumbled into the fresh open. She coughed violently but didn't kneel. Burfi approached her and licked her hand. She shouted at Kunal, 'Where's Snaitun!?'

Kunal pointed to the sky.

Burfi barked as Adira looked up.

The void in the sky consumed Snaitun and the runes, leaving a pulsing black hole in the sky. The hole condensed into a tiny marble that slowly fell to the ground.

Adira's face went pale. 'You need to run.'

The marble thumped on the ground and expanded into a black dome. From within, Snaitun stepped out, still twisted and mutated.

Behind him, a soldier stepped out wearing iron armour similar to Adira's. This one had a pink flower insignia on the breastplate. Snaitun's insignia.

Behind that soldier came more soldiers in perfect formation. An entire battalion marched forward, occupying the warehouse's compound.

Kunal stared with eyes wide open, unwilling to believe what was happening.

He's invading us…

CHAPTER 13
RENDEZVOUS WITH YAMA

SNAITUN LOOKED AT HIS FORCES assembled in the warehouse compound. Clad in gold and white armour, pink flower sigil glimmering on their breasts and flags, his soldiers stood awaiting his commands. He had called forth just one battalion; it would be enough to wreak havoc. From what he had learned, this world was far too weak. Half of the world's kingdoms would probably kneel before him just to avoid clashing swords.

Yes, this world's technology was more advanced, but they had no magic wielders. With the combined forces of his soldiers and mages, Snaitun gauged he would conquer this new world in less than a year. If only his body weren't so twisted…

The night was silent, save for the distant zipping of vehicles and the chatter of humans. Snaitun was eager to plunder this new world, and could almost sense the same from his waiting battalion. But, first, he had to claim his victory. Snaitun had won the game. He had defeated his adversaries, those traitors.

He conjured the runes that he had learned from the Dung Dimension tomes, drawing upon the fabric of this reality with his left hand. Although the runes weren't perfect, they were functional enough.

'Dung Master! I call upon your limitless wisdom and guidance.'

Nothing happened. Snaitun's soldiers stood like statues. Not one of them dared to ask or disturb him. It had been a few minutes, but the sharp spears hadn't budged even a hair's breadth.

The runes faded away. The Dung Master didn't show themself.

This had never happened before. Restlessly, Snaitun redrew the runes, hoping that this time the Dung Master would show.

Nothing again.

Frustrated, his right wing flapped frantically.

'I DEMAND AN AUDIENCE!'

A sudden emptiness filled Snaitun's insides. Body and mind both went numb.

● YOU DARE DEMAND OUR AUDIENCE? ●

The emptiness filled with a nerve-racking fire. Snaitun's body knelt by itself, such was the potential of this eldritch god.

'Pardon my insolence, Dung Master. It stems from excitement.'

● FOOLISH WORM. YOU BELIEVE THIS MEAGRE ACT A VICTORY? ●

'I have defeated my betrayers. I have opened the gates for a new world. An offering in exchange for more power.'

A fire burned within Snaitun's body.

Struggling, he pushed, ***'I won your game.'***

● FALSE. ●

'But...'

● **YOU HAVE NOT WON YET.** ●

'But, I...'

● **THE GAME ENDS WHEN WE SAY IT ENDS. DO YOU UNDERSTAND?** ●

Snaitun paused. *'Understood.'*

Snaitun felt the inside of his skull vibrate with the laughter of the eldritch god.

The laughter faded. The fire within him receded. Snaitun felt drained of all his energy. Even the life force that returned felt somewhat used, ineffective. Snaitun had guessed that regaining his form and bringing his soldiers to this world would have let him win, but the Dung Master didn't agree.

Snaitun looked at the smouldering warehouse. Even if anyone was alive inside, they would either suffocate or burn. But, it was probably a mistake to assume Burfi would die in the fire. Taking his blood wasn't enough. Snaitun cursed his impatience.

Snaitun would've cursed the Dung Master if he weren't afraid of their endless power.

'Fine, I'll finish this.'

He turned to his battalion and raised his hand. They immediately kneeled in a collective thump of heavy armour, heads bowing in wait for a command.

'Sweep the compound. Kill everyone in sight. This world is full of weak heathens. They will...'

A whistling sound distracted him. Snaitun looked up to find a metallic cylinder falling from the sky. Slowly, but steadily, it arced towards them. Snaitun raised his wing to create a force field around him and his soldiers.

The cylinder crashed against the force field. A blinding hot explosion engulfed them all.

Captain Mangesh kicked the door down, letting in a flood of suffocating smoke. Coughing, he quickly slapped his gas mask back on. Luckily the animals hadn't taken away their gear. 'We need to go out. Ana, can you identify where we are?'

'South-east wing,' Lt Ana said as she put on her gas mask, 'Admin building.'

The rest of the Silent Langurs followed suit. They were all looking for an escape route. Unfortunately, they were in a room with barred windows and a centralised AC. There wasn't any plausible escape route, and that would soon lead to the Langurs panicking.

He had to think fast.

'Surya, are you okay?' Captain Mangesh called out. Surya had suffered the worst with the snakes. He was bound to be stripped of his ranks after that episode. If the Captain could keep their weakest link sane, their morale stood a chance. *If we survive this night, that is.*

'Yes, Captain,' Surya said with feigned confidence. The rookie was still shaken and embarrassed about still being shaken.

Captain Mangesh peeped outside the door. Smoke and flames had made the warehouse look like they had descended into hell.

'Come in, Control. Control, do you read me?' Captain Mangesh tried with the comms.

'We're on the opposite side of the extraction point,' Lt Ana announced, 'Assuming extraction is even an option right now.'

The fires crackled loudly. They were loud enough to muffle even gunfire.

Captain Mangesh couldn't confirm if the fight was over. But General Shah had sent reinforcements here, based on all the gunfire they had heard. Why hadn't anyone come looking for them?

He turned to his Langurs and asked, 'Is anyone able to contact Control?'

'Negative, Captain,' Surya said. He looked like he needed something to distract him.

'Surya, keep trying and keep me posted. Lt Ana, lead the way. Everyone else, brace yourselves for melee. No being a hero. Our objective is simple: survive and escape.'

A part of the roof caved, exploding in flames and debris. The AC unit came crashing down in sparks. Wires dangled like spilt innards. Lt Ana shut the door at just the right time. 'I don't think we can escape, Captain.'

'Look for an alternative…'

There had to be a way out. Captain Mangesh tried to calm himself. He had to gather his thoughts and wits. He had to protect his team.

A flash of something dark and void assaulted his mind.

● CAPTAIN MANGESH… ●

Captain Mangesh fell to his feet, clutching his head. The voice was like an atomic explosion in his head. He felt like acid was burning the insides of his stomach.

What is happening….?

● WE HAVE A PROPOSITION FOR YOU. ●

'Captain, are you okay?' Lt Ana asked, rushing to him.

● WE WILL HELP YOU ESCAPE. IN EXCHANGE, YOU MUST DO AS COMMANDED. ●

Foaming at his mouth, Captain Mangesh couldn't believe what he was hearing. Was this one of the enemy's psychological attacks? Was this his dying mind playing tricks on him?

He looked around for something sane, but he could only see death around. His Langurs in gas masks looking at him with what he was certain were worried expressions. He had to save them.

It was not worth dying like this. Not here. Not like this.

Captain Mangesh decided to gamble. He didn't understand magic, but if it meant he'd live to fight another day with his Silent Langurs, it'd be worth it. Painfully, he grumbled, 'Yes…'

● SHOULD WE TAKE THAT AS OUR ANSWER? ●

Captain Mangesh felt the pain recede. He felt like himself again. He quickly scrambled to his feet and looked at his Langurs. With an exhale, he said, 'Get us out of here…'

Kunal ran with all his might, Burfi in his hands. Adira ran with them too, knowing she couldn't stand off against an army.

Battalion. Adira had corrected him.

The primary extraction point was already in flames. Their secondary extraction was the helicopter waiting for them outside the warehouse compound.

As General Shah showered a volley of aerial attacks on Snaitun and his newly arrived battalion, Kunal hurriedly boarded the helicopter and shouted for take-off. He clicked on his harnesses, holding Burfi between his legs.

The helicopter ascended. The wind slapped his face. Beyond falling missiles, dawn teased the horizon.

The missiles crashed into a massive force field. As the dust cleared, Snaitun and his battalion stood unscathed. Burfi barked at them; Kunal had to hold him close to his body so he wouldn't fly out.

Kunal watched General Shah's fighter jets turn for another volley.

Why are they firing? Kunal clicked on his comms and said, 'General Shah! Kunal here! Do you copy?'

Static. Then, *'What is it, boy?'*

'Don't waste your ammo on Snaitun! He's invulnerable!'

'His battalion isn't.'

Kunal chewed on his tongue. He looked at Adira, who just shrugged. He nodded and said, 'We don't know that.'

Adira added, *'Didn't you say you were calling your leaders for backup?'*

There was no response for a moment. Then, General Shah announced, 'The military has been informed, but they can't reach us for at least another hour.'

'Why not?' Kunal pushed.

'Because they need solid proof that an extra-dimensional being is invading our world!' barked General Shah. After a pause, he added, *'Also, some idiot minister is doing a photo-op, so they're preoccupied.'*

'What the hell!? This is a world-ending threat!'

'Boy, if our politicians cared about our country, our people wouldn't be this poor and illiterate.'

He had a point. Kunal clenched his fist and looked out of the window.

'Just get back here, and we'll see what we can do.' Static ended their conversation.

The flaming warehouse drifted away. It looked like even General Shah's jets were retreating. Snaitun's battalion stood their ground, unharmed and ready for invasion.

Kunal felt bile rising again. Burfi barked and licked Kunal's face. The pup looked just as scared as he was. Kunal scruffled Burfi's ears. He watched the dog calm down.

Our saviour...

At that moment, Kunal felt defeated. It had all started

when Burfi came into his life. The chaos, the dread, the end of the world. Burfi whelped in fright, tail tucked between his legs.

But it's not his fault...

● KUNAL... ●

Kunal let go of Burfi.

Burfi landed on the helicopter floor, almost losing his balance. Luckily, Adira grabbed him and held him tight.

She shouted at Kunal, *'What is the matter with you!?'*

Was this another panic attack?

● INTERESTING... ●

Was that a voice in his head? Had he finally sunk into schizophrenia, or was this just his mind coping with something much worse?

Was this Snaitun?

● OUR PRESENCE DOESN'T SEEM TO BOTHER YOU. ●

Kunal clenched his teeth. This had to be Snaitun. Snaitun was playing tricks on him. But it didn't sound like him. It sounded like an old desi uncle asking you uncomfortably personal questions that he has no business asking.

● WE ARE NOT SNAITUN. WE HAVE A PROPOSITION FOR YOU. ●

Kunal shook his head, certain that he was going insane. After everything, his mind was broken.

● YOUR MIND IS NOT BROKEN. ●

'Who's there!?' Kunal shouted.

'Kunal?' Adira asked, leaning forward. Burfi was tucked in her tight embrace. He growled, as if he could sense the evil presence in Kunal's mind.

● WE ARE THE DUNG MASTER. ●

'Like Dunge—'

● WE HAVE SEEN YOUR DEEDS, AND WE HAVE A PROPOSITION FOR YOU. ●

'Adira?'

● DON'T WASTE YOUR BREATH ON HER. ●

'Well, I trust her more than some random voice in my head. Leave me alone!' Kunal screamed.

'Kunal...?' Adira shouted. She harnessed Burfi into a seat and unbuckled herself.

● YOU WOULD NOT EVEN HEAR US? ●

Adira jumped into the seat next to Kunal and held his shoulder, *'Are you okay?'*

'LEAVE ME ALONE!' Kunal shouted, 'I'VE HAD ENOUGH ALREADY! I JUST WANT TO GO HOME AND READ A NICE BOOK AND DRINK HOT CHOCOLATE!'

● VERY WELL... ●

'Did you hear me!? Did you hear me!?'

'Boy, what in god's name is wrong with you?' General Shah barked.

'Dung Master…' Adira said slowly, dread filling her voice. *'That's the Dung Dimension god that Snaitun…'*

'What?' Kunal exclaimed, letting that information sink in. Why hadn't he connected the dots? *Damn!*

Adira shrugged, *'Did they speak with you?'*

'Did you just reject a bloody god's help, boy? If that's the case…'

'SHUT UP, OLD MAN!' Adira shouted over comms. *'Playing the Dung Master's game is what started this whole mess.'*

The comms cut to static.

Adira grabbed Kunal's shoulder firmly and nodded to him. *'You actually rejected the god's proposition?'*

'I guess…?'

Adira stared at him in shock. There was a hopeful glimmer in her eyes.

Burfi woofed, scratching and biting at the harnesses holding him away from Kunal.

Kunal felt proud for a moment, wondering if this was a result of therapy. Then he remembered his desolate mindscape, feeling his pride melt away.

Kunal's eyes grew wide, realising, 'If they contacted me…'

Adira matched his frown as she understood what he was saying. *'There will be others…'*

Captain Mangesh stood outside the warehouse with his Langurs assembled behind him. Doubts and uncertainty were staples of every mission, but his last decision might cost them more than just their lives.

Ironic, because it had saved them from the burning warehouse.

'Captain,' Lt Ana asked with concern, 'How did we…?'

'I don't know,' Captain Mangesh admitted, holding himself back from retching. His entire body felt electrified. 'We're in the middle of a magical crisis.' He considered telling them about the voice, but wasn't sure it was the right thing to do.

Was it even my decision to make?

On the horizon, dawn peeked at them. In the skies, the fighter jets had begun bombarding the compound. One bomb even fell right next to them, but the explosion felt like a light breeze.

They had cowered in panic at first, then slowly recovered with confusion and dread.

'A-are we dead?' Surya had asked, trying to hide the tremble in his voice. Another bomb exploded, but he barely flinched at that.

'No,' Captain Mangesh replied, just as dumbfounded. 'We need to get back. Lt Ana, lead the way.'

'To the extraction point?'

'Wherever!' Captain Mangesh shouted, surprised at the anger in his voice. He had never let his emotions get in the way like this. Never.

'Captain, are you okay?'

Captain Mangesh shook his head, feeling the electricity inside him turn to crackling thunder.

'Yes, I'm sorry. I... we need to go back. Whatever is happening here is beyond us.'

'Copy that, Captain,' Lt Ana said and pointed the way for them to leave.

As they marched away, Captain Mangesh looked at the edge of the compound, where a dome-shaped void stood open. An ancient-looking army was assembled there, clad in iron, wielding spears and pikes. Leading them was a twisted monster that held up a force field protecting them from the assaulting fighter jets.

Something inside him told Captain Mangesh that the twisted monster was their target. Snaitun. He wanted to approach, to attack and neutralize him. But it was too late. Besides, they didn't have any lethal weapons on them.

'Captain...' Surya called, the squad already on their way out.

'Coming,' Captain Mangesh said turning to them.
All eyes were on him.
Surya pointed to Captain Mangesh, dread painting his face. Confused, Captain Mangesh stared back at him, then looked at his hands.
They were changing.

Aisha watched with horror as the aerial assault made zero impact on Snaitun's battalion.
'Target is protected by a force field of some kind,' the fighter pilot announced.
'God damnit!' General Shah screamed, 'Status on the perimeter? We can't let them reach civilisation.'
'The army hasn't sent any backup,' an attendant responded, *'We've sent out emergency requests to the local police. They'll be blocking all major routes, but—'*
'Target on the move,' declared the fighter pilot.
On the blurry projection, Snaitun's battalion moved as one massive beast. At least it appeared so on the video feed.
'Target is moving south-west,' General Shah barked.
Aisha gasped. *They're headed here...*
Alarms blared everywhere. They had to evacuate.
Abbu grabbed Aisha by the shoulders and stood her up, 'There's a bomb shelter underground. Run!'
Aisha nodded and scrambled to leave.
Aisha fell to the floor, face first. Her body froze, feeling empty and void.

⬢ AISHA... ⬢

Aisha felt the air forced out of her lungs.
'Aisha!' she heard Abbu scream.

⬢ WE HAVE A PROPOSITION FOR YOU... ⬢

'What's happening, *beta*?'
Absolute dread. That's what Aisha felt in her heart. Was she going mad? Was she…?
Dung Master…

● YES. ●

Aisha felt suffocated. She forced herself to breathe.

● WE HAVE A PROPOSITION FOR YOU… ●

Aisha stood up and ignored the voice. She turned to Abbu, 'Sorry, I tripped… ugh!'
Abbu grabbed a glass of water for her. She accepted it and pulled a chair to sit down.
'Aisha?' Abbu asked with concern.
She raised her hand to silence him. As she drank, she focused her thoughts.

● AISHA, WE HAVE A PRO— ●

Aisha began singing a terrible Bhojpuri song in her mind. The lyrics were ridiculously sexist and backward, the beats like shrapnel cutting into her ears. But the song did its job by draining out Snaitun's voice.

● WE ARE NOT SNAITUN! ●

The song featured a poor farmer's daughter being harassed—no, flirted with—by a powerful upper-caste man. The man and his gang would harass her every day, demanding she give the man a kiss and more. The woman, finally understanding her place, caved and gave the man what he wants. After all, women were mere objects, weren't they? *Who even makes these songs?*

⬢ AISHA! WE... ⬢

The song played louder, becoming a medley of several problematic-yet-catchy songs that she would never dare listen to in public lest people judge her. Aisha imagined daggers raining on the people who made such songs. She pictured them in hell, tortured for eternity. Her mind spiralled into a maelstrom of everything wrong with Indian society, making her heart race.

Rage filled her, as did disappointment knowing that it probably wouldn't change in her lifetime.

⬢ YOU HUMANS ARE FRUSTRATING... ⬢

Aisha didn't even hear that. She was too busy trying to pacify her enraged mind. She had learned to cull such voices long back and was proud of herself for even drowning out Snaitun's psychological attack.

⬢ WE ARE NOT SNAITUN! YOU BLOODY IMBECILE! HOW... NEVERMIND. ⬢

The void disappeared.

Aisha almost chuckled. She had successfully drowned out the eldritch god that had attempted to assault her mind.

'Aisha?' Abbu was kneeling before her, holding her hands in his. '*Beta*, you're scaring me.'

Aisha licked her lips. 'Sorry... I just...' she closed her eyes and breathed in deeply. 'I can't go...'

'What?'

Aisha opened her eyes, 'Snaitun is coming here. And Kunal is in the middle of all this. And I don't think he responds well to—' she pointed at General Shah.

The General was looking straight at her, a grimace plastered on his face. He just sighed and said, 'I have that effect on people. My husband hates it.'

'Husband?' Aisha asked, slightly taken aback.

General Shah's trademark disgusted look shot back at her that screamed, *'Yes! I have layers too?'*

Suddenly, she had a little more respect for General Shah, maybe even understanding why he was always irritated.

'Aisha, you need to get out of here,' Abbu squeezed her hands, 'Go to the bomb shelter. At least you…'

'No!' Aisha said, 'I'm saying here.'

'But…' Abbu turned to General Shah, 'Say something!'

General Shah shrugged, 'I thought you trusted her.'

Abbu frowned. 'But…'

'My father-in-law didn't trust me with leadership,' General Shah said starting up, 'He dumped it on me with hopes that I'll fail.' He grunted and turned to Aisha, 'She figured out where the animals were. She figured out the pendant thing. She's been a better team member than most of my attendants,' he shot a look at the attendants as they tried to hide their faces. 'I can't believe I'm about to ask… do you have any plans girl?'

Sweat dripped from Aisha's forehead. 'Not yet. But…'

The helicopter pilot spoke over comms, *'Come in Control, this is Garud 02. Requesting permission to land.'*

An attendant responded, 'Negative, Garud 02. The enemy is headed this way. Advise you to head east.'

'Copy that.'

A moment later, Kunal's voice echoed over the speakers, *'Control, this is Kunal. I urge you to let us land.'* He sounded desperate.

General Shah grabbed the mic, 'Are you stupid, boy?'

'General Shah, we need to land at Shri Tranquillity.'

'Snaitun's heading this way! Are you nuts?'

Aisha walked over to the General as if being close to the comms brought her closer to Kunal.

Kunal shouted, *'Exactly! We need to be here when Snaitun*

arrives.'
'Why?'
'Because, I know how we can defeat Snaitun.'

CHAPTER 14
THE PUPPY WAR

AERIAL FOOTAGE SHOWED SNAITUN'S forces marching towards Shri Tranquillity. ETA 10 minutes.

Kunal stood in the conference room. Everyone was concerned about what to do next. For a change, Kunal was the only one not panicking. Not openly at least.

'Are you certain this will work, boy?' General Shah asked. He was sweating profusely. He had admitted this was the most dangerous situation he had ever faced, and he had overseen countless black ops that both started and prevented wars.

'Yes,' Kunal insisted. Burfi barked in agreement, wagging his tail happily.

Being the only one not visibly panicking was strangely empowering. He had just laid out the most ridiculous-sounding plan he could think of, and they had listened to him intently. It was the best shot they had.

'How can you be so sure?' Aisha asked.

'Anyone, have a gun?' Kunal asked.

General Shah took a step back, 'What are you planning, boy?'

'I don't need to hold it. Just do as I say.' He looked straight into General Shah's eyes and said, 'Trust me.'

Gulping, General Shah drew a small gun from his

back. 'What now?'

'Burfi, come here, boy.' Kunal led Burfi to the centre of the room. 'Sit!'

Burfi wagged his tail and sat obediently. He seemed to like the attention.

Kunal turned to General Shah, 'Shoot him.'

General Shah shot Kunal a look that said, *'I'd rather shoot you in the face and get it over with'*. But his mouth simply said, 'Are you sure?'

'100 percent.'

General Shah turned to Adira, 'You're okay with this?'

Adira stood straight with folded arms. Confidently, she said, 'I trust the boy.'

Kunal nodded his thanks. Adira's support and confidence had given Kunal more than he would like to admit. 'Just do it, General.'

Burfi stared mindlessly, his open mouth resembling a smile.

General Shah hesitated, pointing the gun at the puppy. 'Isn't he the saviour, you said?'

Aisha looked at Kunal, worry and sweat drenching her face. Kunal blinked once, reassuring her that he knew what he was doing. Nodding, Aisha said, 'General Shah, just do it.'

An announcement blared. *'ETA for the enemy to arrive, eight minutes.'*

'Fine!' General Shah exclaimed and pulled the trigger. The entire room thundered with the gunshot. Everyone flinched. Burfi yelped as he fell backwards.

The bullet hit Burfi in the chest, then plopped to the floor. Kunal pointed to the flattened bullet.

'What just happened?' General Shah demanded.

'You can't hurt Burfi,' Kunal announced, 'Burfi is— invulnerable. I've seen him getting attacked by stray animals. Clawed, scratched, bitten. I saw fire lick his fur, but he was completely unscathed. Just like…'

'Snaitun!' General Shah finished the sentence. 'Of

course! He's his progeny!'

'Not just that,' Kunal said, kneeling beside Burfi, 'look here.' He scratched Burfi's head and parted bits of his fur around the neck. There were scratches there, some still fresh and moist. 'This is Snaitun's doing.'

General Shah frowned but waited for Kunal's explanation.

Aisha answered, 'So, a bullet is harmless, but Snaitun can hurt Burfi. That means...'

Kunal snapped his fingers at her, 'Exactly!' His exclamation was ill-timed.

The announcement blared. *'ETA for the enemy to arrive, seven minutes.'*

Aisha clapped once and shouted with excitement, 'Burfi can hurt Snaitun!'

Kunal shrugged, 'Exactly!'

'I can confirm,' Adira said, 'Guru and I couldn't hurt Snaitun, but one scratch from Burfi and he flew away.' She shook her head, 'I just wish I had mentioned it earlier.'

'Okay,' General Shah nodded, still lost in thought. 'So, how do we get the dog to attack the pigeon monster?'

'Great question! I was thinking—'

'Just get to the point, boy!'

Kunal felt disappointed at not being able to explain in detail. But they were running short of time, so he couldn't complain. 'Burfi listens to me. Stand up!' Burfi stood up. Kunal knelt and raised his hand, 'Hi-five!' Burfi raised his paw and slapped it against Kunal's.

'Killer tricks!' General Shah said sardonically, 'Can he chase his own tail?'

Kunal stood up, 'He listens to me. When the strays chased us, when Snaitun was attacking us...'

'He's right,' Adira said walking over to stand next to Kunal, 'Burfi is just a baby, but in the dog's body, he seems to have gained some of a dog's survival instincts.'

'And a small street dog can kill that monster pigeon

mutant thing outside!?'

Adira pointed to Burfi, who raised his snout to sniff at her hand. She petted him gently, 'This is our only attempt. As a warrior who's seen her share of bloodshed, I wouldn't risk it. But as someone who knows Snaitun personally, he is too proud. He likes the spectacle as much as the victory. If we can get him to duel against Burfi—'

'ETA for the enemy to arrive, six minutes.'

'And who's going to persuade that monster?' General Shah asked.

'I'll do it,' Kunal said, his heartbeat rising. Panic gripped his throat, but he faked it nonetheless. 'It has to be me. He'll have his guard down if I'm facing him.'

Adira sighed and nodded. 'We'll have to lure him away from the main fight, away from his soldiers. Once we're in the clear, we can—'

'This is stupid!' General Shah slammed his fist on the table.

'That's what I said when Adira and Guru first approached me!' Kunal pushed, trying not to think of his actual exchange verbatim. 'This isn't your everyday shoot and bomb the enemy to the stone age battle! This is a fantasy showdown.' He looked at Aisha.

Aisha added, 'Trust us, General Shah. Give us half an hour to engage. If that fails, we'll go ahead with your plan.'

'You don't really think I'm going to listen to you kids, do you?' General Shah picked up the comms, 'The only way to stop that pigeon thing is to drop a nuclear warhead on…'

Dr Raza raised his beefy hand punched General Shah.

No one saw General Shah dodge the punch; they only saw Dr Raza smack his fist onto the wall and groan in pain.

General Shah had a disgusted look on his face. 'You don't really think you're the first to attempt that, do you, Raza?'

Dr Raza was shaking his palm. His knuckles were red. Stifling a scream, he grumbled. 'Why are you so difficult?'

'Do what I've been doing for decades and you'll know why!' General Shah sighed. He began rubbing his eyes.

'General Shah, please!' Kunal pleaded.

'We have a plan!' Aisha added, standing next to Kunal and doing her best to look confident. 'We've—'

ETA for the enemy to arrive, five minutes.

General Shah looked at his watch.

Burfi twitched restlessly. He began barking and continued to bark, directed straight at the General.

General Shah was looking at Burfi now. He briefly glanced at the pistol on the table, then said, 'Bulletproof dog... who would've thought?'

Kunal felt hope kindle in his stomach. 'General?'

'Tonight's been the weirdest night of my career. Bah!'

If he was saying what Kunal thought he was saying, Kunal would've hugged General Shah in gratitude; the man's repulsive expression told him not to.

General Shah pointed to Kunal and Aisha, 'You two are civilians. If anything happens to either of you...'

'I'll be right here!' Aisha said, 'I'll be Kunal's POC.'

Kunal blushed.

'What do you mean POC? I can't let him in the fi—'

'There's no one else Burfi trusts!' Kunal said. Burfi barked in agreement. He even wagged his tail once.

'I'll be there protecting them,' Adira declared, instinctively reaching for her empty pommel. She looked at her belt, then said, 'I need a weapon though.'

General Shah nodded and ordered one of the attendants, 'Get this woman a...' he thought for a second, 'Get her a *Vajra*.'

'2.5 or 2.6?' an attendant asked.

'I don't care!' the General yelled, prompting the poor attendant to run out of the room. He turned his gaze to Kunal, 'I'm trusting you, son.'

Kunal gulped. 'Yes, sir!'

Another attendant rushed into the room and called, 'General Shah, there's someone at the gate…'

'Snaitun!?' panic painted everyone's face.

'No…' the attendant pulled up the feed.

The last person Kunal wanted to see at that moment was his landlord.

Mr Tambe stood wearing a military helmet and a bulletproof vest. Behind him were a hundred SUVs, all full of youngsters with hockey sticks, cricket bats, swords and other makeshift weaponry. Kunal hated how common such things were in his country. The Kunal from twelve hours ago would've panicked and run away thinking they were here to beat him up. The new and improved Kunal of the present panicked and only *thought* of running away.

'Mr Tambe, what are you doing here!?' Kunal shouted, trying to ignore the fleet of SUVs behind Mr Tambe.

'I told you I'll help,' Mr Tambe said twirling his walrus moustache. His military helmet didn't look real.

'But… how did you track me?'

'I tracked your phone!' a thirteen-year-old boy whose voice still hadn't broken out announced happily. He had a cricket bat leaning over his shoulder.

That is disturbing.

Mr Tambe was looking around Shri Tranquillity's complex with the same fascination as an adult presented with a lucrative investment opportunity. 'Do you have an apartment here, Kunal? What's the going rate here?'

'I don't…' Kunal had to remind himself that there were more pressing matters at hand. 'Mr Tambe, Snaitun—'

'ETA three minutes,' General Shah roared over comms, *'You can see them in the distance.'*

'Is that the rakshas?' Mr Tambe asked, pointing with a rifle at the rising cloud of dust. 'See there, just across the tennis court. The rent here must be steep.'

Kunal ignored that last bit and said, 'Yes, that's Snaitun. The rakshas who kidnapped you.' He held back questions on why his landlord owned a rifle. This wasn't the US or Uttar Pradesh.

Mr Tambe laughed nervously. 'Good, good. Now, I'll have my revenge!' His supporters whooped. Mr Tambe wiped away his sweat.'

They didn't have much time. Kunal clicked on his comms, 'General Shah?'

No response. The comms went silent. His mind thought of the worst possible scenario. 'Guys?' Kunal asked to confirm.

General Shah sat rubbing his temple, groaning. 'You're mad!'

'It's perfect!' Aisha yelled, 'The military's at least half an hour away, and your soldiers aren't nearly enough.'

'They're untrained civilians.'

'They're a community. Probably all distant cousins who've grown up together. Ready to die for each other. Best alternative to trained soldiers in my opinion.' Aisha looked at the fleet of SUVs that had filled up Shri Tranquillity's compound. She would normally be frightened of all these SUVs with fluttering flags of their deities and politicians but, at that moment, she saw them as godsend.

General Shah looked at the same screen and winced. 'I don't trust them. They are foolish locals with zero combat experience. Worse, they're foolish Mumbaikars!'

Aisha smirked, 'Spirit of Mumbai, am I right?'

General Shah shot her a glare.

Dr Raza raised his hand, 'Two minutes.'

'What?' General Shah asked annoyedly.

Dr Raza pointed to the monitors, 'The enemy will be here in two minutes.'

General Shah ground his teeth, and sunk into his

chair, 'I can't believe what my life has come to!'

Aisha unfolded her arms, feeling sympathy for the hateful general. 'Look, General Shah, neither of us know what we're doing. But, so far, Kunal and I have figured out more of this puzzle than any of your scientists!'

General Shah groaned. 'Girl, I already let you take the reins. But this…'

'It's better than risking your soldiers, right?'

General Shah shrugged. 'But they don't know what they're…'

Aisha raised her hand to silence him. 'Mr Tambe—the guy Kunal was talking to—was kidnapped by Snaitun. I'm sure he has already explained the risks to his cousins.'

General Shah scoffed.

Aisha pushed, 'We don't have much time. Let's use them!'

General Shah muttered curses under his breath. Finally, he said, 'I've spearheaded more operations than you could ever study in years of training. Not once have I risked civilians by involving them.'

Aisha frowned. 'I'm a civilian, and you used my plan.'

General Shah sighed. 'Touché.' He gestured to the mic. 'Go ahead.'

'Seriously!?'

General Shah rolled his eyes and slumped into his chair. 'For god's sake, just do it!' He turned to the attendants, 'If anyone asks, they held me at gunpoint and forced me to surrender.'

Dr Raza clicked his tongue, 'As if anyone's going to believe that.'

General Shah groaned and waved him off.

Aisha rushed over to comms. 'Kunal, do you trust me?'

Kunal sounded glad to hear her voice, *'Always!'*

'Then get into Mr Tambe's car, and do as I say.'

Adira stood atop the building's roof, wielding one of this world's strangest weapons. It was a long stick with some device at the edge that shocked enemies in contact.

A few more soldiers entered the roof, taking positions to cover all directions. Adira couldn't talk to them because none of them had the translator earplugs. But they seemed to recognise her.

The soldiers pulled out slim cannons with longer barrels and aimed at the approaching battalion in the distance. They would reach Shri Tranquillity any minute now.

Below, Adira spotted several cars—these vehicles were bigger and louder than the one Kunal had driven— packed with soldiers. It seemed that Kunal had amassed the support of the locals. *I was wrong about him...*

'Adira!'

'Aisha?'

'I need you to keep an eye on Kunal and Burfi,' Aisha commanded.

'Where are they?'

'He'll be in one of the cars below,' Aisha paused. *'Snaitun will be looking for him.'*

'You want me to prevent that?'

'No,' Aisha said, *'You need to make sure Snaitun finds them.'*

'Did you misspeak, Aisha?'

'Just trust me!'

Kunal sat in the middle of two fat uncles, each wielding a sword. To Kunal's left sat Burfi on one uncle's lap, head outside the window, tongue lolling. His tail did not wag however, as though he understood that he had a duty to perform.

'Comfortable?' one of the uncles asked Kunal with a wide grin.

Kunal smiled politely.

'I heard your parents' building also got raided?' Mr Tambe asked nonchalantly, 'I'm sorry to hear that.'

Kunal smiled again, thinking to himself that it was Mr Tambe's squealing that led to the attack. *No. It's not his fault. Snaitun infiltrated his mindscape. He couldn't have helped it.*

'Are they safe?' Mr Tambe asked nervously.

Kunal nodded. 'They're inside, actually.'

'Oh, good,' Mr Tambe nodded. 'Very good.' After what wasn't really a pause, but brief enough silence to change the subject, Mr Tambe asked, 'Once this is over, can you check with the committee how much an apartment here would cost? This looks like a really good residential complex.'

'I... don't think they're for sale.'

Snaitun's army made itself visible. They were marching at a steady pace, a massive cloud of dirt and dust trailing behind them. The sun had just peeked over the horizon, sending a dim grey glow over the world.

Snaitun used a volley of flames to melt down Shri Tranquillity's gates. With a mighty swoop of his wing, he knocked them out of their place, leaving the path open for his forces to enter.

'Wow!' Mr Tambe exclaimed, 'Those gates couldn't even hold back this rakshas. I bet I can use that to bring the price down! Kunal?'

Kunal ignored him. He was too busy holding back his anxieties. Despite their primitive weapons and armour, Snaitun's soldiers looked invincible. Was he making a mistake in trying to win this? Maybe submission was the better option.

No! He'll kill you no matter what. Might as well go down fighting.

Kunal reminded himself what Aisha had said. *We need to separate Snaitun from his forces. That's the only way the military can eliminate his numbers.*

'I think he's scared stiff,' Mr Tambe chuckled, wiping away his sweat and poorly pretending to stay calm.

'Can I start driving now?' Dilip asked. He was Mr Tambe's cousin. He was allegedly the leader of the SUV fleet, a local politician-gangster with enough clout to make Kunal disappear if he offended him.

Burfi barked, shuffling at the window.

Kunal snapped back to reality. 'Wait for the signal,' Kunal told Dilip, ignoring his racing heart. Hopefully, that wasn't too firm for Dilip. Kunal couldn't afford to deal with a politician-gangster after this whole ordeal.

'What signal?' Dilip asked with the characteristic ignorance of a politician. Gangsters are always better informed.

'My signal.' Kunal held back. He was dangerously within slashing range of the uncles' swords. 'I'll tell you. Just...' *Patience, Kunal. Patience.*

'ETA sixty seconds,' Aisha's voice announced. Kunal held his breath unconsciously. 'Kunal, get going! NOW!'

Kunal leaned forward and shouted, 'Go, go, go!'

Dilip cheered, 'Finally! Some action!' He put his head out of the window and yelled orders to the other cars. His gang scrambled into their SUVs and slammed their doors shut. A chorus of diesel engines revved to life. Headlights flashed. Horns blared.

'GANPATI BAPPA!' Dilip screamed.

His army replied, 'MORYA!'

The air burgeoned with the smell of burning diesel and testosterone. Dilip slammed the accelerator.

Kunal felt a jerk as the car sped forward. Around them, the other SUVs revved together in an almost post-apocalyptic scene.

One of the SUVs had giant speakers mounted in the back. It began playing a gully rap song that was strangely catchy. No misogyny, no discrimination, just pure rage against the unfair society that kept its people poor, illiterate and forever subservient.

If they survived this, Kunal made a mental note to ask for the song's name and read the lyrics.

Snaitun's battalion continued their steady march. Snaitun's glowing red eyes seemed to search for something. He spotted the approaching vehicles. With a raised hand and a war cry barely audible over the SUVs' gully rap tracks, Snaitun commanded his soldiers to raise their spears in defence.

The locals in the SUVs, however, were drunk on power and testosterone. They screamed insults and curses as the cars rapidly closed the distance between them and Snaitun's soldiers. The drivers ignored all lawns and gardens, using their off-roading skills honed by Mumbai's bad roads.

Who knew that the BMC's incompetence would equip people with skills useful in tackling world-ending threats?

One car raced forward, aiming straight for the pigeon-human monster at the head. Snaitun opened his beak and sprayed it with a lance of flames.

The car didn't stop. It continued to race forward until…

The car slammed into Snaitun and shoved him back into his battalion. Spears stabbed into the car, but the car ran over five soldiers, scattering the rest.

Their position was broken. Before the battalion could react, the other SUVs slammed into their formations, knocking some soldiers off their feet, running over others.

Dilip drifted just in time, skirting the enemy's formation. Even Burfi switched sides to look out the right window as Kunal caught a glimpse of Snaitun being run over.

Obviously, nothing would happen to him. But the delay was enough to buy them more time.

Burfi barked at the enemies. The uncle on his side had to hold Burfi's collar to stop him from jumping out.

As they were crossing, one of the SUVs drove next to them. Adira climbed out of its window and perched on the carrier. 'SNAITUN!' She grabbed a dagger and threw it straight at the dark lord.

Adira, the legendary warrior that she was, hit Snaitun straight in the face. The dagger bounced off his pigeon face. His glowing rage-filled eyes spotted her.

Immediately, and with inhuman speed, Snaitun

sprung out of the chaos of the battlefield, landing closer to them.

Adira jumped off her SUV and landed on top of Kunal's. She leaned down and screamed, 'Keep going!'

'Keep going!' Kunal repeated to Dilip.

'You really think I was going to stop, kid?' Dilip snapped, hitting the accelerator.

Kunal pointed towards the shattered gate, 'Out of the complex! Away from the battle!'

'I know!' Dilip said, looking straight at Kunal. 'I heard your plan the first time!' he turned to Mr Tambe, 'These rich kids have no respect for their elders.'

Mr Tambe didn't respond. His eyes were fixed on Snaitun, fear painting his face white. 'That's the rakshas?' he asked no one in particular, 'Panduranga! Give me strength!' He raised his rifle and shot.

The recoil and boom were deafening. Even Burfi shrieked in fear.

Kunal clapped his ears shut. The tinnitus in them was just what he needed at that moment.

'Did I get him?' Mr Tambe's hopeless voice asked. It sounded muffled to Kunal's ears.

'No,' Dilip's muffled voice responded, 'Let the others do the shooting.' He turned to the uncles, 'Why are you holding swords? I paid good money for those rifles!'

Kunal looked around in a daze, spotting the shattered gate. They had reached an open ground.

The ringing in Kunal's ears had started to fade. Almost clearly, he heard one uncle respond, 'We look very cool. Like Chhatrapati Shivaji Maharaj!'

'If you don't pick up those rifles and shoot, I'll send you to Shivaji myself!' Dilip commanded.

Rifles replaced swords. Kunal cupped his ears again as Mr Tambe and the two uncles fired at Snaitun. Some bullets hit their mark.

Snaitun was entirely unbothered. He was focused on someone else, eyes gleaming red, fire blooming in his throat.

'ADIRA! I WILL HAVE YOUR HEAD.'

'WHAT WAS THAT!?' Dilip shouted.

'That's the rakshas who kidnapped me,' Mr Tambe replied in a strangely vindictive voice. 'Still think I was being a coward?'

Dilip, pale as a ghost, just shook his head. 'Just keep shooting!'

Burfi jumped into the backseat, barking at the rear window. Kunal turned and found Snaitun closing in. He was about to catch up to them.

Snaitun pounced. Adira flung her electric baton towards him.

Fire erupted from Snaitun's beak.

The baton went straight into his mouth, erupting in a cloud of thunder and flames.

Burfi barked as Snaitun crashed into the rough ground. Dust clouds engulfed him as Dilip's SUV sped on.

Snaitun took a moment to recover, then shot forward like a rocket bursting from its launch pad. The SUV couldn't outrun him.

'Drift!' Kunal shouted.

Dilip pulled the handbrake and swerved to the side. They watched Snaitun fly past, angry glowing eyes not leaving them for even a heartbeat. He disappeared into the dust cloud rising from the sudden drift.

Adira watched as Snaitun's arm reached out of the dust cloud and grabbed the carrier. With a quick jerk, he pulled himself up. His eyes were fixed on her.

'You will die for this!'

Before Adira could react, Snaitun shot flames straight at her. She dove forward, the flames singing her back. She kicked the vehicle's roof and speared him in the torso. The two fell on the bonnet of the car. The vehicle slid to a halt, throwing them both onto the ground.

'Adira!' someone called from the vehicle, tossing a

sword at her. It was a weak sword, forged by an incompetent swordsmith.

But it would do for now.

Adira snatched it out of the air and swerved it straight into Snaitun's chest. 'I will not stand by and watch as you destroy another world!' Adira screamed. She was foaming with rage, eyes bloodshot and ready to kill.

'You have no power over me.'

Snaitun dodged her slashes as if they were butterflies hovering around him. Finally, he clutched the sword with his bare hand and crushed it. Shards of weak metal dropped to the ground. Snaitun's hand was unhurt.

'Weakli—'

A vehicle slammed into Snaitun, rocking up and down as it drove over his body. Snaitun's wing twisted at odd angles. His legs too. Feathers exploded in the air as the vehicle drove a further distance and halted. Snaitun's twisted—more than before—body rolled to a halt.

An ordinary man would groan with pain. Snaitun bawled with rage.

With a burst of flames, Snaitun was standing again. His twisted bones mended themselves, his broken wing growing feathers anew.

'Enough games...'

Snaitun flew straight at Adira, grabbing her by the throat. Adira clutched his hand and punched him in his hideous pigeon face. Undeterred, Snaitun shot upwards.

Adira felt her feet lift off the ground. She kicked in the air. Her surroundings grew colder, the air she inhaled was thinner. From their height, she saw the sun rising. Bright warm light melting away the inky violet of night.

So, this is it...

'Die... Adira...'

Adira closed her eyes and accepted her fate. *I'm trusting you, Kunal...*

Something slammed into them. Something rock solid and warm. Adira felt Snaitun's arm leave her throat, the breath of cold air harsh but welcome.

Adira felt something hold her. She opened her eyes to see—

Dust clouds wafted all around them. Dawn made the dust appear gold. Drenched in sweat and full of anxiety, Kunal frantically searched for Snaitun in the sky.

'What in god's name is happening!' Mr Tambe shouted, aiming the rifle up at the clouds.

'You were always bad at hunting,' Dilip mocked, failing to find the pigeon-human monster with his own rifle.

Kunal found two black spots in the sky. Snaitun and Adira.

And then there was a third spot. The third spot rapidly closed in on the other two and hauled one of them out of the air.

Now the three spots were falling to the ground, slowly. As they fell, they grew more discernible. Kunal clicked into comms, 'Aisha, are you seeing this?'

'No, I don't have eyes outside the complex. What is it?'

'There's…'

Something thudded on top of their parked SUV. Not one of the spots. But eerily similar to one of them, albeit much larger than Kunal had expected.

The four uncles instinctively turned their rifles to aim at the arrival.

Kunal took a step back, clutching Burfi's collar tighter. Burfi barked, threatening to charge at the arrival. Kunal had to hold him back.

The giant grey langur in black military fatigues before them roared and bared its razor-sharp fangs. It loomed over nine feet tall, its midnight black visage made it look like an ancient old man. The dawn's light made its silver-grey hair look golden and sacred.

Kunal had never seen a langur in his life, let alone one that was almost twice his height. Another nightmare from the other dimension?

'Bajrang Bali!' Dilip screamed, falling to his floor, 'Bajrang Bali has come to save us!'

'Am I dreaming!?' Mr Tambe gasped, lowering his rifle.

Kunal doubted this was the monkey god. The atheist in him refused to believe it, but maybe the uncles were on to something.

The four middle-aged men prostrated before the arrival, praying to protect them.

'Save us, Bajrang Bali!' they chanted in unison.

'Slay that rakshas like you did Ravan!' Dilip yelled.

'Idiot! Hanuman didn't kill Ravan,' Mr Tambe reprimanded.

The langur hissed.

'Don't make him angry!' Mr Tambe yelled, then screamed, 'Forgive my brother, Bajrang Bali. He's not…'

The langur launched forward and grabbed Mr Tambe, tossing him straight into the SUV.

He fell with a thud, leaving behind a Mr Tambe-sized dent in the SUV's side.

'Giant langur…' Kunal shouted in a panic, struggling to keep Burfi from attacking. 'This is Snaitun's doing!'

Before Dilip could react, the langur lifted and tossed him to the side. The plump man plopped to the ground in a cloud of dust. He skidded to a halt and whimpered prayers for his own soul.

'Giant grey langur… wearing black military fatigues…'

The langur turned to face Kunal.

Kunal took half a step back, just as Burfi launched forward. 'No! Burfi, back! Run! Danger! HELP!'

The langur bared his teeth at them and jumped forward. Kunal leaned back and fell on his backside.

He watched the langur fly past overhead, continuing to chase the other two fleeing uncles. Their rifles lay discarded next to the SUV (and Mr Tambe's groaning body).

'Kunal, what the hell is happening!?'

'I...' Kunal could feel his heartbeat in his throat. 'don't... know...'

'Boy, we don't have eyes on your location!' General Shah barked, *'What is your status!?'*

Kunal gulped and reported. 'Giant grey langur. Nine feet tall. Attacked us.'

'One of Snaitun's?'

'I don't know...' Kunal took in a deep breath trying to regulate his breathing. 'I don't know... It... military fatigues... black ops...'

There was a gasp over comms. *'Black Ops? Like...?'*

'We've got eyes,' Abbu announced as the attendants put up the drone feed.

Aisha rushed to the screen, 'Do you see any langurs?' General Shah was right behind her.

'Negative,' Abbu replied.

Aisha was right. Separating Snaitun from his army had left his army vulnerable. She just hadn't expected their bane to be local SUVs blaring gully rap. Snaitun's forces had been reduced by a third. It had been an almost equal fight, and the Indian army's arrival in twenty minutes would mean a certain victory.

But the langurs had arrived before them.

Aisha watched in horror as giant grey langurs wreaked havoc on the battlefield. There were six of them, attacking cars and iron-clad soldiers alike. The SUVs that had survived the road rash assault fled outwards. Snaitun's remaining forces rallied into smaller companies, trying to hold their ground.

'Are they wearing...?' Abbu gasped in horror.

'Yes. One attacked Kunal's SUV too...'

'Looks like the Silent Langurs...' General Shah said softly. He stared at the screen with a frown.

Abbu asked, 'Did Snaitun...?'

Or the eldritch god... Aisha grabbed General Shah's arm,

'Maybe we can talk to them? What channel are they on?'

'The channel's dead,' General Shah replied almost instantly, 'Their comms were fried when they were captured by that monster.'

Aisha felt panic rising. 'Okay, we can do this. This is just like any video game. When the final boss is vulnerable, the game launches additional forces to complicate the gameplay.'

She expected some kind of gen-Z-bashing comment, but both the men before her stayed silent.

'We have to think of something…'

'The langurs are unnaturally powerful,' Abbu said.

'And they're trained soldiers,' General Shah said, sinking into a chair, 'What do you expect?'

Aisha tried to keep the conversation going. Maybe that would lead to some kind of solution, 'It looks like a chaotic attack. No pattern, no plan, no leadership.' Aisha thought hard. They didn't have much time to rethink their strategy. 'Ignore the langurs. We need to focus on Snaitun…'

'I've located Adira,' an attendant informed. She changed to another feed displaying the warrior.

Aisha watched as Adira was being hauled by a single grey langur. *Is that—?*

Captain Mangesh crashed into the ground. He tossed the warrior woman away. As they rolled to a halt, he quickly jumped to his feet and searched for her. He screamed in his langur voice, 'I'm sorry! The… god… rakshas… evil…' It was of no use. The woman probably didn't understand him. He himself could barely recognise the coarse sounds his throat produced.

The warrior woman scrambled backwards, trying to put some distance between them. There was no fear in her eyes, only conviction. Captain Mangesh had seen this look before. Often when missions led to melee combat. She was looking for a way to beat him. To kill him.

He had the advantage of standing against the morning sun. The warrior woman probably saw him as a frightening shadow. But it didn't matter.

Captain Mangesh persevered, 'They made us do this! Please! I don't want to hurt you!' he raised his lanky arms before him. The woman raised her arms defensively.

The warrior woman found a broken brick and tossed it straight at Captain Mangesh's head. He saw stars and spots. The woman shouted something in a language he didn't understand.

'Please...' Captain Mangesh begged, regaining his balance.

The warrior woman lurched forward, clutching Captain Mangesh by his silver mane. She was fierce and strong, impossibly so. Despite his beastly strength, he struggled to stand. She climbed onto Captain Mangesh's back and crunched her elbow straight into his skull. A sharp pain pierced through his forehead.

'Woman... please... I am not your enemy...'

The warrior woman scrambled again, this time putting her arm around his neck in a chokehold. She squeezed, and immediately Captain Mangesh felt the air supply cut off. He struggled to get up, swaying this way and that. The sunlight slapped his face with one step, and went dark with the other. He had to calm down.

I will not die this way...

With his lanky long arms, he grabbed onto the warrior woman's tunic and pulled at her. A few tugs later, he gave up and jumped high in the air hoping his plan worked. As they descended, he twisted himself to fall back-first. They slammed into the ground with a sharp crack; he felt the warrior woman's iron armour cut into his back.

She groaned and shouted something.

'I can't... understand...' Captain Mangesh struggled. 'Please...'

The warrior woman's arm wrapped around his neck yet again, her legs a vice grip around his torso.

'Goddamnit!' Captain Mangesh screamed.

Her grip suddenly went loose. He faintly heard her speak his name.

Suddenly, the woman let go and scrambled to her feet. She took a defensive stance as Captain Mangesh stood up weakly. 'Thank you...' He raised his langur arms up in surrender, 'I don't want to hurt you.'

His skull reverberated with the deafening howls of a black hole. His body froze, unresponsive.

● YOU PROMISED US, CAPTAIN MANGESH. YOU HAVE TO KEEP YOUR END OF THE BARGAIN. ●

There was no tricking this accursed god. Captain Mangesh had axed himself in the foot by accepting the god's proposition. Would he be branded a traitor? Would they give him a chance to explain?

No time to think of all that.

Captain Mangesh looked at the warrior woman, realising she was superior to him in every aspect. There was no way he could defeat her.

But, I'm not my normal self.

Captain Mangesh took on an offensive position. 'I'm sorry...' He lunged forward with inhuman speed. The woman dodged with almost equal nimbleness. But he was a beast now. With all his might he launched a volley of punches and scratches at the woman, cursing and apologising with every swerve.

'I'm sorry... but I have to do this...'

Captain Mangesh grabbed the warrior woman and launched himself up. He raised the woman above his head just as he stopped ascending, then threw her straight at the ground. Her body shot up a cloud of dust as it crashed.

Forgive me...

Snaitun eyed the giant grey langur blocking his way. He debated whether or not to kill it.

'WHAT IS THE MEANING OF THIS?'

● **YOU DARE QUESTION US?** ●

Snaitun considered his response. *Is this another hurdle I must cross?*

● **YOUR FIGHT IS LACKLUSTRE. WE DEMAND BETTER ENTERTAINMENT.** ●

Snaitun sighed. *'Mindless chaos is entertaining?'* He felt the void chuckle in his mind.

● **IT IS MORE AMUSING.** ●

'Where is my son?'

● **RIGHT OVER THERE...** ●

Snaitun looked and found the sun's rays guiding him. The dawn's light shone over the shattering grounds, reflecting against the white vehicle next to which stood the boy Kunal holding onto his son's collar.

In a single leap, Snaitun flew over to them.

Burfi barked at him incessantly. It appeared that he was ready for attack.

Snaitun landed before Kunal and demanded, *'Hand me my son.'*

The boy turned pale with fright. His heart raced faster than a charging war horse.

Snaitun did not care. He took a threatening step forward, *'I will not repeat myself.'*

This was it. The final battle. The final test.

Burfi's collar cut into Kunal's grip. He had to let Burfi go. He had to let the end commence.

'What are you going to do with him?' Kunal stalled. He needed time.

Snaitun clenched his fist. '***None of your business.***'

'Will you hurt him!?' Kunal shouted, hoping Snaitun didn't see his free hand. It was hard keeping Burfi from running forward.

'You are stalling. You—'

Kunal found the dagger and threw it at Snaitun to distract him. At the same moment, Kunal let go of Burfi's collar.

Burfi dashed forward and leapt at his father.

Burfi watched the evil pigeon-man block the attack with his wing. Burfi snapped his maw into the wing, chomping into flesh and feathers, forcing a pained scream from the pigeon-man.

'Let go of me you stupid dog!'

Burfi barked ferociously. *NO!*

'I'm your father!'

Burfi didn't understand; he didn't care. The human–pigeon struggled to flap his wings, shaking Burfi in the air. Burfi felt like he was flying.

This was fun!

The pigeon-man flung Burfi away. Burfi landed on his back and rolled over in the dirt. His mouth was full of pigeon meat and feathers. He spat and coughed, hating the taste. Burfi quickly rose to his feet and shook the dirt away.

He heard Kunal shout, 'Here boy! Burfi! Here!'

Burfi frantically looked around until he spotted Kunal and zoomed towards him. The pigeon-man landed between them, making Burfi flinch. He barked at the monster to shoo him away. It didn't work. The pigeon-man could sense Burfi's fear.

Whelping, Burfi backed away. He wanted to run.

'Burfi! Attack!' Kunal shouted from behind the monster. 'Bite him, Burfi!' Kunal's mouth snapped with his teeth bared wide.

If Kunal was saying it, it must be possible. Burfi's newfound motivation made him bark more aggressively, growling and baring his teeth to hide his fear.

The pigeon-man was unmoved. He raised his hand to strike, grey light glowing at the back of his mouth.

'Don't you dare...'

Burfi shot forward. The pigeon-man opened his beak, spewing flames into the air.

Burfi slowed down, retreating a few steps. The heat coming from the pigeon-man hurt Burfi.

Suddenly, the pigeon-man stumbled and fell to the ground. Burfi watched with surprise as Kunal wrestled with the pigeon-man, smashing a rock onto his head and torso.

The pigeon-man flapped his wing, shooting the rock into the sky. He grabbed Kunal by the neck and brought his face closer to that ugly pigeon head.

Burfi shivered. But, more importantly, Burfi grew restless with anger.

Kunal was in danger. He had to save Kunal!

Without thinking, Burfi shot forward and jumped up, mouth open and ready to bite.

The pigeon-man flapped his wing, slapping Burfi away.

'Are you really going to hurt your father?'

Burfi fell, rolled, recovered and darted again.

'Bu'ur'feil'aal!'

Burfi jumped again, scratching the wing that blocked the attack.

Kunal... I save you... I...

Burfi jumped for another attack.

The pigeon-man flung Kunal far away and grabbed Burfi in mid-air.

'ENOUGH!'

Burfi scrambled, scratching and biting without success.

'I said ENOUGH! It is a shame that you disobey me!'

Burfi barked. When that didn't work, he growled. And when that failed too, he barked again just in case it worked this time.

It didn't.

The pigeon-man looked like he was done playing games. Burfi glared at him, wondering what he would do next.

'Why do you hate me, Bu'ur'feil'aal? You would risk your life for a mortal from a world that isn't even ours?'

Burfi didn't understand anything. He growled in confusion, hoping it was the right threatening response. His little doggie legs scratched at the pigeon-man's chest, leaving dark grey marks. But the pigeon-man didn't seem to care.

The pigeon-man's twisted shoulders slumped.

'I am sorry, little one.'

The pigeon-man's glowing grey eyes pulsed. He raised Burfi in the air.

'I need your blood to make things right.'

The grip around Burfi's neck tightened. He scrambled to break free, but it was useless. The pigeon-man was too strong. Burfi panicked and scratched at the pigeon-man's arm, drawing dark grey blood. But it wasn't enough. The pigeon-man's nails dug into Burfi's flesh, sending a searing pain throughout his body. Burfi wailed for help, tried to bark but couldn't. He couldn't breathe. He was feeling weaker...

'I wish you were a better son.'

Adira coughed and crawled out of the cloud of dust.

Suddenly, she felt the weight of the giant langur crash against her. Her armour, her muscles, all felt like wet clay against the iron hide of the beast attacking her. She let out an agonised wail, trying her best to reorient herself.

She had to persevere.

The langur leapt and beat its chest. Was it enjoying this battle? Was it goading Adira to attack?

Adira staggered forward, trying to figure out how she could attack it. The langur had easily soared into the air like a bird, its leap and strength far superior. There was something there she could use. But what?

Adira had enough experience fighting beasts in her world. If she could tame wild elephants in her youth, she could sure as hell knock out this langur. Even if it was a special soldier from this world.

The langur was wearing black garb. Aisha had informed her that this was possibly the leader of the special soldiers that had been first sent to kill Snaitun. Captain Mangesh, his name was, and he was probably under Snaitun's control.

Snaitun... Dung Master... I don't care.

Adira growled at the langur, mocking it, urging it to attack. The langur hissed back at her. Its searching yellow eyes like a pair of moons amidst its midnight visage threatened to freeze her in a trance. Adira emptied her mind and let her warrior's body take control.

There was no strategy to be adopted here. The langur was stronger. The langur was faster. The langur was even larger than Adira. The only thing Adira could hope to do was outlast it on the battlefield.

The langur raised its hands again, and Adira shot forward. Fists clenched, she feigned right and dove under the langur's left arm. Using its black garb as grip, Adira climbed onto the langur's back and held it in a chokehold yet again. She knew this was one weak spot that she could exploit.

But the langur could jump into the air. And it could slam her into the ground yet again.

Just like before, the langur shot up into the air. Adira felt emptiness around her.

The langur growled in pain, scratching at Adira's arm.

They stopped ascending. The ground rushed at them.

Adira braced herself as they crashed. Her armour cracked. She felt a tooth chip off as well. But her grip was firm. She didn't let go.

The langur tried to shake her off, growling and roaring bestially. But it didn't stagger Adira. Spitting out the chip, she tightened the grip on the langur's throat, growling, 'Die, you monster!'

The langur slowly scrambled to its feet and prepared to jump yet again. Unable to breathe, it was growing frantic, and weak.

This time, Adira braced herself. They ascended into the air, grew still for a heartbeat, then began their descent.

Adira looked through narrow eyes and just at the right moment twisted her body with all her might.

They swerved; the langur panicked.

They crashed onto the ground. This time, Adira was on top. The langur's head crashed straight into the ground with a loud thud. Its body slumped unconscious.

Adira let go and scooted backwards.

The langur was still alive, but it wouldn't be a problem. Not for some time at least.

Dusting herself, she stretched the pain out of her muscles and clicked into the bean in her ear. 'Aisha, where's Burfi!?'

'East!'

Adira looked east and found Snaitun with his hand raised. In his clutches was a tiny dog that looked like it was struggling.

Adira started dashing forward, but her legs gave way. She crashed to the ground, feeling just a little lightheaded.

No...

She had exhausted way too much energy in fighting the langur. Her insides screamed for respite. Her body ached with the familiarity of incessant battle.

Adira persevered. Groaning, welcoming the pain,

Adira rose to her feet and treaded east. She glanced once towards the langur, glad that it was still immobile, and focused her attention on Snaitun. And Burfi.

Where's Kunal?

Kunal felt his bones ache. His body was still recovering from the shock of his crash. He couldn't believe what he had done. But he didn't have time to think.

Burfi was in danger. He slowly trudged towards Snaitun, trying to reach Burfi, trying to save him.

But they were too far away. Kunal had failed.

Despite the fact that Burfi had managed to hurt Snaitun, it wasn't enough. The plan was to overwhelm Snaitun once he was hurt, but the attack from the giant langurs had foiled their plan.

Now it was just Burfi and Kunal against Snaitun.

And Snaitun already had the upper hand. He was holding Burfi by the neck, and the pup's movements were slowing down.

He's strangling him!

Kunal upped his pace, shouting after them, 'Snaitun! SNAITUN!'

Snaitun ignored him. His twisted form standing against the morning sun shed a menacing shadow upon Kunal's face. The world was blindingly bright, but Snaitun choking Burfi was clearly visible to him. As visible as could be to his teary eyes.

Kunal couldn't walk anymore. He fell to his knees just a few steps away from Snaitun. He could hear Burfi wailing.

'Snaitun, please…'

Snaitun continued to strangle Burfi. Burfi's whimpers grew weaker.

Kunal's gut wrenched. He felt pain like never before. He had been with Burfi for less than a day, and yet seeing the pup like that made him feel worse than anything he had ever experienced in his life. And it was all Kunal's fault.

He would do anything to protect the dog.

● ANYTHING...? ●

Kunal felt the eldritch god's presence in his skull.
Dung Master...
He didn't have time. 'Please, just don't kill Burfi...'

● WE CAN HELP YOU... BUT IT WILL COST YOU... ●

Burfi wailed, almost falling unconscious.
'What do you want from me...!?'

● THE DOG WILL LIVE. BUT SOMEONE ELSE FROM YOUR LIFE MUST DIE... ●

'No...'

● CHOOSE, KUNAL. THE DOG, OR SOMEONE ELSE FROM YOUR LIFE. ●

Burfi had stopped moving. Tears flowed down Kunal's cheeks. He was choking with shock and pain. 'No...' He couldn't breathe. He had to remind himself to breathe.

Four seconds inhale, seven hold, eight exhale.

● CHOOSE, KUNAL. YOU DON'T HAVE MUCH TIME... ●

Four seconds inhale, seven hold, eight exhale.

How could he sacrifice someone else? How? Kunal cleared his throat and grumbled, 'Take me.'

● THAT'S NOT HOW IT WORKS. ●

'I can't let anyone else die…' Burfi's legs still twitched. There was still time. But not enough.

● YOU MUST CHOOSE SOMEONE ELSE FROM YOUR LIFE. THAT IS THE CONDITION… ●

How was that a fair choice? How could a god even offer such an evil choice?

Burfi wouldn't survive too long.

● YOU'RE RUNNING OUT OF TIME. ●

Kunal thought about it. Choose someone else from his life, but who? Dad? Mom? They were old. They had ruined his childhood, given him a ton of mental health issues, but that didn't mean he wanted them dead.

Burfi braved a wail. Kunal started panicking. He couldn't afford to overthink it.

Aisha? Dr Raza? Mr Tambe? General Shah?

The faces and names of people from his life passed through his mind. Seeing them, remembering them, Kunal realised he couldn't sacrifice anyone.

But if he didn't, Burfi would die. And Snaitun would take over the world.

That was the real choice. Snaitun's victory, or Kunal's loss. But, how was he supposed to live with himself knowing he had been responsible for an innocent's death?

The god had said 'The dog, or someone else in your life.' But did he really mean *anyone*?

What did the Dung Master even have in mind? What fate lay ahead for the person he chose?

A wild idea struck Kunal. He looked at Burfi's unmoving body and decided to gamble it.

'Anyone from my life?' he asked, '*Anyone?*'

● **YES...** ●

Kunal decided to risk it. He yelled, 'Then I choose Snaitun!'
There was silence from the eldritch god. Then, the blackness filled his mind.

● **THAT'S...** ●

'You didn't give any other condition!' Kunal shouted, trying to keep a hold of himself. Even Snaitun turned to look at him with suspicion. 'Snaitun is a person from my life. I choose him!'
A cosmic sigh shook his entire world, sending shivers of doom through every pore of his skin. The dawn seemed just a little dimmer, the winds just a little colder.

● **WE DO NOT APPRECIATE BEING OUTSMARTED...** ●

Kunal ignored it, shouting again, 'I CHOOSE SNAITUN!'

● **VERY WELL. THIS COULD BE INTERESTING...** ●

The god's presence disappeared from Kunal's skull. It was a much welcome vacancy, one that brought with it a peace that Kunal hadn't felt in ages. Was this what it felt like to live without anxiety?
He looked on as Snaitun's grip on Burfi weakened. This was working, but what exactly would happen?

Snaitun couldn't feel his body anymore. He watched Burfi

fall to the ground. Kunal ran over to Burfi and cradled him in his arms.

'What is happening...?'

● **THE BOY HAS MANAGED TO DO WHAT YOU COULDN'T...** ●

Dread, unlike any before, filled Snaitun's very soul. A mere cowardly boy had handed over the world to the Dung Master? How? What power did the boy command? How was he able to beat Snaitun without even—? *'You favour the boy?'*

● **NO, WE OFFERED HIM A CHOICE. HE CHOSE WELL.** ●

'You would betray me? AFTER ALL I HAVE DONE?'

● **WE ARE ONLY MAKING THINGS INTERESTING.** ●

Silence filled the world. The Dung Master wouldn't even grace Snaitun with a fair explanation. This was how he was to die?

Snaitun felt his energy fade. His body began crumbling.

'NOOOOOO!'

Snaitun didn't have much time. He had to do something. He wouldn't let the Dung Master win. Not like this.

Snaitun's wing and hand had already become dust. He wouldn't be able to use any runic magic.

Snaitun called upon the weave of this new world. With his mind, he began twisting it as best he could. Snaitun didn't have time. He picked his assault. Picked his weave. He just needed a vessel to imprint on. And the vessel was just a step away. Snaitun's legs faded away, his torso crashing to the ground. He had to hurry.

Snaitun began breaking down the threads of reality. The weave of magic twisted until it formed an astral passage for his soul to survive.

'BOY!! YOU WILL SUFFER FOR WHAT YOU HAVE DONE!!'

Screaming his threat, Snaitun pulled on the threads, breaking reality. The rent sent shockwaves outwards.

Kunal and Burfi were thrown off their feet.

Focusing on the boy, Snaitun projected his mind upon him. The astral passage locked onto the boy's soul.

Snaitun's torso had faded to dust. Only his neck, shoulder and head remained.

'I WILL NOT DIE THAT EASILY.'

He watched as the boy fell to the ground, clutching his head. Burfi's blood was on his hands.

'Perfect...'

Snaitun ruptured the connection between his soul and his body just in time. His head burst out in a cloud of dust. Snaitun's astral projection shot towards Kunal.

Snaitun laughed as his soul engulfed Kunal's body in a shimmering explosion of stars and abyss. He watched the boy cower and shake as his body convulsed with the new presence breaking into it.

Snaitun had to be careful. If he damaged the body too much, it would all be for nothing...

'Snaitun!'

Snaitun's attention turned to Adira. She was jogging forward. She looked hurt, but the pain was nothing compared to her rage that was focused just on him.

He didn't have time. He had to do it now.

Snaitun commanded the lifeforce wafting out of Burfi's spilt blood and began burrowing himself inside Kunal's soul.

Something was wrong... It wasn't working...

Burfi's blood...

'No...'

As Snaitun's soul completely immersed itself into Kunal's form, another soul merged within their spiritual soup.

'No...'

Together, the three spiralled out of reality and fell straight into a void that Snaitun didn't recognise.

The world was fractured. A starless abyss floated in the background, its midnight inkiness far more menacing than the emptiness of space. Chunks of rocks floated around them. They held caves blocked by boulders, holding back mysteriously terrifying droning.

Snaitun, Kunal and Burfi—the three of them were on a platform, a flat rock suspended in nothing.

Snaitun looked around, feeling the same kind of dread he had felt every time the Dung Master made their presence felt to him.

'Is this the Dung Master's domain...?'

'No...' Kunal grunted as he stood up straight. 'You're in a place far worse than any eldritch god's domain.'

Worry gripped Snaitun. Fear, confusion, anxiety. The place reeked of them all, and they doused Snaitun in their essence. Trembling, he asked, **'Where are we...?'**

Kunal smirked and answered, 'My mindscape.'

CHAPTER 15
MEMORIES OF FRIGHT

KUNAL COULDN'T BELIEVE what he was looking at. Guru had brought him here twice in the past twelve hours. The plain of existence that haunted him all his life, the playground of his perpetual suffering once again sprawled before him in all its cosmic terror.

In this plain of existence, you are in absolute control. Guru's voice echoed in his mind. So did the cosmic groaning of his traumas.

Kunal's mindscape was darker than he remembered. He had expected the progress he made in the past few hours to have undone some of his trauma, but there didn't seem to be even one new speck of light in the darkness. The void still floated around him, the abyssal mountains with caves of muffled trauma blocked by boulders of suppression still littered the grounds of his mind. This place was still just as dangerous.

And to make matters worse, Burfi was here too. If it was just Snaitun, maybe Kunal could've done something, but having Burfi here was a risk. He couldn't let the chosen one perish inside an anxiety-ridden mindscape.

Kunal didn't know what magical trick Snaitun was playing, but it had brought them all to his mindscape. He was in his bad place. *They* were in his bad place.

But it was unfortunate for Snaitun as he could not anticipate how dark this place could be.

'Is this the Dung Master's domain?'

Kunal grinned. For the first time since this whole mess had started, he had the upper hand.

'No…' Kunal grunted, standing up tall. 'You're in a place far worse than any eldritch god's domain.'

'Where are we?' Snaitun sounded puzzled. Kunal could feel a rush of thrill in his body.

Kunal smirked and answered, 'My mindscape.'

Snaitun straightened and looked around. **'Of course…'**

Snaitun looked different though. He wasn't the twisted human-pigeon hybrid anymore. He was actually a handsome man, lean and fit with a striking face. His dark hair hung loosely over his shoulders and bare torso. His pants looked tattered but his body was unscathed. This was probably his original body. If it weren't for his soul-piercing voice, Kunal wouldn't have recognised him.

'I didn't expect your mind to be so…'

'Dangerous? Dark? Dis…'

'Rotten.'

Kunal frowned. Yes, he had issues. And he was working on them. But his mind wasn't rotten. Not yet, at least. And he wasn't going to let some evil dark lord make him feel bad about himself, not when they stood in his own mindscape at least.

⬢ **THIS IS INTERESTING.** ⬢

Kunal looked around, searching for the Dung Master. But nothing showed itself.

⬢ **WE DID NOT EXPECT THIS PLACE TO BE SO…** ⬢

'ROTTEN?' Kunal shouted.

⬢ HOMELY. ⬢

'You hear them too?' Snaitun asked.

Burfi woofed, standing between them and barking at nothingness.

Why is he still a dog?
'Why is my son still a dog?'
Burfi bared his teeth and growled at Snaitun.

'Because that's how I've known him to be,' Kunal answered, recollecting what Guru had told him the first time he had come here, 'But why are you…' he gestured to Snaitun and said with a grimace, '… handsome?'

Snaitun groaned and ignored him. **'Doesn't matter… now that we're here…'** Snaitun looked up at the void, **'WHAT DO YOU WANT FROM US?'**

⬢ FIGHT. TO THE DEATH. ⬢

Kunal and Snaitun glared at each other. Burfi snarled.
'I thought you would get rid of Snaitun! Why didn't you?' Kunal searched his void for the eldritch god.

⬢ WE TOOK AWAY HIS PHYSICAL BODY. BUT HE CAN ONLY BE KILLED BY HIS SON. THAT WAS THE CONDITION WITH WHICH HE ARRIVED IN YOUR WORLD. THE CONDITION STAYS. ⬢

'You lied!' Kunal screamed.

⬢ WE DO NOT LIE. ⬢

'How do you expect us to kill his soul!? Was this all a trick!?'

A cosmic sniggering shook Kunal's mindscape. Even Snaitun looked unsettled.

● **WE EXPECTED SNAITUN TO DO SOMETHING. BUT THIS…? THIS WAS A WELCOME SURPRISE.** ●

Kunal clenched his fist. 'But…'

● **ENOUGH! FIGHT NOW.** ●

Kunal gulped. Burfi whelped.
Snaitun roared and lunged forward. Kunal watched the handsome, toned man close in. His perfect jaw opened bestially, his muscular arms spread and ready for violence.
Burfi barked and readied himself to jump, but there was no way Kunal and Burfi could overpower Snaitun. But this was Kunal's mindscape.
I'm in control.
Before Snaitun could lay his hands on him, Kunal turned to look at one of the many dark caves scattered around the void. He picked one belonging to his childhood and shattered the boulder blocking it. He then leapt forward and grabbed Burfi just in time. The cave spewed a flash of blinding light, engulfing everything in his mindscape.

Kunal was five. Mom had to take him to a wedding, but it was too far away and they were getting late. Kunal was too young to understand the urgency, but he trusted Mom to know what she was doing, trusted her to protect him.

Mom said the fastest way to their destination was by train. Kunal, who loved trains, was excited. He had two train sets and they were his favourite toys. Their functioning, how they glided smoothly over their tracks, switched lanes and halted on time at the platforms always fascinated him. He wondered how trains in the real world operated. He didn't know it then, but his toy trains were modelled after sophisticated Japanese bullet trains. But Mom wasn't taking him to Japan; she was taking him to Goregaon Station.

Kunal's toy trains were nothing like the cruel Mumbai Locals.

Goregaon Station was full of people—smelly, sweaty and restless people. Barbarians pushing and shoving for an inch of space. The platforms looked like gates to hell, and they were jam-packed. The commuters stood agitatedly, half of them leaning over the tracks to see the approaching metal monster.

Kunal clutched Mom's hand tightly, worried someone would kidnap him. After all, some had already stepped on his tiny feet and pushed him around mindless of the fact that he was just a kid. One man had even pinched his backside a little too forcefully.

Kunal prayed silently for the train to arrive.

Another train announced its arrival on a different platform. Its horn blared deafeningly; it was nothing like what he had seen before. It was an ugly monster. Old paint full of dirt and paan *stains. People hung out of the doors like clothes outside windows. They wouldn't even wait for the train to stop before jumping in and out. Kunal wondered if he would see dead bodies once the train left and the crowd cleared. But the crowd never cleared. It was always full.*

Complete chaos.

Was this the spirit of Mumbai or the ghost of Mumbai's decency? Kunal wanted to leave the platform. He wanted to cower behind Mom. He wanted to go home.

He even cried but Mom yelled at him to shut up, because that's how you deal with a troublesome *kid, right? Stupid kid! Can't he see that his fear and anxiety are a major inconvenience to people, especially to his parents? Stupid Kunal!*

When their train finally arrived, Kunal was partially certain it would leap off the tracks and run them all over. He imagined the train transforming into a hungry rakshas and devouring them. He clutched Mom's leg and closed his eyes, screaming.

He didn't want to die...

The train was going to hit them all...

The train was going to run them over...

The train was going to eat them…
IT'S GOING TO KILL ME!!!
Kunal screamed. But his scream was drowned out by the train's horn that continued to blare incessantly.

The train slammed into Snaitun. Its horn blared incessantly, louder than even the explosion of its crash into one of the floating rocks in the sky. Metal and rock collided into an explosion, leaving a sharp screeching echo. The sight was as gory and brutal as Kunal had imagined in his worst nightmares.

Kunal held Burfi close to his chest, petting his warm and bristly fur to calm him down. 'It's okay,' he said, 'We've got this!'

Burfi woofed and licked Kunal's face.

Train carriages disintegrated into nothingness. The flames were consumed by dark smoke and soot. Snaitun lay pinned to the rock in the sky, disoriented and out of breath. **'What was…'**

'You think you can conquer us!?' Kunal shouted, 'I've braved the monstrosity of Mumbai's public transport many more times than you can count!'

Before Snaitun could react, Kunal shattered another blocking boulder, summoning a double-decker bus that sped forward uncaringly. Snaitun raised his arms before him as the red BEST bus crashed into him.

Another explosion. More floating debris.

Snaitun fell on the massive platform, just far enough for Kunal to conjure his fears of commercial airlines.

Kunal let go of Burfi and commanded him to stay. Burfi obeyed and stood sentinel next to him. His eyes were fixed on Snaitun, ready to dart forward the moment Kunal ordered him. Kunal scruffled his ears. 'Good boy.' He turned to Snaitun and said, 'Now, let's make this more interesting…'

Three commercial planes kamikazed one after the other right where Snaitun knelt. The explosions shook

Kunal's very soul. His heart pounded inside his chest, not from anxiety, but from excitement. For once, he was in control. And he was going to save the world!

He watched the explosions light up his dark mindscape. Arid, lifeless, but it didn't look that bad anymore. This was his playground now. Hunting ground, he corrected himself and refocused on the rising mushrooms of fire and smoke.

Out of the flames, Snaitun stumbled forward, **'You can't hurt me, Kunal!'**

'Snaitun,' Kunal said with as much smugness as he could manage, 'You're seriously underestimating how dangerously messed up my mind is…'

Burfi barked and growled threateningly. It was the perfect punctuation for Kunal's threat.

The ground rumbled, spewing magma right onto Snaitun.

'Fire can't burn me, you fool! Not in this plain of existe—'

A giant centipede with a million teeth and a billion wriggling legs broke out of the ground. It wrapped its segmented body around Snaitun and bit his head. It bit and chewed at Snaitun's spotless face. It did not damage him externally, but it looked painful enough.

Snaitun screamed like a madman.

Finally, the centipede vomited acid onto Snaitun's head and tossed him forward. Snaitun slid to a halt just in front of Kunal.

Snaitun coughed acid out of his mouth. He looked miserable, nothing like the dark lord or god-emperor that he was. But he wasn't broken yet. No, Kunal's traumas had barely started to rub off on him.

The centipede vanished, and Kunal replaced it with the worst possible horror anyone could ever foresee—

Another boulder exploded in the distance and the contents of its cave spewed out in pixelated flashes. They assaulted Snaitun's face, enveloping his body in a cocoon of screens.

Snaitun screamed with confusion, **'What is this?'**

Kunal faked a laugh. Burfi looked at him with concern, ears flopping. Kunal scratched his head once and turned to Snaitun. Monsters were nothing compared to the trauma of the Indian workplace. And the worst of them all was—'a work email'.

'What in the hell is a "worky mail"?'

The office was small, as all spaces in Mumbai are. A small office meant even smaller workstations. Worse, Kunal's office didn't even have designated workstations, just long benches where people sat and worked side by side. Now, Kunal's colleagues were decent people who minded their own business. But their manager?

The fat piece of junk trotted over to Kunal and began assaulting him verbally. His hairy fist was clenched, ready to punch and smack Kunal without warning.

Kunal held his tongue. What could he even say?

Kunal stood up from his chair and looked at his feet defeatedly, trying to hold his composure. If he cried now, everyone would laugh at him. Or, worse, pity him. Or think of him as a weakling.

Of all the drawbacks of the Indian workplace, apathy was the worst. And the abysmally low salary. The rich grow richer on the backbreaking labour of the poor and the middle class.

The manager continued to scream at him. The transgression wasn't even half the value of the reprimand, but it didn't matter. A minor inconvenience to the boss is worse than a worker losing his life.

'I told you I needed a day more. You…'

'DON'T TALK BACK TO ME!' his boss barked, 'A college student could do this job in a single night. And it'd cost me half your salary!'

Kunal felt a punch in his gut. He knew it wasn't true, but it still hurt. 'I had a family emergency. I told you I needed…'

'I don't care if your mother died. She doesn't pay your salary, you worthless loser! Get this done by the end of the day, or I'll ruin your bloody life. You got me?'

Mom wasn't dying, but she had fallen down the stairs. Dad was on a business trip, and no one could've taken her to the hospital. Couldn't his manager understand that simple detail? It's not like Kunal hadn't informed anyone about it. He'd even relayed the urgent tasks to his colleagues. Why not yell at them for not following through?

Kunal wanted to scream back. Kunal wanted to grab his work laptop—a hefty old machine that shouldn't be in use—and smack it across his manager's fat face. But he didn't want to get jailed for manslaughter.

Kunal hated his job, this toxic, underpaying worthless waste of his time and life. But he needed the money. And the job market had been down for a long time. Desperation was what led him to keep his job. Desperation and weakness were why he kept his mouth shut.

Kunal clenched his jaw and nodded. The tears came, however. And his colleagues saw. They watched, and they kept silent.

Because they too wanted to keep their jobs.

Kunal's heart ached to have to endure such humiliation. And he was too underconfident to quit and look for anything better.

Maybe he deserved this.

Kunal wiped away a tear as he projected the memory onto Snaitun. He had overcome most of the trauma of that workplace, but Snaitun hadn't had the luxury of therapy. Kunal watched Snaitun fall to his knees, his entire body convulsing, as if every single artery and vein were coursing with pure cortisol.

Snaitun screamed, clutching his head. **'So... much... cruelty...'**

Kunal was surprised. *Even the dark lord has more empathy than Indian workplaces...*

At this point, even Burfi looked frightened. He sat still, but his legs were trembling lightly. Was he scared of Kunal?

Kunal put his hand forth to pet him, but he flinched. Kunal frowned, 'No... Burfi...'

Burfi whimpered. Kunal knelt beside him and offered his hand. Burfi sniffed it suspiciously. After ample inspection, he finally licked it.

Kunal hugged him and said, 'I'm sorry you have to see all this, Burfi. But we need to incapacitate Snaitun.' *It's the only way to defeat him.*

● THIS IS AMUSING… ●

Snaitun shoved the laptop aside. It crashed and—as Kunal had imagined in some nightmares—it shattered into small dagger-like shards. All the shards—like in Kunal's nightmares—shot straight at Snaitun.

Before Snaitun could recover from the thousand stabs, a fat balding man appeared next to Snaitun. 'WHY DID YOU NOT RESPOND TO MY EMAIL? ARE YOU SLACKING OFF? YOU WORTHLESS PIECE OF—'

Snaitun punched Kunal's former manager in the face. He pounced on him and continued to beat him to a pulp. Seeing his manager fall and writhe in pain was a tad bit therapeutic for Kunal.

But it would've been more fun if the manager transformed into a twisted monster of epic proportions.

So, that's what Kunal visualised.

His former manager's body convulsed, becoming a hybrid of insects, snakes, slugs and every creepy-crawly creature Kunal hated.

● INTERESTING… ●

The giant moth that fluttered in his room when he was six.

The four-hundred and thirty-six cockroaches that infested his new apartment because his landlord had skimped out on pest control.

The butterflies that he felt in his stomach when he saw butterflies. Kunal never understood why people loved those ugly bugs.

Burfi stood up, barking in fear. Kunal held him and pet his head. 'Calm down, boy. Not yet.' Burfi moved to run, but Kunal held him back. 'Stay! I'll tell you when it's time.'

Burfi sat down, tail between his legs. Kunal stood up and called upon his traumatic memories, everything he had faced and conquered in therapy. Everything he was yet to face and conquer.

No happy thoughts. No happy thoughts.

The monster bulged and grew cosmic in size. And the more it grew, the more frightened Snaitun looked. **'What is the meaning of all this?'**

'You thought me to be a weakling, didn't you?' Kunal asked, transporting right next to the shivering dark lord. Burfi barked, wagging his tail.

Snaitun reached out to attack, but his body refused to obey. **'YOU—'**

'Sleep paralysis…' Kunal said, sounding prouder than he should have. 'It gets worse, Snaitun…'

Kunal sat in an underground temple. There were cockroaches everywhere.

But his fright had no sway over his parents' blind faith.

'This will bring us good fortune!' Mom had told him.

'I just need his blessings for my business,' Dad had said half-heartedly.

Kunal didn't want to be a part of it. But, being the youngest—and allegedly purest—soul in their family, he was forced to perform the puja.

'Are you dumb, boy? Can't you hear what I told you to do?' the priest was a nasty man. He looked like his hobbies included chewing paan *and abducting children.*

'Sorry…' Kunal said with a bowed head. There was no point arguing. If he did, his parents would fight with him, yell at him, guilt him into believing he was wrong to disobey them. After all, they were his elders and elders deserved respect irrespective of their morality.

Kunal tried to focus on the lifeless stone before him, but he couldn't take his mind off the cockroaches on the walls. Why did they have to build this altar underground? How did they know this was an actual temple, and the idol hadn't just fallen into an ancient potty?

Kunal didn't even believe in those gods. He didn't believe in any god, but the one time he had expressed his feelings, it had brought a hailstorm of guilt, emotional blackmail and slaps across the face. Since then, he decided that he'd rather pretend to believe than speak his mind honestly.

That was until he felt a cockroach run over his foot. The brown piece of flattened turd with legs sent pangs of disgust throughout Kunal's body.

'I don't want to do this...' Kunal screamed, 'THERE'S COCKROACHES EVERYWHERE! WHAT KIND OF GOD LIVES AMONG COCKROACHES!'

'An indiscriminate one,' the priest said quietly, 'stop insulting our god, or he will curse you.'

Kunal couldn't control his anger and frustration. He spat in the priest's face.

Big mistake...

It was a surprise that no news outlet covered the beating up of a ten-year-old boy by the staff and patrons of that tiny temple.

Kunal had hoped his parents would be by his side, but they weren't. They didn't file a police complaint. They didn't fight for justice. They didn't do anything.

As much as the priests and patrons had insulted him, his intelligence, his character and his family in ways that no god could condone, his parents had done more or less the same, only this time in private. Typical.

Kunal had turned ten just two months ago, but he felt like the burden of the world was on his shoulders now. Well, it was just the burden of his parents' expectations, but stories had taught him that parents were supposed to be a child's world, so technically it was the world's weight.

That night, Kunal stayed awake wallowing in thoughts of hate. Predominantly self-hate, bordering on self-harm.

He was powerless in this world.

He was powerless in his own family.

For the first time in his life, he hated his parents. For the first time in his life, he wished he had never been born.

And these feelings lodged deep within his soul. They were a parasite that sucked his energy every so often. Years passed, his traumas grew more solid, his doubts piled up and Kunal's life grew bleaker and bleaker.

His mindscape that once housed lush gardens and open fields, castles and spaceships, dragons and aliens, slowly grew dark and desolate.

It faded.
To black.

'STOP IT! PLEASE! STOP!' Snaitun begged. **'I can't take it anymore...'** Tears flowed from his sapphire eyes as his trembling hands joined before him. **'Please... no more...'**

Kunal felt...

Sad.

The dark lord had crumbled before him. He was on his knees begging for mercy. Kunal took a step forward, 'Give up, Snaitun.'

Burfi barked at him aggressively.

There was no remorse in Burfi's bark. He wanted to attack Snaitun. Wanted to...

Was Snaitun a bad father?

Of course, he was! He was willing to sacrifice... *kill*... his son for personal gain. For more power. There's no justifying those actions.

'Forgive me, Bu'ur'feil'aal... I wish I could have been a better father to you...'

Kunal looked on suspiciously. What was Snaitun playing at? Was he truly repentant, or was this a ploy to lower their guard?

Burfi grew tired of barking but stood his ground.

'Enough, Snaitun!' Kunal shouted, 'What do you want?'

Snaitun looked at Kunal with innocent eyes. **'Forgive**

me, Kunal...'

Suddenly, Snaitun leapt forward with red glowing eyes. Fire trickled out of his mouth. He was ready to consume Kunal.

Kunal raised his hands up instinctively. *Damnit!*

Burfi jumped in the way, maw open wide. It shut right at Snaitun's neck, pushing him off his trajectory.

Kunal fell on the platform and watched Snaitun and Burfi crash beside him. Burfi ripped Snaitun's throat, a wet gurgling growl filling Kunal's mindscape.

Snaitun's eyes stopped glowing red.

When Burfi pulled up, it was like watching a carnivorous animal in a wildlife documentary feasting on its prey.

Burfi is a dog... he's a carnivorous animal...

Snaitun coughed, **'No...'**

Kunal ran forward. He watched Snaitun's wounds tearing wider. The dark lord looked like he was in pain. He wasn't healing now. Was this it?

Burfi leapt forward again, scratching and biting the man.

Everything Kunal feared about having a dog, all his worst nightmares, were now manifesting before him.

Except Burfi wasn't doing it to Kunal, he was doing it to protect Kunal.

Was this Burfi's animal instinct kicking in? Was this him seeking revenge for a lifetime of pain?

Kunal had his problems with his parents, but his parents hadn't sought the aid of an other-dimensional deity and risked the existence of two worlds just for their selfish needs.

Kunal wanted to go and hug his parents. He wanted to tell them that he loved and adored them despite their shortcomings.

Snaitun convulsed. **'Stop... please...'**

Burfi was relentless. He continued to torment Snaitun. He was a dog. He didn't know better.

'Burfi!' Kunal said, voice almost breaking in pity, 'Stop it!'

Burfi stopped, sitting obediently. Red dripped from his open jaw and lolling tongue.

'Thank y—'

'Snaitun,' Kunal cut in, 'You will free us from this place.'

Snaitun looked at Kunal with one good eye. Kunal avoided the other that Burfi had mauled. **'If I...'**

'Consider yourself lucky,' Kunal pushed, 'After all the suffering you've wrought upon your world and ours, this release is too easy.'

Wow, where did that come from?

Snaitun, broken and defeated, coughed out blood and said, **'Fine...'**

With twisted, scarred hands he began casting his spell.

Kunal watched as stars blossomed in the void of his mindscape. The floating rocks crumbled to glitter, swirling together to form an astral passage.

'But remember one thing...' Snaitun said with a cough, **'I will always be within your mindscape...'**

Burfi barked and advanced.

'NO! STOP!'

Burfi stopped and looked at Kunal with confusion.

'You didn't think I'd let you win so easily...'

'Win?' Kunal shouted, 'This isn't a bloody game!'

'For the powerful, everything is a game.'

Kunal looked at the astral passage. He could go back to his life. But Snaitun would be within his mindscape, forever plotting an escape. Or something worse.

He looked at the void and shouted, 'DUNG MASTER! Will Snaitun remain in my mindscape if we leave?'

● **YES.** ●

Kunal gulped. 'But we defeated him!'

⬢ YOU HAVE NOT KILLED HIM. ⬢

'You said defeat…' *No. He said fight to the death.* There was no other way.

'How do I kill him? He's in my mindscape without a body!'

'CHEATER!' Snaitun yelled painfully. His voice was as broken as his body.

Kunal ignored him. But the Dung Master seemed to be ignoring Kunal too.

He had to figure it out himself.

Kunal looked at Snaitun and conjured shackles. They latched onto Snaitun's limbs and spread them out wide. 'Burfi…' he couldn't bring himself to do it. How could he?

Kunal looked at Burfi's innocent face staring back at him. How could he make this innocent little pup commit such a heinous act? If he made Burfi kill Snaitun, Burfi's mind might forever be plagued with those haunting images.

Kunal hadn't seen death that early in life, but he'd experienced enough trauma to know that he didn't want anyone to suffer like that. Especially not Burfi.

Kunal gulped and turned to the void again. 'Dung Master! We have brutalised him enough. Call it a win and end this!'

⬢ NO. ⬢

'Please!'

⬢ WHAT'S THE FUN IN THAT? ⬢

Kunal frowned. 'You want fun?' He looked at the miserable dark lord and the scared pup next to him. *Think,*

Kunal. Think!

How could he kill Snaitun without leaving the trauma of the act on Burfi's mind?

And then it struck him. 'I have a proposal!'

● NO PROPOSALS. ●

'Just hear me out!' Kunal demanded, and explained his idea without being told to. He explained it in excruciating detail, how this fate was much more punishing for Snaitun than any other death. He elaborated everything minutely, his descriptions making Snaitun beg for mercy.

Kunal felt sympathetic. But he persevered. If he could convince the Dung Master that this was a crueller ending, he could actually save Burfi from killing his father.

● YOU ARE CRUEL. ●

'Do we have a deal?' Kunal asked. His heart raced. He didn't want to jinx his prospects.

There was no response.

'Just kill me! Please!' Snaitun screamed. He was breathing heavily, but he wasn't dying. Not yet.

'Dung Master! Do we have a deal?'

● FINE. ●

Snaitun's body shone with stars. When the stars faded, his wounds had all healed. He was his old handsome self. He was also paralysed, as requested.

'Kunal, please…' Snaitun's voice wasn't dark and demonic anymore. He sounded like any other human being.

Kunal clenched his teeth, feeling guilty for the first time. He wasn't assisting the death of a dark lord. He was assisting the death of another human being. *One who is a threat to reality itself. This has to be done.*

'Burfi…' he pointed to Snaitun and said, 'Fetch!'

Burfi lanced towards Snaitun and grabbed him by the hand. Kunal grabbed Snaitun's feet and the two began dragging him towards the portal.

Burfi doesn't have to do it alone. 'Good boy, Burfi! Good job!'

The dog's tail wagged happily.

'NO!' Snaitun screamed, but he couldn't do anything. The Dung Master had taken away his powers. Once across the portal, Snaitun's soul would disintegrate one particle at a time. A painful passing that would take less than a few seconds, but, for Snaitun, it would seemingly last an eternity.

'Please!' Snaitun begged.

Kunal ignored him, inching closer to the portal. It was time.

'Burfi, stay!'

Burfi halted, but didn't drop Snaitun's legs down.

Kunal began swinging his body.

'Kunal, please! I beg of you! I possess the wisdom of two worlds! More! I can…'

'SHUT UP!' Kunal snapped, using all his might to swing the body.

'One… two… three! Drop it!' Kunal let go. So did Burfi.

Snaitun's body entered the portal. As the void of Kunal's mindscape shone blindingly, Snaitun's body withered away. One particle at a time, each exploding in a flash of pretty lights. For Burfi, they would be simple grey fireworks. But Kunal knew the brutal truth of it.

He turned to check on Burfi. The pup's eyes were mesmerised by the explosions. He looked at them like a baby. *He is a baby…*

Kunal turned towards the fireworks too. A trillion deaths—that's what they really were. And all within a few heartbeats.

Snaitun's scream was unlike anything Kunal had heard before. And it echoed long past the death of his last particle.

Kunal watched him fade to nothing. Then he looked at Burfi and petted him lovingly. 'We did it! We did it!' They celebrated. Jumping up and down, Burfi woofed and wagged his tail, entirely unaware of the brutality they had just committed. *I hope he doesn't remember this for what it really is.* Kunal embraced the dog tightly. 'Okay, we have to leave.'

Kunal got up and began walking towards the portal. Burfi was right next to him. He stepped in and gestured for Burfi to enter. Hesitating, Burfi dipped one foot into the astral passage, decided it was safe and hopped in.

They reached the end of the passage, the white light blinding and frightening. Beyond was their world. *Kunal's* world.

Home.

But Kunal wasn't scared. He just looked at Burfi, who was gently wagging his tail. 'Go, boy. Go in there!'

Burfi kept staring.

'Together?'

Burfi's tail wagged faster.

'On three. One... two... three.' Kunal leapt into the white at the same time as Burfi.

CHAPTER 16
SO LONG, AND THANKS FOR ALL THE CRISES

KUNAL OPENED HIS EYES to the morning sky.

It was quite a pleasant morning, to be honest. The sunlight was like a warm embrace in the middle of a strong and cold breeze. The grass was just about dewy enough to make the picturesque landscape of Igatpuri look dreamlike. Of course, that picturesque tableau was bookended with soldiers of the Indian Army. They had probably arrived when Kunal was inside his mindscape.

Which begged the question—*how long was I inside?*

He clicked his comms, 'Aisha, you there?'

Burfi started barking. Before Kunal could turn, something tackled him to the ground, clutching him and squeezing the air out of him. He slapped and punched his attacker frantically, only to get slapped back.

'What is wrong with you!?' Aisha screamed, then immediately changed her stance and hugged him tightly. 'Sorry, I was... I thought you were dead!' She sounded like she had been crying.

'Well...' Kunal started, but didn't know how to continue.

Burfi barked and tried to join the embrace. Or maybe he was just jealous of someone else hugging Kunal. He realised he had never hugged anyone in front of Burfi before.

Aisha, however, ignored Burfi's protests. She screeched with joy, 'You're alive! Thank god!' and with that, Aisha planted wet kisses all over Kunal's dirty face. She stopped after the fourth and spat out the dirt.

Aisha let him go. Burfi stepped in between them and sprawled on the ground, making sure they wouldn't leave him out again.

Kunal welcomed the space as he took in his surroundings. The army was busy rounding up Snaitun's soldiers. Of the thousand, Kunal was certain a lot had perished in the battle. *I need to thank Mr Tambe and Dilip for that.*

He looked at his dirty hands to make sure he was all there. Aisha's kisses were real enough to ground him back to reality, but he still wanted to double-check.

Finally, he looked at Burfi and petted him. 'Good boy.'

Burfi took that as a sign for a hug and pounced on Kunal. He licked Kunal's face and didn't even bother to spit out the dirt. He continued to shower his love on him. And when he got tired of licking, he sneezed and barked and wagged his tail, all the while jumping around Kunal.

How could anyone love someone so much? Kunal grabbed the dog and hugged him tightly, welcoming the second round of sniffs and kisses.

Okay, he really has no idea what he's done. That's a relief!

Kunal looked up to find Adira standing next to them. Arms bruised and bandaged, armour cracked, she looked badly beaten up. She even had a black eye. Kunal opened his mouth, and his absolute lack of social skills weighed his tongue down. Like an idiot, he said, 'I hope Burfi's dog instincts don't stay with him for life. Wouldn't want him licking us when he's grown up. He he…' *Why did I say that?*

'That is if we can go back,' Adira said and looked away.

Kunal frowned.

They had to go back. This wasn't their home. He had almost forgotten.

Burfi, sensing the change in the air, stopped wagging his tail. He sat down obediently and looked at them with his beady eyes.

'I'm sure you have a way back,' Aisha said, 'I mean, Snaitun's soldiers are all still here... even the portal at the warehouse seems open. We can...'

'How certain are you that the portal will lead us back home?' Adira asked, 'Sorry, but that portal is Snaitun's work. I do not trust him or anything that has his stench.' There was an aggressive growl in her voice. 'He even turned your own soldiers against us.'

Wasn't that the Dung Master's doing? Kunal tried to distract himself by petting Burfi. They had just defeated a dark lord. He wanted to relish the victory. But something was amiss.

Kunal had a hard time giving himself credit. He rarely was able to relish his victories. But this wasn't one of those moments. This didn't remotely feel like a victory, and that was stranger than him not wanting to take any credit.

'Prepare the captives for transit,' General Shah said over comms. After a brief pause, he added, *'Adira and Burfi too.'*

Kunal looked into Burfi's beady eyes, into their limitless love and affection, and instantly realised why this didn't feel like a victory.

And with that came a sinking feeling that made him tear up.

Half an hour later, military trucks had lined up outside the burnt-down warehouse. Kunal stood at the edge of its ashen compound, looking at the midnight dome portal that Snaitun had opened. The very light of the sun seemed to get sucked into its abyssal depths.

Adira and Aisha were busy confirming the captives' numbers. Burfi and Kunal stood alone. Burfi was taking in the view of that morning. The lines of extra-dimensional captives in chains, the Indian army and their near-perfect discipline in managing the captives, all against the backdrop of a balmy morning.

Kunal clutched Burfi's leash tightly in his hand. He felt a gentle squeeze on his shoulder.

'It's best they leave as soon as possible,' Aisha said, walking towards them, 'General Shah's orders.'

Kunal nodded. If the higher-ups got a hold of the soldiers or Burfi, they'd undoubtedly subject them to off-the-books experiments. Besides, there was the hypothesis that the portal might close only after all extra-dimensional beings had left their world. Kunal looked at the body bags being carted towards the portal, hoping there hadn't been any mistake during clean-up.

Adira walked over to them, announcing, 'Every soldier is accounted for. It's time.'

Aisha nodded and clicked into comms, 'Preparing transfer.'

Burfi yelped. Kunal swallowed his words. He knelt down and began petting Burfi for what would probably be the last time.

Adira asked the Indian troops to release their captives, then commanded one of Snaitun's soldiers to walk into the void. Hesitantly, he obeyed. The shackles obstructed his walk, but he managed to trot over slowly. When he passed into the dome, nothing happened. The darkness consumed him without any change in sight or sound. He simply vanished.

'That was uneventful,' Adira said, then ordered the rest of the soldiers to cross the portal.

The remainder of Snaitun's battalion started marching into the void, into nothingness. Supposedly, they were going back home, but were they really? What if the void disintegrated them? Mini fireworks of excruciating death, just like Snaitun.

Kunal shook his head, trying not to let his anxieties ruin this moment. This was going to be an important moment for him. As it is, he was terrible at saying goodbyes.

Kunal watched Snaitun's ironclad soldiers cross back into their world. He noticed that the dome grew visibly smaller every time someone passed through. And with every shrinking moment, he felt his farewell coming closer.

You can do this. You can do this. Be brave. For Burfi.

By the time the last soldier crossed, the void was barely bigger than a kiddie pool. This was it.

Adira voiced her concern about the state of affairs back home. She put on a brave face to avoid discussing it at length. But that didn't stop Kunal's mind from pulling at those threads of worry. What state was their world in? How much time had passed since they left it? So many unanswered questions, but...

Focus, Kunal. Focus. It's not your responsibility.

Finally, when everyone had left, Adira prepared to enter the portal.

'Wait...' Kunal said, feeling the need to say a proper farewell to her.

After everything that had happened, he owed it to her. After everything that had happened, he needed it.

'Adira...' and that's when his inability to speak normally assaulted his tongue. His mind went blank, unable to process words and thoughts as smoothly as he had just moments ago. He swallowed the lump in his throat and continued, 'Thank you for everything. Our worlds are safe because of you.'

Adira stepped forward and squeezed Kunal's shoulder. Although she was much taller than him, he didn't feel like she was looking down on him. Not anymore. She had pride in her eyes, 'I was wrong about you, Kunal. And I didn't save our worlds; *you* did.'

Kunal smiled weakly and said, 'Take care of Burfi for me, will you?'

Adira smiled, a strange and unusual sight from the

warrior. 'Of course. He's my nephew after all.'

Kunal's eyes bulged. 'Nephew!?'

Adira looked away, 'Snaitun was my brother-in-law...'

'Why didn't you tell us!?'

'Why would I?'

'Why tell us now?'

'Who knows when we'll meet next?' Adira said, then hugged Kunal. Awkwardly, and too tight for his preference. 'You will be missed.'

'You too,' Kunal managed to croak, clenching his jaw shut.

'Farewell, Kunal.' Adira turned to Aisha, 'You have what it takes to lead and inspire people, Aisha. I wish you luck and success.' With that, Adira walked into the void.

Burfi woofed at Adira, but didn't run behind her.

Oh god...

Burfi sat obediently next to Kunal. The pup made eye contact with him, then yawned widely, ears pulling back.

I don't know if I will ever see him again...

Pangs of pain bore a hole in Kunal's heart. It hadn't even been twenty-four hours. Burfi hadn't even left yet. Why was he feeling such intense loss? The void portal was shrinking, but the void in Kunal's heart was sorely growing.

He hadn't felt half this bad when he had moved out of his parents' house. He hadn't felt even a fraction of this during his first breakup, and he'd dated that girl for a long time.

Kunal knelt down and scratched Burfi's head. 'My baby...' he didn't care how ridiculous it sounded. He was going to miss this doggo. 'My baby...' he pulled Burfi into an embrace. Burfi raised his forelegs in an awkward embrace. Kunal felt his rough tongue lick at the back of his neck and ears.

It tickled. It drew tears from Kunal's eyes.

'Don't you forget me, Burfi...' Kunal said wiping away his tears. Finally, Kunal let go.

Burfi woofed and licked his face, wiping away the remaining tears.

'I just wish I had more time to get to know you... hopefully, we'll see each other again. Right?'

Burfi woofed happily, his tail wagging, eyes beholding Kunal with love and affection.

Kunal embraced Burfi one last time. When he broke the embrace, Burfi rolled over on his back, prompting Kunal to rub his belly. After a few final head scratches, Kunal got up and wiped his tears. 'Okay, Burfi. Time to go.'

Burfi's wagging tail stopped. He wailed once, then barked.

'I'll always remember you. See you soon...'

Burfi howled like a puppy in an attempt to say 'goodbye', then reluctantly walked towards the void. The pup turned once looking straight at Kunal.

Kunal waved him forward, feigning a smile.

Burfi woofed again and entered.

The void imploded with a soft pop, and disappeared. The portal connecting Kunal's world with Burfi's was closed.

Probably forever.

Kunal felt Aisha's hand hold his palm, her fingers intertwining with his. 'It's okay.'

Kunal knelt a little and rested his head on her shoulder. The awkward position slowly transposed into a full hug with Aisha slowly running her fingers through Kunal's hair.

This was the second time Kunal had broken down, the first being at the beginning of this entire adventure. When it had started, he was begging for it to end. Now that it was over, why did it hurt so much?

This was perfect. No more adventure. No more world-ending threats.

Then why?

'It's all right...' Aisha said, 'He's back home. Back

where he'll be happy.'

'I've only known him for a few hours... why does it hurt...?' Kunal sniffled.

'Because,' Aisha said, 'That's what happens when you love someone unconditionally.' She pulled him to face her, 'Besides, the two of you saved our whole goddamn world. That's a lot for one person to handle. And you didn't even get a chance to celebrate!' Aisha cupped his face, 'Once all this mess is cleared, we'll do that, yeah?'

Kunal nodded, snorted embarrassingly loudly and wiped away tears. 'Yeah.'

Aisha ignored his snot and tears. Instead, she just asked, 'What do you want to do after we're done?'

Kunal sniffled and smiled at the thought, 'Hot chocolate.'

Aisha laughed and hugged him. 'Let's go back?'

'Yeah...' Kunal said, taking in a deep breath. 'What else do we have to do?'

'I'm sure there's still some mess to clear up,' Aisha said, then checked with her father on comms.

Dr Raza spoke on the public channel, *'All good here, guys. General Shah's handling everything. We should be relieved by EOD.'*

Kunal felt a flutter in his stomach. He couldn't wait to go back home and...

The flutter in his heart turned into an ache in his entire body. He fell to the ground, clutching his heart.

Was he having a heart attack?

● **NOT AN ATTACK.** ●

'Kunal?' Aisha asked, holding his back, 'What's—'

● **FORGIVE US.** ●

The pain receded.

'Kunal!?' Aisha screamed, 'What is happening?'

Kunal inhaled slowly. Then groaned, 'Dung Master…'

Aisha went pale. 'They're...'

A few Indian soldiers rushed over to them too. 'Is there a problem, ma'am?' Kunal had almost forgotten about them. But even if they were here, there was nothing they could do to stop the Dung Master. Why was the eldritch god still here?

● **WE MUST GO TOO. OUR TIME IS NEARLY UP.** ●

Kunal sat up and shouted to the sky, 'Why are you bothering me!?'

● **YOU SUCCEEDED WHERE SNAITUN FAILED.** ●

What was the god even talking about?

● **WE WANTED ENTERTAINMENT. YOU GAVE US THAT. IN RETURN, WE OFFER YOU A BOON. ASK AND YOU SHALL RECEIVE.** ●

Kunal went pale. '*Anything?*'

● **YES.** ●

'Kunal!' Aisha said, looking pale with shock. 'Refuse to play their game, Kunal. You can't!'

● **THAT ALSO IS A CHOICE, IF YOU LIKE.** ●

Kunal looked at Aisha, worry painting her pale. Behind her, even the soldiers looked alarmed, one of them having drawn a handgun for safety.

Kunal gulped and thought about it. Maybe this wasn't a game. Maybe the Dung Master really did want to reward Kunal.

But all rewards come at a cost…

⬢ YOU HAVE ALREADY PAID YOUR DUES, KUNAL. ⬢

Right.

'Kun—'

'LET ME THINK!' Kunal yelled. He looked at Aisha flinching, and immediately felt horrible. 'I'm sorry… I-I just… I'm sorry… please… let me think…'

Aisha nodded and took a step back. 'I trust you,' she said and continued to look at him with concern.

'Can you… not look? Please?' he requested nervously.

She clicked her tongue and turned around.

'Thank you,' he said, then closed his eyes. *Think, Kunal, think!*

Luckily, the Dung Master was being patient. Kunal tried to weigh his options, which were basically ask for a boon or refuse to interact with the Dung Master. His gut told him that he could once again use the first option to do something good. But Aisha wasn't wrong in not wanting to play this game. Who knew what trick the Dung Master would play on them?

But, if this wasn't a trick, maybe he could ask for a way to contact Burfi and Adira whenever he wanted. Or all the riches in the world. Or happiness.

Or was there a catch? Things he couldn't ask for?

And then it hit him. 'Dung Master!' he called.

The Dung Master's presence made itself felt inside Kunal's skull.

'I can ask for anything?'

● YES. ●

Aisha turned to look at him. Her eyes were bulging with shock and fear.

Kunal closed his eyes and said, 'Dung Master, I want you to leave our world and never come back. EVER!'

Aisha's mouth opened with awe.

Pain punched outwards from inside Kunal's chest.

● YOU ARE A CONNIVING FOX. ●

'That is what I want. I never want to feel your presence in this world, or have you interfere in its doings ever, no matter what!'

A cosmic sigh relieved his pain.

● VERY WELL. ●

With a soft pop inside his skull, the Dung Master's presence vanished. Kunal let out a sigh and let himself fall back onto the ground. Aisha rushed over to him, 'Are you okay?'

'Yeah...'

'Did it work?'

'I guess. I don't know.'

Aisha closed her eyes and laid next to him. 'God...'

Kunal burst out laughing. He couldn't help himself. After everything, he'd managed to outsmart the Dung Master. Twice. He pounded his hand onto the charred ground and continued to howl.

Aisha looked at him all puzzled at first. But his laughter was contagious. She saw his bliss and joined in.

It's over. It really is over.

Back in Shri Tranquillity, Mom hugged Kunal, kissing him on the head and cheeks, all the while crying with relief. Dad stood on the side, making sure he was around to share the moment.

All around them, Shri Tranquillity's workers were being redirected back to their stations for briefing. The relief on their faces was negated by their reluctance to resume work.

Kunal and his parents were the only ones who seemed to be beaming with emotion and life, which was why they were asked to stay within a room as the workers marched in double files. Can't let them miss their own families after everything, at least not until the end of their shifts.

The room was plain white and empty, save for some old boxes and paint cans. It didn't matter though; Kunal and his parents were there for each other.

'I can't believe you did it!' Mom croaked, 'My baby is a hero!'

Dad added with the bare minimum emotion required, 'Good job.'

'It wasn't just me, everyone contributed,' Kunal said sincerely. He hated being the centre of attention.

'Yes, but you were the one who fought that pigeon monster Snaitun!'

Kunal decided not to tell them about the Dung Master. Snaitun had them worked up enough. They didn't need to know about something a million times worse.

'Can we go home now?' Dad asked.

Kunal shrugged, 'I don't know. I'll have to check with the authorities.'

'Aah, yes,' Mom said, wiping away tears with her dupatta, 'General Shah will probably find some excuse to keep us all here. I didn't get a good vibe from him.'

'Someone needs to smack him across the face,' Dad added.

Kunal scratched his head, 'He's not that bad, to be honest.'

'What are you saying? The man is...'

'Misunderstood,' Kunal said, 'He's a good leader.'

Dad looked at Kunal with narrow eyes, then nodded. 'Good, good. We need good leaders.'

Kunal smiled.

'Where's Burfi?' Mom asked, 'I hope he's safe...'

Kunal frowned. Realising what it meant, his parent's expressions changed.

'I'm so sorry, *beta*...' Mom said.

Dad looked down and asked, 'Did Snaitun kill him?'

'What? No!' Kunal shook his head, 'Burfi's fine! He just... went back home. *His* home.'

'Oh right,' Dad nodded, 'Yes, they weren't from our world. I forgot about that.'

'Well, I'm sure he's happy,' Mom said, cupping Kunal's face, 'And I'm sure he'll be missing you.'

For once, Kunal didn't mind being treated like a child. He needed the comfort of home. He couldn't believe what he was about to ask, 'After all this is done, can I stay with you guys for a few days?'

His parents exchanged a look. Mom hugged him tightly and said, 'Of course, you can! You're always welcome, *beta*.'

Dad cleared his throat, then said awkwardly, 'Bring Aisha too, if you want.' He looked at Mom's scandalised face and shrugged, 'Let's not pretend he's still a kid.'

Mom wasn't fully convinced, but she decided not to make a scene at that moment, 'Of course. Separate rooms though.'

Dad chuckled, 'Like that would've stopped you—'

Mom punched his arm.

'Excuse me?' Kunal said, 'What did you say?'

'Nothing!' Mom said.

Dad continued to chuckle, 'We had our share of fun when we were your age, Kunal. It's a surprise your Nana agreed to our marriage.'

'Nana *agreed*? Didn't you have an arranged marriage?' Kunal asked.

'Son,' Dad grabbed his shoulder, 'I don't know what we did to make you think that. But no.'

Kunal needed a moment to process that. He had lived a quarter of a century not knowing his parents had a love marriage. What else were they hiding from him?

Kunal blinked rapidly and smiled, 'Okay, we need to talk. And *really* talk, okay? No more secrets for the sake of modesty.'

Mom went red. Dad laughed out loud and slapped Kunal on the back, 'As you say, son!'

They held each other for a little while longer. This was the family Kunal wished he had grown up in. He almost felt bad for moving out.

Dad broke the silence, asking, 'By the way, where's my car?'

Once the military returned to Shri Tranquillity, General Shah spoke to every concerned person of interest, team leaders, managers, attendants, and perused every report presented to him with absolute attention. By the end of it, his notes were extensive enough to fill up two fat dossiers. He spent three hours reviewing all the information, then held a meeting with the higher-ups. After all, they needed to know what the hell had happened. He didn't look very happy about the meeting but did it anyway.

During all this, Captain Mangesh and his Silent Langurs were put under observation to see if their temporary transformations had left any kind of long-lasting effects on their bodies. Captain Mangesh wondered how many months they'd be behind glass cages. Which was why he was surprised when General Shah cleared him for a meeting.

Captain Mangesh entered General Shah's cabin and saluted him. 'Sir!'

'At ease, soldier,' General Shah gestured. He looked inhumanly exhausted.

Captain Mangesh changed his stance and clasped his

hands behind his back. 'Sir, the scientists...'

'I cleared you already.'

'But...'

'They didn't find anything, did they? I don't see the point of keeping some of my best soldiers off duty.'

Captain Mangesh nodded. He didn't agree with General Shah, but also knew it was pointless to argue.

However, it did feel strange to see that the civilians who had interacted with the extra-dimensional beings were allowed to roam free, while the Silent Langurs were kept under strict observation.

'May I ask why I was called, General?'

He turned to Captain Mangesh, 'I heard you and your team have consented to let the scientists do their tests on you.'

'It's our duty, sir. Besides, it's better to spot any kind of threat right now. In fact—'

'Spare me the details,' General Shah waved him off, 'I'll make sure the scientists don't overstep their boundaries. Feel free to punch anyone in the face if they do. Say I ordered you to,' he shook a fist before him.

'Yes, sir!' Captain Mangesh saluted him again.

General Shah steepled his fingers, 'I called you to discuss your actions as the transformed langurs.' He paused, 'I couldn't get hold of you because of those stupid tests.'

Captain Mangesh nodded. There was no escaping it. He had gambled with a god to protect his team, and that had led them to transform into beasts, forced to do the god's bidding. He narrated his ordeal and his psychological encounter with the god.

General Shah nodded quietly throughout the narration. Surprisingly, he didn't ask any questions. Captain Mangesh was used to giving thorough mission reports, and he assumed that was the reason.

In the end, General Shah leaned back in his chair and asked, 'So, you were in complete control throughout the whole ordeal?'

Captain Mangesh swallowed the lump in his throat. 'Yes and no.' He paused to let the General ask questions. When none came, he continued, 'We were in control of our faculties, but the moment we tried to act contrary to the god's whim, we were subjected to excruciating pain. I believe...'

'Illusion of choice. Not mind-controlled, like the stray animals; but forced to act of your own volition. That's...' he sighed. He really was exhausted, despite the steely demeanour he tried to display. 'What a fix!' he finally exclaimed. 'You and your team will probably be tried for treason. You'll need legal advisors to help you fight that. These higher-ups love to mince words.' There was disgust plastered on his face, 'And, lastly, you will have to go through a whole ordeal. Psych-eval, medical tests, blah, blah, blah. You're a veteran, you know the circus.'

'I do, sir.' Captain Mangesh said.

'Last thing, do you think this whole episode with the other world was the last?'

Captain Mangesh thought about it. The magic, the absolute power of the eldritch god, their world was far too weak compared to the magic-wielders. Even with its technological prowess, it was lacking. 'No, sir. We couldn't even imagine something like this would happen. The possibilities of other-worldly interactions—and intrusions—are limitless.'

'Exactly what I was thinking,' General Shah said.

'You have something in mind, sir?'

Kunal, Aisha and Dr Raza were summoned into General Shah's cabin. They were hesitant to visit him, especially knowing he had been in a gruelling three-hour meeting with the higher-ups just half an hour ago. However, refusing or being late would probably be just as bad, so they hurried off.

Captain Mangesh was already in there. He was back

in his human form.

Once the doors were closed, General Shah got straight to the point, 'The higher-ups aren't happy with what happened last night. I've managed to pacify them for the moment, but they're going to raise some issues over it. Sooner if not later.'

General Shah turned to the others, 'Now, coming to the more important matter. The higher-ups can never be convinced that we're safe from extra-dimensional threats. And I'm inclined to agree with them. This incident has shown us that we aren't alone. And we need to be prepared for any and all possibilities. We're putting together a team of experts who can deal with any future infringements.'

Kunal smiled. *I knew it!*

'Did I say something funny?' General Shah grimaced. But it was harder to hate him now, having seen his good side.

'No, sir,' Kunal said, standing up straight.

The General shook his head and continued, 'As I was saying, we're putting together a team of experts. Since the three of you were involved in last night's incident, I'm putting in a special recommendation for you three to come onboard. As consultants.'

Kunal and Aisha exchanged glances.

'Can we think about it?' Dr Raza asked.

'Dr Raza, you can take all the time to think about it. That's going to be your job anyway.'

'Okay, Abbu's an astrophysicist. But why us?' Aisha asked.

'Do you really want me to spell this out for you?' General Shah rolled his eyes.

'Yes,' Aisha replied.

The General groaned and said, 'You showed commendable leadership and problem-solving skills. Kunal was closer to the extra-dimensional beings than anyone else involved. Do I really need to add two and two here for you?'

'No,' Aisha replied, looking at her feet. She was clutching her hands nervously.

'And, in case you're wondering,' the General continued, 'Captain Mangesh and his Silent Langurs will be transferred over to our team once the scientists relieve them. Knowing how this department functions, you'll be called in for duty in about two weeks' time. Consider it your vacation. You aren't going to get one in a long time.'

'But we haven't accepted your request,' Dr Raza said.

General Shah leaned back in his chair, 'I wasn't requesting.'

A knock on the door caught their attention. Before General Shah could respond, the door opened and Mr Tambe barged in with Dilip and three of his goons. He smiled with all his teeth and greeted everyone, 'Hello, I heard you're the owner here.'

'Who let these clowns in!?' General Shah barked.

Ignoring his demeanour, Mr Tambe dumped a folder in front of General Shah.

'What in the hell is this? Security!'

Kunal saw attendants and security trying to stop Mr Tambe, but Dilip's goons held them back.

'This is a proposal,' Dilip said, 'This place is majestic. We'd like to buy a few apartments here.' He leaned forward and said, 'You know, like an investment.'

General Shah started up, 'Get the hell out of my cabin!'

'At least look at my proposal, sir,' Mr Tambe pleaded, 'I have the down payment ready. Just let me...'

'GET OUT!'

By noon, all the news channels reported an unfathomable phenomenon. One of the country's top ministers posted a video lip-syncing and dancing to a trending K-pop song. It was sweet and cringe all at once. Debates erupted around the country questioning said minister's masculinity, modesty and responsibilities towards the people of the country.

For all their faults, Indian news reporters were experts when it came to covering up the real news.

Strangely enough, there wasn't any mention of the strays or the mind-controlling rakshas. Maybe the strays didn't care to involve themselves with human matters. Maybe they were just happy to be rid of Snaitun's influence. Kunal found it strange that there was no lasting effect. They'd find out eventually.

He decided not to bother himself with those fears. Not now, at least.

After their meeting with General Shah ended, Kunal had to report to the medical bay, where he was subjected to preventive shots. Six, to be precise. Even after felling a god-emperor from another dimension and outsmarting an eldritch god twice, a single needle scared him stiff.

The only saving grace was that he didn't cry. He just closed his eyes and let the doctors stab him.

After finishing a very late lunch, Kunal and Aisha snuck out to the roof to enjoy some peace and quietude. The only drinks Aisha managed to find were hot coffees. Kunal didn't complain, knowing they'd be free to leave soon.

The world looked fairly peaceful now. Kunal tried really hard to not think of anything and just take in the view, but it was impossible. Shri Tranquillity's compound was one of the most beautiful places Kunal had seen in his life. It was also entirely ravaged by their battle. The fate of their world had been decided on the very landscape Kunal was beholding at that moment.

The damage to the grounds would be explained away as the doing of rowdy locals running illegal races. Most of the battles had luckily happened away from civilisation. But there were still some locals who claimed to have seen magical lights shooting in the sky, along with shadow demons and giant monkeys. Kunal was certain that those incidents would somehow become justified as holy sightings of Lord Hanuman, Garuda and other gods.

'I can't believe Mr Tambe just tried to buy an apartment here.'

Aisha chuckled, 'I guess no one told him they're not for sale.'

Kunal sipped his coffee. No sugar, just as he liked it. He didn't say anything more. He continued to look at the view from that height. The beautiful evening, the ravaged complex and broken gates, the scenic horizon curtained with mountains. It was beautiful.

'How are you feeling?' Aisha asked gulping the last of her coffee.

'I don't know…' Kunal said, 'I feel like more has happened in the last twenty-four hours than I've seen happen in my entire life.' Kunal sipped on his coffee, reliving all of it. He was surprised at how well he had handled it, despite all the anxiety.

Aisha tucked in a loose strand of hair, 'I know. I can't believe it either. It's… a lot.' She played with her empty cup. 'I wonder how this is going to affect us.'

'What do you mean?' Kunal said, turning to her, 'You don't mean…' he waved his hand back and forth between them.

'I… no!' Aisha sat up straight and clasped his hand, 'Not *us*. I meant… like… our lives. Our jobs.'

'Shit!' Kunal said, pulling out his phone. 'I never logged out last night! I completely forgot…'

Kunal opened the email app on his phone. He had made it a point to not be logged into any work-related accounts on his phone, a simple measure to draw boundaries between work and personal life.

However, there was an unread email from his boss sent to his personal email. Hesitantly, Kunal read it.

Subject: *Checking In*

Hey Kunal,

You went offline in the morning and never came back online. You even missed a couple of client calls. You never do that.

Then Risabh mentioned some trouble in your city. I'm just checking in to make sure everything is all right. Please respond to this email whenever you see it.

Thanks,
Don K
Marketing Mastermind

Kunal read the email a second time. Then a third.

In his former job, being offline for half an hour could prompt the managers to send a blast of disciplinary emails. But here, his boss was actually just checking in. He responded immediately confirming his safety and stating he'd need some days off to clear the mess.

As he hit send, Kunal wondered what condition his laptop and apartment were in. Thoughts of cleaning up and all the servicing fees began overwhelming him.

Kunal took in a deep breath and decided to deal with it later. Besides, he might have to move out of his apartment if he were to join General Shah's team, so it really wasn't something worth stressing over anymore. He deserved some rest.

Surprisingly, the thoughts stopped bothering him. They didn't vanish; they just didn't have any power over him. At least for the moment.

Kunal had been through enough. He turned to Aisha, trying to return to the moment. 'Sorry, I just...'

'All okay?'

'Yeah, I'm not used to this much empathy,' Kunal said shaking his phone at her.

Aisha smiled, 'I know.'

'What were we talking about?'

'Our future,' Aisha said, then added, '*Professional* future.' She giggled.

'I guess we'll have to quit our jobs and become full-time consultants here, no? You heard General Shah.' Kunal did his best impression of the General's gruff voice, 'Commendable leadership and problem-solving skills.'

'No one else was taking charge! And General Shah seemed like a fish out of water in this situation,' Aisha said, 'I'll admit, playing all those video games did help.'

Kunal sneered, 'Yes, but you also showed your worth. Aisha, you stepped up when needed, you held your ground and came out unscathed. That deserves some recognition, right?'

'I guess…'

'Why do you never give yourself credit?'

'Childhood trauma, I guess?' Aisha said, then faked a laugh.

'Yeah, I get that,' Kunal said. He sipped the last of his coffee and crushed the cup.

Kunal wondered what value he'd bring to this team. At least Aisha had her archaeology background. Kunal was a useless marketing strategist.

No, I refuse to use such hurtful language when talking about myself.

Kunal emptied his mind. He would deal with his anxieties and feelings of inferiority later. He was given a special recommendation, and he should really be giving himself some credit.

The more he thought about it, he was able to convince himself that he did, in fact, deserve it. He had actually defeated Snaitun. And he had outsmarted an eldritch god. Twice.

'Kunal?' Aisha broke his train of thought. She grasped his hand, 'You aren't second-guessing your place here, right? You were just as involved in this mess as the rest of us.'

'Actually,' Kunal said, trying to think of something funny. He decided to just state the truth. 'I was more involved than any of you. In case you forgot, the animals approached me first.'

Aisha giggled, 'You're right.' She was considering something. After a few awkward moments, she said, 'I'm sorry. I left Burfi with you and...'

'No!' Kunal raised his hands, 'No, don't apologise.'

'But... your anxiety... and you almost died...'

'But I didn't!' Kunal said, 'And I always wanted a dog and Burfi made me realise... I actually can take care of a dog. It was scary at first, yes, but it was also...' Kunal thought about Burfi, about holding him and hugging him and his rough tongue on Kunal's face. '... it was the best feeling ever!'

Aisha giggled, 'Of course. If only the dark lord hadn't ambushed and almost killed you...'

'Yeah, wouldn't want to do that part again,' Kunal said, hoping he nailed the delivery.

Aisha laughed. Kunal laughed with her.

Finally, he said, 'You know, whatever happens next, I'm sure we'll figure it out.'

'And if we don't?' Aisha asked.

Kunal shrugged, 'Then we'll figure something else out.'

A crow fluttered onto the rooftop. Kunal flinched as it tossed something at him.

'Relax!' Aisha said, picking it up, 'It's just a bottle cap.'

'Why?' Kunal asked as another bottle cap tumbled next to him. Another crow perched nearby. Before they knew it, hundreds of crows had begun dumping tiny trinkets at them. Not at them, around them, as if they were offerings. With the crows came pigeons, sparrows and other birds. They all cawed and cheeped in a chorus that was frighteningly powerful.

'What's happening!?' Kunal said, panic gripping him.

Aisha just looked around with fascination. She smiled and said, 'I think they're trying to thank us.'

She got up and looked around as the birds flapped and continued to sing. From the roof, she spotted clusters of dogs and cats approaching the building. All howling and screaming.

No… they weren't threatening the humans. They were thanking them. Thanking *him*.

Aisha turned to Kunal and said, 'Guess there's going to be another news report about the mind-controlling rakshas.'

Kunal stepped beside her and marvelled at the sight. He'd seen strays gathered below his building before. And that was a nightmare.

This, however, was magical.

EPILOGUE

ADIRA STOOD IN THE ROYAL palace's gallery beholding her world. The smell of freedom wasn't as fresh as one would expect, but bloody freedom was better than any kind of enslavement. Ironically, their freedom had now put Snaitun's forces in chains.

The skies were bright, the lands near-desolate. But the people, they were beaming with joy. Celebrations were in full swing as music and dance filled the air, masking the gory residue of their revolt. The god-emperor Snaitun was dead. A real golden age of prosperity and peace was dawning upon their world.

Adira couldn't remember the last time she felt such relief and happiness. But it wasn't without its dues.

Snaitun was gone. Guru and the other rebel leaders were gone too. That meant it was Adira's head burdened to wear the crown.

However, Adira didn't feel the power rot her mind. She wasn't ruling because she believed it was her right, nor did she believe she earned it; she was ruling because it was her duty. Adira hoped that a better leader would take over from her, so she could go back to being a warrior. She wasn't built for ruling, even as a regent.

Adira had learned that in life one has to often take up roles and responsibilities that they aren't fully prepared for. It's rarely a choice, but always a necessity. Adira watched her soldiers separate Snaitun's forces into smaller groups, to be led to their respective fates.

Half of Snaitun's forces surrendered with reduced punishments. The other half was sentenced to death. It was an extreme measure, but Adira had to make sure none of them would even dream of following in her brother-in-law's footsteps. By the end of the decade, the very name of Snaitun would be synonymous with evil and ruthlessness in her world.

She couldn't afford another mishap like Snaitun's. Enough people had died for his power struggle. Enough worlds had suffered.

No more.

Being a ruler was hard. Worse, being a ruler was boring. It was less about gaining power and more about upholding the peace. And, as ruler of her entire world, the scope of Adira's responsibilities was beyond what she was prepared for.

If not me, then who?

'Empress Regent Adira,' a servant called out to her, 'Crown Prince Burfi seeks your attention.'

That was the only responsibility she liked about being a regent. At least she got to spend time with Burfi.

Unlike Snaitun, Adira would raise him right. She would give Burfi everything he would need to become a better ruler, and, more importantly, a better person.

Adira walked into Burfi's chamber, where he sat on the ground playing with his toys. His soft and milky skin in velvet royal garbs made him look like a little marble boy. His radiant black eyes, beady like a puppy's, and that innocent smile with chubby cheeks always melted Adira's heart. He opened his mouth wide and howled at her in welcome. Then, he grabbed one of his toys with his mouth and shook his head like a dog.

Some things are going to take time to change…

'Adira!' Burfi exclaimed and rushed over to her. On

all fours.

Adira picked him up and cradled him on her side, 'Burfi, you need to walk on your feet now.

'Woof!' Burfi said, then sniggered. He was just teasing her. She hoped.

Adira chuckled and kissed him on the cheek. At least now he was listening to her.

'Mischievous devil!' Adira smiled and tickled him.

'Woof! Woof!' Burfi said again, then laughed out loud.

Adira took him back to his play area and sat down on the soft carpet. Burfi stayed in her lap. 'What do you want to do, Burfi?'

'Woof! Woof!' he sniggered, then said, 'Story! Woof!'

'What story would you like to hear?'

'Woof! Woof!'

Sigh. *I can't wait for this to phase out.*

'Prince and dog!'

Again!? Raising children was hard. Harder than ruling empires even. Adira shook her head and smiled, 'Of course.'

'Woof!'

Adira cleared her throat and recollected the story. 'Once upon a time, there was a brave and strong prince.'

'Woof! Kunal! Kunal!'

Adira smiled. 'Yes, Prince Kunal.'

*

Kunal entered his apartment to find it in an impeccably clean condition.

'Oh, I didn't know you were coming today!' Mr Tambe popped his head out of the kitchen.

'Hello, Kunal!' Dilip waved his meaty hand as he supervised a guy mopping the floor. Others from his gang were dusting and packing up trash bags. They'd even fixed the windows.

'Wow!' Kunal exclaimed, still reeling from the shock.

He hadn't expected this at all. And Aisha was going to arrive any minute. Would Mr Tambe complain again?

Kunal shook his head. *Not now. Relax. Just breathe.*

Kunal had to get them out. Then he saw Mr Tambe washing some vessels and a horrid scene from a daily soap flashed before Kunal's eyes, 'My laptop?!'

'On your desk,' Mr Tambe pointed, 'Couldn't find a bag, so I just covered it with a cloth.'

Kunal walked over to his desk, where his laptop lay under a lacy cover that looked like it was made for old TVs. 'Thanks!' he called out, checking to see if the laptop was still working.

Thankfully, it was working fine and was fully charged. He glanced at the folder titled "Kunal's Sci Fi Epic", and wondered if he had the time to write it now. After all, he did have a ton of inspiration.

Kunal made a mental note to thank Mr Tambe for everything. He shut down his laptop without opening any apps or checking any messages. He had earned his time off.

'All done here, Pakya,' Dilip told Mr Tambe, 'I'll wait downstairs.' The rest of his men followed.

Mr Tambe walked out of the kitchen wiping his hands on a white handkerchief. 'All done here, *beta*. How are you feeling?'

'All good, Mr Tambe,' Kunal replied politely. 'Why did you...?'

'You saved the world, didn't you?' Mr Tambe said, shoving his damp handkerchief into his back pocket, 'I faced that rakshas. It's no easy task.' He patted Kunal on the shoulder, 'Good job, Kunal.'

'Are you—?'

'They made us sign an NDA,' Mr Tambe leaned in and whispered, 'And paid us for our silence.' He sniggered. 'I just wish they had at least looked at our proposal. That Shri Tranquillity complex is a gold mine, you know that?'

Kunal smiled, 'I know...'

'Why is the door... Mr Tambe!' Aisha stopped, doing a poor job of hiding her shock. 'Didn't expect you here.'

'Hi, *beta*,' Mr Tambe waved, 'I'm just on my way out. Kunal, take care, okay? And if you need anything, just send me a message. Okay?'

'Sure!' Kunal said, 'Thanks for cleaning up, and for charging my laptop.'

'Least I could do,' Mr Tambe smiled and walked over to the main door. He slipped on his sandals, then said rather sternly, 'By the way, rent is due next week. Don't be late.' Then he smiled, 'Bye!'

'What was that?' Aisha asked, closing the door.

'He just... cleaned up. I guess as a gesture of gratitude.' Kunal looked around his apartment. It hadn't ever looked this clean. Not even at the time he had come to see it before signing the rent agreement. Everything was in its place, carefully organised. He spotted the pink basket that Burfi had come in. It didn't make him feel sad anymore.

Damn, I miss that dog!

Not a dog.

Aisha put down the two brown paper bags in the kitchen and produced two cardboard cups out of them.

'Great!' Aisha said, handing one cup to Kunal, 'Here's your hot chocolate.'

Finally! 'Thanks! Is it—?'

'Lavender mint, just as you like it,' Aisha replied with a smirk. 'And...' she removed another thing from the bag, 'a little present.'

'A book!' Kunal exclaimed, snatching it from her hand. 'Why?'

Aisha shrugged, 'Just. You kept saying you wanted to read a book and drink hot chocolate. So...'

'But... I thought we were going to hang out...'

Aisha produced a second book from the bag, 'I have my own, don't worry.'

Kunal placed the hot chocolate down and went to

embrace Aisha. He kissed her and held her tightly, 'I wish we could stay like this forever.'

'Yeah, forever's going to have to end soon. I need to go pee.'

Kunal let go, 'And you say I'm not romantic.'

'Shut up ya, Kunal,' Aisha said, pulling his cheeks.

Kunal read through the book's blurb and the first few pages as he waited for Aisha to return. He didn't even realise he had plopped onto his couch and settled in.

'Wow, you started without me,' Aisha said grabbing her book and joining him on the couch.

Kunal took a sip of the hot chocolate, a dash of sweet lavender and a hint of mint adding the perfect flavour to the otherwise bitter chocolate. This was the stuff of Kunal's dreams, exactly what he had been craving for all this time.

Aisha cuddled up to him and they continued to read their books in silence. They'd pause in between just for a quick discussion on something interesting, or simply a peck of affection.

'This is perfect,' Kunal said with a smile. He was home, and he was comfortable.

For the first time in ages, Kunal felt at peace.

FIN

ABOUT THE AUTHOR

Ronit J is a fantasy author and indie filmmaker. He decided to write fantasy books at the age of 11, and finally—just a few months before his 30th birthday—he's publishing his debut fantasy novel (the one you just read).

He's a fantasy nerd with big dreams and bigger anxieties, all struggling to make themselves be heard within the existential maelstrom that is his mind. He also loves world cinema, chess, beer, food, and annoying his loving wife.

He's constantly working on stories (2 at the time of writing this bio), and plans on publishing them soon.

THANK YOU FOR READING!

I'm genuinely grateful that you read my book, and I hope you had a good time.

If you enjoyed this book, please consider leaving a review on Goodreads, Amazon, or any of the other platforms you use for book reviews. For a first-time author like me, reviews from awesome readers like you can make the world of a difference.

Lastly, if you'd like to stay up to date with my writing, you can sign up to my newsletter. I don't send out too many, and it's a great way to get news about giveaways, deals, and upcoming projects.

You can sign up on my website: www.ronitjauthor.com

Or follow me on social media: @ronitjauthor

Once again, thank you for reading!

Printed in Great Britain
by Amazon